HIGHLAND

PROTECTOR

HIGHLAND

PROTECTOR

BY

CATHERINE BYBEE

Book Five in the
MacCoinnich Time Travels

Highland Protector

Cover Art by Crystal Posey

Visit the author at www.CatherineByee.com

Publishing History
First Edition, 2013
Published by Catherine Bybee
Print ISBN 978-0985088873

Published in the United States of America

Dedication

This one is for The Chatty Cathy's
The best street team evah!

Acknowledgments

For every whip-cracking fan of this series, thank you! Seriously, all those emails... as in daily emails, about the dark hero that Amber would marry were a welcome sight. At one point my assistant Crystal threatened to start handing out flaming pitchforks if I didn't finish this book. "You will not write another book before Amber is done, Catherine!" Crystal home schools four kids and she used *that* voice. So, yeah... I had to finish Amber.

I do realize the wait for you, dear reader, has been long. Imagine the wait in my head once I placed Amber's hero in the ending of Highland Shifter. Gavin Kincaid eluded me for a time, he'd swing back around and wave, and then run away again. He's here now and more than ready for all of you to read his story.

I know the minute my whip-cracking fans finish this latest book there will be a mass dump in my inbox asking for the next book. And that fact makes this author *squee* with delight. So keep the emails coming. Crack that virtual whip and tap those fingers.

Cian, dear reader, will be worth the wait.

Chapter One

1686, MacCoinnich Keep Scotland

Fighting with a sword ranked up there with having sex without an orgasm. Holding the damn thing took too much energy and the end-result was anticlimactic and messy. Kincaid's free hand itched to pull any one of his hidden weapons from the pockets of his modified seventeenth century clothes and finish off his opponent. The man's death was inevitable. He had no earthly prayer of taking Kincaid. Even without the use of Kincaid's gift, the kilted Scot had two fatal flaws working against him. One, he underestimated his opponent, never a good thing in battle. Two, Kincaid's Druid gift would prevent any fatal blow from reaching his skin. He was damn near immortal.

Kincaid missed being skewered by the Scot's blade by lunging to his right and placing one foot on the edge of the Keep's massive stairs. Above him, other men fought, some with powers, a few without. Preventing the ancient Keep from falling into any hands that didn't belong to descendants of the original owners, wasn't going to happen. These missions were planned and orchestrated with extreme caution and precision.

The Scot advanced again—sweat falling from his brow with the effort of the fight.

"Kincaid!" He heard his name from the floor above, but didn't make the mistake of looking up.

"I'm busy." He blocked his opponent's sword again, locked the man's free arm, and attempted to pull it behind his back.

Kincaid was rewarded by taking an elbow in the ribs and having the wind knocked from his lungs.

"Finish him already. We need to move on."

Moving on was his queue that their time was nearly up.

"I guess…" He shoved the Scot a foot away and lifted his sword high. "That means we're done here."

"Your confidence will be your downfall," the Scot said.

Kincaid motioned the man forward. *…said the spider to the fly…*

The Scot advanced with a surge of strength and determination.

Kincaid held his ground, threw up his Druid shield, and watched as shock filled the man's gaze when his sword bounced off the shield and opened him up for Kincaid's final blow.

Killing never sat well with him. But he was a warrior and killing was part of his soul. Damn shame that.

Kincaid heard his name called again, and he took the familiar stairs two at a time to reach the others. From the corner of his eye, his gaze met a painting on the wall, one he'd not seen before.

His steps faltered as he connected with the haunting gaze of the most beautiful woman he'd ever seen. Didn't matter that the painting was one dimensional, or that the woman was most likely dead…even in this century. He did a quick inventory of the other images on the walls and recognized only one. The same painting hung in that very space on the wall, so many years in the future. But this one…the picture of the woman with her long dark hair and pained focus as she attempted to smile, beckoned him. This painting he'd never seen.

"Kincaid! Dammit man, get your ass up here!"

Kincaid shook away the woman's soulful gaze, bounded up the stairs, and trailed his band of men up the spiral staircase of the turret.

As they moved to the privacy of the bricked room, he noticed the small face of one of the Keep's youngest occupants watching from behind an adjacent door.

Rory moved to close the door when Kincaid motioned toward their witness.

The child, a girl not more than ten years old watched with wide eyes. She didn't appear frightened in the least.

"Is she..."

Rory lifted his hand, palm up, and from it, a small ball of fire swirled from nothing and hung suspended.

The girl's wide eyes lifted and a small smile inched at the side of her lips. She lifted her hand and a sputtering of fire sprang from her fingertips.

Kincaid felt his pulse dip as he lifted his finger to his lips "Shh," he whispered with what he hoped looked like a friendly smile.

Noise from the long staircase met their ears. Rory ushered them inside and closed the door. Before the noise from below became another battle, Kincaid closed his eyes, lifted his shield, and spread it over his small party...then he began to chant and time slid away.

****

Current Day, Los Angeles

Amber MacCoinnich endured the weight of emotional pain that surrounded every moment of her life for as long as she could stand it before slipping from her bath. Though she enjoyed the freedom of a quick shower from time to time, she endured the splitting headache that swam up her spine once she removed her protective cloak. The soothing water in the hot tub came at a price, but Amber was willing to pay the price at least once a week. As a sixteenth century woman living in the twenty-first century, there were some habits she brought with her.

Unlike MacCoinnich Keep in the Highlands of Scotland, the place she'd grown up, Mrs. Dawson's Southern California home was virtually empty of inhabitants. Mrs. Dawson herself lived in chambers that had been moved to the bottom floor to aid her failing joints. Although age might be robbing her of her ability to take the stairs as often as she used to, her mind was sharp, and her wit always made Amber smile.

Simon, her cousin of sorts, and Helen, his wife, took over several rooms on the second floor while Amber took one of the many rooms on the third floor. Up here, the weight of emotions from those below only penetrated her mind and her soul when she removed her cloak. Up here, she could manage several hours of sleep if she exhausted herself during her day. Up here, she could breathe. Or so was the case when she'd first arrived in this century. As her days wore on the cloak began to lose its power and Amber began to long for a fourth floor.

Long before she heard her name called, she felt Helen's intent...an enormous emotional wave of energy surged from below. Though she wasn't positive what caused Helen's happiness, she experienced it...and knew Helen's intention was to share it.

The fall night gave the house a slight chill, which suited Amber well when she covered her pale skin with a long nightgown and the warm cloak that served as a temporary emotional shield.

Instantly, the threads of the magic woven into the long garment muted the outside emotions until they dulled the building headache inside her skull.

A long-winded sigh escaped her lips. "'Tis better," she whispered to herself.

Helen's soft knock on the door brought a smile to Amber's lips. "Come in, Helen."

She opened the door and bounced in the room like a young child, the smile on her lips lifted the fatigue from Amber's heart. "I still can't get over how you know anytime one of us is nearby."

"I've been here for two moons...months," Amber corrected herself in an attempt to use the proper words from this century. "What has you so joyous?"

Helen's eyes swept up her frame. "It can wait until you've dried your hair. Besides, Simon and I wanted to tell you and Mrs. Dawson together."

Amber lifted a brush and stroked the ends of her hair. She probably should cut the locks short but she couldn't bring herself to the task. Every part of her life had changed, and her appearance in the mirror was one of the only things that reminded her who she was and where she came from...of her home. "News worthy of an audience?"

"The best. Ten minutes?" Helen asked.

"If you won't mind damp hair, I'll be down in five."

"Awesome." Helen moved forward, as if she were going to embrace Amber. She hesitated, nearly tripping over her feet and sighed. "Five minutes," she said before turning and leaving.

Amber's own sorrow filled her heart as Helen fled the room. A simple expression of love, of joy, a hug wasn't something given freely to her because of the emotional attack on her system.

Most Druid gifts were a blessing. If managed, those gifts were used to protect and serve the recipient of the gifts...and their families. Amber's gift had served a useful purpose for years. Something easily managed and controlled. Until her family battled with Grainna and the power inside her tripled. It was as if she'd drawn in the sinister side of Grainna's power. The thought left something inside Amber cold and dead. She wanted nothing of the powerful Druid's essence inside of her. Yet she knew something leaked into her with the woman's death.

Once Amber ran a brush through her hair, she tied it back in a silk ribbon, placed a pair of slippers on her feet, and descended the stairs.

She found Helen and Simon in the kitchen, a place she seldom visited when living with her parents in the sixteenth century. In this time, it seemed most of their conversations were around the stone island.

Simon stood beside Helen who was perched on the edge of a stool, his arm draped lovingly over her shoulders. The love radiating off the two of them penetrated the cloak and made Amber smile. When he nuzzled the side of Helen's neck, Amber cleared her throat. "Perhaps I should leave and come back another time?" she asked with a grin.

Helen laughed and pushed Simon playfully away. "Don't be silly."

"There you are." Mrs. Dawson walked into the room. The cane in her hand was a constant companion after the three o'clock hour. Seemed her legs grew weaker as the day grew long.

Simon pulled out a chair for Mrs. Dawson.

"Thank you." She patted Simon's hand before folding her hands together in her lap. "So what has prompted this family meeting?"

Amber glanced between Helen, Simon, and Mrs. Dawson, her new family, and waited.

Helen nodded toward her husband. "You tell them."

Simon stood behind Helen with his hands on her shoulders, his lips pulled back into a huge smile. "Helen is pregnant with our child."

"Oh, Simon." Amber moved around the counter, pushed back her worry about touching others, and wrapped her arms around Simon. His strong arms folded her in and his warmth filled her with hope. "I'm so happy for you both."

Mrs. Dawson moved from her chair to hug Helen before Amber switched places with the older woman.

"I cannot wait for tiny feet to run around the house," Amber told Helen when she hugged her. "I think I miss the children of my father's home most of all."

"I'm going to need some serious help," Helen said. "I know nothing about babies."

"The baby will teach you everything you need to know," Simon said.

Still, Amber could feel Helen's worry lacing her joy. "I can help," Amber told her.

Mrs. Dawson sat again. "Will you find out the sex of the baby before you give birth...or wait?"

Helen shrugged. "I see no reason to wait. The doctor said we'll be able to tell in a couple of months."

"Would you like to know now?" Amber asked.

Simon pulled in a breath. "I completely forgot that you were able to guess the baby's sex back home."

Simon referred to their sixteenth century life as if their mutual family lived in another town and not another time.

"You can do that?" Helen asked.

"I can. 'Tis one of the more useful sides of my gift."

Helen sent a hopeful smile to Simon, who nodded.

"Let's do it," Simon said.

"Shall we move to the living room? I need you to lie down so I can touch your belly."

Even through Helen's hopeful smile, a measure of concern pushed beyond the barrier of the cloak. "Won't that hurt you?"

Amber swallowed and offered a convincing lie. "'Tis not that bad today. I'll be fine."

She followed the others into the larger room and instructed Helen to lie on her back and bare her abdomen so she might search out the newest member of their family.

Helen used Simon's lap as a pillow while Mrs. Dawson sat in a chair on the other side of the room.

"Is this good?" Helen lifted her shirt and slid the edge of her jeans down.

"Perfect." Moisture gathered on Amber's forehead even before she reached to remove her cloak. Moving slowly at first, the cloak slid off her shoulder and the first wave of emotions of those in the room hit her. Excitement radiated from Helen. That joy kept Amber in motion. She didn't need Helen worrying about her. Simon agonized under his pretend smile. He, of all people, knew this caused her pain. Mrs. Dawson, the dear, had a unique ability to feel like a gentle wave upon the ocean. Amber

7

knew she was there…that she cared…but her emotions only truly shot through Amber when the woman didn't think Amber was near.

Amber gathered the cloak in her hands and kept it close to her body as several waves descended upon her from every direction. Someone close by emitted the pain of loss, their heart was broken and nearly made Amber whimper. Another neighbor fretted over money and a child was frightened of the darkness. She closed her eyes for a moment and sat.

"Are you okay?"

"Fine. I just need a moment." Amber thought of Mrs. Dawson's gentle wave and attempted to mute the neighbors' misery. Her attempt to beat the emotions surrounding her into silence only muffled them slightly. When she opened her eyes again, she smiled and rubbed her hands together with fake confidence. "Ready?"

Helen nodded and reached for Simon's hand.

Amber knelt at the side of the sofa and gently lowered her hands to Helen's stomach.

So much love and happiness helped deafen the unpleasant thoughts of all the others. Once again, Amber closed her eyes as she envisioned the tiny life blooming inside her friend.

"Try and relax," Amber told her. "I can do this."

"Reading minds now, Amber?" Helen asked with a laugh.

"You're worried I won't be able to do this and that it will hurt me too much. Let that go. Help me connect with your child."

Come now little one… Where are you?

Helen's tension eased and a flicker of another soul radiated. "Ahh, there you are."

Amber hushed those in the room before they could ask questions.

So comfortable and loved. How an unborn child felt loved Amber couldn't guess, but this child knew he was coming into a world of unconditional love and devotion. Then the strangest thing happened, he sensed Amber's probe and kicked against her as if to say he was very happy where he was, thank you very much, and to leave him alone until he was ready for the world. *All right, lad...I'm leaving now.* But before Amber let the connection completely go, she searched for anything dark...anything of concern.

Blissful silence met her mind. It only lasted a moment, but it was there. Reluctantly, she removed her hands from Helen's belly and opened her eyes.

Three sets of expectant eyes looked her way.

Amber connected her gaze to Simon. "Congratulations, Simon. Your wife will bear a healthy baby boy."

Moisture gathered in Simon's eyes and happiness punched Amber low in her gut.

Helen gasped. "He's healthy? You can tell that?"

"I can. He's very happy where he is for now."

While Helen and Simon embraced, a strange wave of sorrow emitted from Mrs. Dawson. The sorrow was directed at Amber, for her loss of ever having the joy of a child of her own. Withstanding the bare touch of anyone proved difficult, anything more intimate she would forego. No, Amber knew she would have to enjoy the children of others.

When she moved to stand, all the emotions she'd pushed aside to search for Helen's child struck her like a fist. She stumbled and fell into the table, knocking a lamp to the floor.

Simon hurried to her side and attempted to steady her. Her head swam, and nausea filled her throat.

"Her cloak," Helen said.

Simon swiveled, grasped the cloak, and threw it over Amber's shoulders.

She tightened the edges of the garment around her, muffling the outside world. It took several minutes before

Amber could speak. "Don't feel guilty, Helen. I wanted to do this for you. For Simon."

"But you're hurting."

"I'm fine. Just a passing discomfort." Only Amber knew it was more. Each time she attempted to live outside the cloak was worse than the last.

She knew her smile didn't hide the pain in her eyes, but she kept it there anyway.

Chapter Two

2231, Los Angeles

Kincaid shed his costume, and removed the weapons strapped all over his body. He tossed the clothes down the chute to the cleaning room where someone would wash and mend any damage from the day's battle. After stepping into the shower stall, he closed the door sealing him in.

He considered his choices for cleaning off the day's battle, skipped over the dry shower, and hit the water button. It would take more than chemicals to wash the dead from his skin today. As the hot water poured from the rain shower, Kincaid tilted his head into the spray. He groaned and let the water remove the grime. Though he would have loved to stay in the hot spray for hours, he couldn't be that selfish with all the others in the fortress.

He waved a hand over the chemical spray and let it shoot antibacterial disinfectant over his skin, and turned into the spray to catch the other side. After washing his hair the old-fashioned way, with soap, he rinsed it clean and watched the remaining water circle the drain. He could hear the pumps below the stall as it already worked on recycling the cast-off liquid.

He stepped from the shower minutes later and shook the water from his dark hair. It was getting a little long. Short cuts were a luxury he didn't afford very often. It was hard to blend with warriors of the past with a haircut of the current century. He took a moment in front of the mirror to trim the thin goatee he preferred on his face before finishing his ritual. The light in the adjoining bedroom switched on as he walked through and stretched out on his bed. "Video display?" he called into the empty room.

From the hologram projector positioned above his bed, a digital screen lit the wall across the room.

"What can I do for you, Kincaid?" The voice of the room control was that of a woman. Her soft-spoken words always made him envision a long-legged brunette with bright red painted lips behind the voice. Problem was, the voice was probably computer generated, and his vision shouldn't be anything other than soundboards and computer chips. But it still didn't stop him from his daily fantasy.

"KTLA news."

"Would you like me to interrupt the current broadcast or play from the recording?"

"Recording."

He had at least thirty minutes before any of his team would be called for a debriefing of the evening's events. Catching up on what had happened during his brief voyage through time was essential to his psyche. He needed to know that he was actually in his time...that the world hadn't dramatically changed because of their interference.

The bright colored lights of the broadcast flashed on the wall. The polished anchorman sat behind the desk wearing a sleek coat without a collar over a turtleneck sweater. At his side, his co-anchor sported an over-puffed jacket with awkward shoulder pads. They wore plastic smiles and spoke false truths. There was no reason to believe the news would deliver facts...they hadn't in some one hundred and fifty years...probably longer. But they did send out recordings of events...and with enough practice, Kincaid could peer through those events and pick out certain truths.

After introductions and short laughter about the unseasonably cool weather, they jumped into current events. "The president of Texas made a surprise appearance at the Governor's State of the State dinner which took place in Westridge. It appears that both the governors of Northern California and Southern California are once again talking about following Texas in seceding from the Union."

"Which would result in a civil war," Kincaid said to himself. Though the secession was inevitable. History repeated itself…always.

Confident his latest trip in time didn't result in anything catastrophic, he released a long sigh, threw his arm over his eyes, and let his mind empty. When it did, his memory of the painting he'd seen while fleeing up the MacCoinnich Keep's massive stairs settled into his system. The woman's troubled gaze followed him, made his heart rate climb. She was hauntingly familiar yet he couldn't place her from his history studies. Was she from the original family? A grandchild to the first time travelers? *Who is she?* Or more precisely, *who was she?*

Unable to tune the image out of his brain, he gave up his quest for sleep, turned off the news, and left his room.

He passed the main living room where he heard several of his team talking among themselves while the same broadcast he'd been watching in his room blared in the background. Savory smells from the kitchen told him the cooks were working late to feed them after their battle. His stomach made a sound of protest when he turned down the short hall and into the fortress library.

The room hadn't changed in centuries. Oiled oak bookshelves lined each wall from floor to ceiling. Each shelf housed books in all shapes and sizes. The collection wasn't filled with fiction and fluff, but history and folklore. To the uneducated eye, some of the books might look like fantasy and nonsense, but Kincaid knew each book held the history of his people. There were books of witchcraft and sorcery, ancient beings and shape shifters…and yes, even time travelers.

He moved to the center of the library where a large table housed two computer stations. Each book had been carefully categorized and input into the data system. With any luck, the image in his head would be somewhere in the

CATHERINE BYBEE

library and he could put a name to the face he'd seen on the wall of the Keep.

He sat in front of the computerized station and placed his palm on the monitor screen.

"How can I assist you, Kincaid?"

The computer's voice was that of Giles, the keeper of the books, and often the teacher of everything Druid to those who lived in the house.

"Search artwork in MacCoinnich Keep in the seventeen hundreds."

"Can we narrow the search, Kincaid?"

"Portraits."

A giant image of a book circled on the massive screen while the computer searched its database.

Early portraits began to appear, which he flipped through one at a time. As always, the image of Ian and Lora started off the art. That painting still hung on the wall in the Scotland fortress and Kincaid had seen it several times in person both in the past and in his time.

There were very few portraits of the MacCoinnich family in their early years. In the mid sixteenth century, Kincaid knew paintings started to fill space on the walls of the staircase. Though from his memory, most were of children. Apparently, those images were some of the only ones in the computer system. He was midway through the images of the seventeenth century when the door to the library opened.

"I thought I saw a light on in here." Giles, the man and not the computer, brought his lean frame into the room and pushed his glasses up onto his nose. Why he didn't just have the corrective surgery performed on his vision, Kincaid would never know.

"I'm borrowing your space," he said.

Giles set the book he carried into the room on the table beside Kincaid and peered over his shoulder at the monitor. "Anything I can help you with?"

He wasn't sure how to answer the man. To tell him

14

the image of a long-dead woman on a wall back in time made his heart skip a beat might sound a little obsessive. Unstable even. Then again, following instinct was something every Druid man and woman was taught to do from birth.

"I noticed a portrait on the walls of MacCoinnich Keep as we were leaving, one that I'd not seen before. I thought maybe we had some reference of it."

"A portrait of a child?" Giles asked.

"No. A woman."

Giles lips lifted slightly as he glanced his way. The man was too perceptive. His Druid gift did make him the perfect historian. He had an ability to file away nearly every word he'd ever read. He seldom used the computer unless he was inputting data. The man didn't need it.

"What did this woman look like?"

"Long dark hair, sad eyes." *Sad beautiful eyes.*

Giles tapped his chin as he thought. "What style of dress?"

Kincaid closed his eyes and tried to picture what the woman was wearing. All he could see was her high cheekbones and full lips. "I'm not into women's fashion."

"Did she wear a hat? Was her hair bound?" Giles walked across the room, pulled the ladder along the bookshelf, and proceeded to climb to reach the top shelf.

"No hat. Her hair was down. She wore a long dress if that helps." He gave up searching the computer files and let Giles do what he did best.

"And this was a woman, not a teenager?"

Kincaid shuddered. "No. She was a woman."

Giles retrieved a leather-bound tome that was half the size of him. "That's odd. Most women in that time wore their hair bound, unless they were unwed."

"And most of the women were married early..." Kincaid said his thoughts aloud.

"Precisely."

"Was the woman unattractive? Some alarming feature

that might have made her an unlikely candidate for marriage?"

He rubbed the heat from the back of his neck and tried to appear unaffected. "She was beautiful." He couldn't imagine the men of the time looking past her. If she were a direct descendent from the MacCoinnich's, she may have had a long list of must-haves in a potential spouse. Kincaid couldn't imagine any of the original family letting their children marry just anyone. The family was much too private to marry outside their inner circle.

Giles opened the large book and proceeded to turn the pages.

"There you are!" From the door, Rory called out to him and beckoned him with a wave of his hand. "We're waiting on you."

Kincaid pushed from the chair. "Coming." He patted Giles on his back. "I'll be back after the briefing."

"Yeah, yeah." Giles was already moving to the bookcase in search of some lead only he saw.

The entire basement had been converted into a safe room years before. The far end of the massive room held their armory, both modern and ancient. The center of the room held a conference table and a monitoring system that linked them into the safe houses abroad so they might be able to obtain reinforcements if needed.

Kincaid stood before a chair between Rory and Colin. Across from them sat Allen and Joshua with Colleen standing at the head of the table. "Nice of you to join us." Colleen scolded.

Dressed in full skintight leather with a body that would rock many a man's world, Colleen's cold stare was meant to intimidate. Only it took more than her piercing steel gray eyes to move him.

"I was following up on something."

She tilted her head to the side at the same time the door to the safe room closed with a loud bang and the lock clicked into place. Colleen flexed her Druid powers without blinking an eye.

"Something important?"

"I don't know yet."

Just when he thought she'd pitch a bitch-fit, she folded into her chair and expected him to settle.

He did.

"Do you have the report?"

Colin, Colleen's twin leaned back in his chair and grinned at his sister. The two of them were quite a pair. They'd run the fortress for as long as Kincaid had been there and neither of them appeared to age a day. Colin didn't always lead the expeditions in time, but he nearly always accompanied them. Colleen would love to join them, from what Kincaid could see, but she wouldn't blend well on a battlefield in a time where men ruled and women stayed behind to pine and worry over their men's fate. It killed her and she took great pleasure in flexing her power whenever they returned to remind them all that she was just as powerful as they were, even if she was a woman.

Truth was Kincaid would welcome Colleen in battle any day of the week if given a choice. He'd seen her in action and knew she brought more cunning and power than many of the men in the room.

He also thought she'd relax a little if she'd just get laid.

Colin started talking, removing thoughts of Colleen doing the nasty, and reminding himself of their battle. "Everything was just as expected. While the men were outside the Keep battling their known enemy, the walls inside were breached and the women were vulnerable."

"Did you arrive in time?"

Kincaid envisioned their arrival to the seventeenth century, his short trip down the stairway and straight into the path of a distant Highland clan who wanted to claim MacCoinnich Keep as their own. They were beyond surprised to find able-bodied men inside the walls of the

Scottish fortress willing to fight to preserve the lives of those who lived there.

"We kicked ass."

"Were there any witnesses?"

"Of the battle, no," Kincaid told her.

Colleen's gaze narrowed. "But someone saw you."

It wasn't a question.

"A child," Rory reported. "A girl, not more than eight or ten. She saw us entering the tower."

"And?" Colleen asked.

"Druid. No doubt. Rory pulled a fireball in his palm and she attempted to do the same, smiled, and kept silent," Kincaid reported.

Colleen once again moved her eyes to him. "You've spoken with Giles about the girls?"

Kincaid nodded. "I have."

Rory nudged his arm. "What about them?"

Without waiting for Colleen to elaborate, Kincaid did. "Giles recently discovered first hand accounts of several children—all girls—who've reported time traveling warriors who helped in battles from the past."

"We're just learning about this now?" Allen asked.

Colleen leaned forward. "I've known about them for some time. But until now, we didn't know if the girls actually interacted with any of us. Guess now we know."

"I thought we have always been invisible," Owen said.

"If we were completely invisible we would never know exactly when we were needed," Colleen told them.

"I thought your visions told us where to go, where to fight." Rory's normal smile fell as he spoke.

"They do. But I have often had Giles consult his books to double check the time period. Make sure."

This was news to Kincaid. If their trips in time were recorded somewhere they could be traced and attacked by the Others. Any of their trips in time could be virtual traps. The thought left him cold. He glanced at Colin, who didn't

18

seem fazed by the news. "You knew about this?"

He shrugged. "We're twins. Little happens I don't know about."

"So we've been watched?"

Colleen shook her head. "Not watched. Seen. There are vague references of traveling warriors, who understood the *family*, who arrived long enough to help, and then left." She lifted her fingers and quoted the word family in the air. "The references in the books came from mother to daughter and no one else."

"You mean these girls never told their fathers…brothers?"

"Not that we can determine at this point. Giles is cross-referencing his books." Colleen once again pinned her gaze on her brother. "I didn't know Giles told anyone else about his discovery. I told him to keep the information between the two of us."

"Give the man a break, Colleen. I walked into the library and found him frantically turning pages," Kincaid told her. Others in the room laughed. All of them knew Giles' perplexity when he worked on a puzzle in his books and how very narrow minded he became when he wanted to determine the end point. "He started rambling about the children knowing we were there, and how he swore he'd never read or heard of this before. I asked what he was talking about and Giles, being Giles, rambled on long enough for me to understand the situation. I suppose it's impossible for us to have gone back in time as many times as we have without ever being discovered."

Owen leaned back, ran a hand over his bald head. "I'm surprised there aren't tapestries with all our mugs stitched on them."

"Who says there aren't?" Colin teased.

The conversation went around the table like that for several minutes, the men laughing and decompressing from their battle. When it became apparent there wasn't more to report, Colleen dismissed the lot of them.

They moved to the dining room where they filled their stomachs and shared battle stories. The men in Kincaid's century weren't terribly different than those in the time from which they'd all just returned.

Except he and his men were much better armed.

Chapter Three

Mrs. Dawson hunched over several books in her library, carefully searching for something that would help Amber with her plight. "Oh, Frank," she said to her long-dead husband in a whisper. "We should have made some order of these old books while you were alive."

She could practically hear her late husband's gruff voice saying they had plenty of time for such menial tasks. He'd been a collector, not a reader. Oh, he'd enjoyed many of the books in the room, but there was no possible way he could have read them all even if he had lived four hundred years. As it turned out, he lived a lively seventy-six years before leaving her alone in the big house filled with books.

After pushing the fourth book away, and reaching for the fifth, Mrs. Dawson decided warm tea might aide in her search. Ever since Helen, Simon, and Amber came to be a part of her family...her home, she limited the time her hired help stayed in the house. The result was moving her old bones more than she'd have liked.

She was walking back into the library with her tea, trying her best to keep the contents in her cup from spilling when Helen intercepted in the hall. "Let me take that for you."

"Thanks, dear. I'm not as steady as I used to be I'm afraid."

Helen was the closest thing to a daughter she'd ever had. They'd met years before when she stumbled upon the auction house where Helen worked. Helen, having no family of her own, developed a kinship to Mrs. Dawson and from there the two of them became fast friends.

"Where are we headed?" Helen asked as she moved aside to let Mrs. Dawson lead the way.

"The library."

Helen placed the tea on the table where a stack of books took up most of the room.

"Looking for anything in particular?"

Mrs. Dawson settled into her chair with a heavy sigh. "I was hoping to find something to ease Amber's suffering."

Helen eyes drifted toward the ceiling. "She really is hurting, isn't she?"

"Yes. And it's getting worse."

Helen sat in an opposite chair. "She hasn't left her room since she told us about the baby." That had been days ago.

Mrs. Dawson reached over and patted Helen's hand. "Don't blame yourself. We have to believe she'll find something to ease her pain. Her mother was adamant she stay in this time to find a cure." Lora MacCoinnich's gift of premonition spoke of Amber's demise if she stayed in the sixteenth century, which was why Lora and Ian had entrusted their daughter to Simon's care in the twenty-first century.

"How can a Druid gift have a cure? And why would any of our gifts cripple us like hers is doing?"

"I wish I knew. All the years I've sat among these books and never really understood the messages within the pages. Mr. Dawson and I collected them, but didn't read nearly enough of them."

Helen glanced up at the bookshelves and stood. "Maybe I can find the answer…if it's here." The greatest Druid gift Helen possessed was her ability to find missing objects and even people.

"I should have thought about that before searching myself," Mrs. Dawson said as she sat back and sipped her tea.

Helen stood before one of the shelves, closed her eyes, and lifted her hands. Mrs. Dawson had witnessed her searching for answers with her Druid gift before. Helen moved slowly about the room in complete silence for several minutes. She paused in front of the wall of windows and lifted both of her hands before clutching both hands into fists. "This is the only space I feel any energy."

In front of the window were two high back chairs and a single lamp.

Helen lifted the cushion of the chair as if perhaps there were a hidden book under the fabric. "Nothing," she whispered.

"You felt something."

"Yes, but obviously not the right thing. Unless you have a hidden floor vault."

Mrs. Dawson smiled. "Not in this room." There was one in the room Helen now shared with Simon, and another in the basement safe room.

Helen twisted back to the window, opened the pane, and reached beyond the opening. She moved her hands back inside and shook her head. "No. It's inside."

Mrs. Dawson pushed from her chair and made her way to Helen's side. "Shall we try and ask for help. Like Simon taught us?"

Actively using their Druid gifts was new for both of them. Simon had shown them how to work together and ask the Ancients for help with life's more difficult problems.

"Do you think we can do that without Simon? He'll be home in a couple of hours."

"I don't see why we should wait. If it doesn't work, we can try again when he's here." According to Simon, the more Druid power used the better chances of achieving success.

Helen shrugged and moved about the room to arrange several candles in a circle surrounding the reading chairs by the window. After closing the blinds, Helen placed a finger to each of the candles and sparked the wicks to life.

"You've gotten better at that," Mrs. Dawson said.

"Simon is a good teacher. I still can't do it from

across the room like he does."

"Give it time."

With the candles lit, Helen clasped hands with Mrs. Dawson and shrugged. "Here goes nothing."

Mrs. Dawson closed her eyes and thought of Amber while Helen chose her words carefully.

"In this day and in this hour, we ask the Ancients for their power. Bring to me what I can't see, to help ease Amber's misery."

A familiar breeze lifted the hair on Mrs. Dawson's neck and the hair on her arms stood on end. She opened her eyes to find Helen looking around the room. Energy bounced around the space, shifting the curtains and the flames from the candles. Yet nothing else happened.

"Please."

"Are you sure we're in the right spot?" Mrs. Dawson asked.

"Yes."

The room kept up a constant buzz, not letting go of their power. It was as if the Ancients were waiting for the right request to give them what they needed.

Mrs. Dawson tried her own appeal. "In this day and in this hour, we beg the Ancients for their power. Whether from the future, present, or past, bring us the knowledge that this spot possesses."

A blinding light filled the room with a crack of lightning.

Mrs. Dawson's heart leapt and Helen let go of her hands to circle protective arms around her.

As quickly as the room exploded with noise, it stopped and silence filled every corner.

Mrs. Dawson hadn't realized she'd closed her eyes until she opened them. Her gaze fell on a lone man calmly sitting in one of the reading chairs with glasses perched on his nose and a large book tipping from his fingertips.

"Well, that was a whole lot of noise for nothing," Helen said.

"Um, dear?" Mrs. Dawson nodded behind Helen toward the man. When Helen turned around, she gasped.

****

Kincaid found Giles where he'd left him. He sat with a book in his lap, his head buried in the pages.

"Find anything?" Kincaid asked as he walked in the room and closed the door behind him. The others had gone to bed and only a small watch kept their eyes on the compound.

"Nothing about a painting of a single woman as you described. I've dug further back to see if there is any reference to it."

Disappointment filled Kincaid's heart. If anyone could find out who the woman was, it would be Giles.

Giles turned the pages in his book and delivered a brief history lesson. "You see, back in the times you just visited, tapestries were often used to record the people, the history. Only the very rich and nobility could afford portraits. And we know our ancestors were private people."

"Because they risked persecution."

"Some things don't change. The difference between then and now is that back when Druids were accused of witchcraft, they faced being murdered, burned, or beheaded. The last few hundred years we've been used as lab rats, held hostage and studied." Giles didn't need to remind him of these facts. Kincaid understood why they lived outside the normal population.

"Are you suggesting the portrait I saw was of a non-Druid woman?"

"I suppose it's possible, but I doubt it."

Kincaid leaned against the center table, crossed his arms over his chest. "There are very few unwed descendants of the MacCoinnich's through the generations leading up to the seventeen hundreds. Maybe the woman died before she could marry?"

"I thought of that." Giles turned another page, barely

25

glancing over the book to capture Kincaid's gaze. "Which is why I'm searching for the life spans of the family. The problem is, we can't be sure the family members died young, or if they traveled to a different time. We know the first time travelers were direct descendants of Ian and Lora. It's said that all their children traveled in time at one point. Duncan and Finlay were the oldest, the first to move forward in time and back again."

Kincaid knew the story well. Duncan and Finlay MacCoinnich had been instructed by the Ancient Ones to protect their world by finding Grainna, the most powerful, greedy, evil Druid ever known and stopping her from destroying every Druid and thousands of innocent lives. Most of the missions Kincaid and his men undertook also protected the lineage of this family. But none of them took them back to the time of Grainna, ever. It was hypothesized their interference might change the outcome of that final battle. They couldn't risk that Grainna would become the victor, and not the MacCoinnich's. Travel to the late fifteen hundreds was off limits. Always.

"I remember the stories, Giles. If I'm not mistaken, the middle sister married a knight."

"Right. And there is some speculation the youngest sister died in the final battle, though some reports state she survived the battle, only to die later after a long illness." Giles lifted the book in his lap. "This book has references from the first families' grandchildren. I'm searching to see if they document anything about their direct aunts and uncles."

"What happened to the youngest brother?"

"It's vague. But it could be because the family clouded themselves in secrecy, or perhaps it could be he traveled beyond their time. I'm hoping to find the answer here. If not, I'll call the Keep in the morning and request a link into their database."

Kincaid ran a hand over his face, smoothed down the hair on his chin. "I can't shake the feeling I saw that painting for a reason." And he couldn't. During their dinner, he kept picturing the woman, her eyes.

The hair on his arms stood on end.

"I'll find out who she is, Kincaid."

He turned to leave Giles to his work. "Oh, Giles...what were the names of the MacCoinnich daughters again?"

"Myra was the oldest." Kincaid glanced over his shoulder to find Giles turning pages of the book. "Amber was the youngest. The one we think died young."

Amber?

The air in the room changed with the mention of Amber's name. Kincaid's palms started to itch.

He looked over at Giles whose attention shifted from the book to the fireplace as it burst into white-hot flames. Before Kincaid could ask if Giles summoned the fire, the room rumbled and Giles—along with his book—disappeared.

Chapter Four

Amber shot up from her bed when the house shook. Very few things caused the world to upend as they just had. She paused, briefly, felt the presence of someone unfamiliar, and forced herself from her seclusion.

The pain in her head peaked as she descended the stairs. Anxiety, hers and several others in the house, assaulted her system and made her shake.

Helen and Mrs. Dawson stood in silence when Amber rushed into the library. Their eyes locked with a stranger sitting in one of Mrs. Dawson's reading chairs.

All eyes swung to her.

The man surged to his feet, the book in his lap dropped to the floor. Amber clutched the edges of her cloak and stepped back. Though she didn't think the man meant her any harm, her instinct kicked in. Every candle in the room lit, and the fireplace roared to life.

He didn't stop staring at her.

Helen pulled Mrs. Dawson beside her until the three of them stood in unity. "Who are you?" Helen asked.

The man switched his attention to Helen then back to Amber. "I-I'm Giles." He blinked a few times and reached down to pick up the book that had fallen to the floor. He waved a hand in the air, and the candles sitting on the floor blew out. He stepped over them, placed the book on a table, and proceeded to study the walls in the room. "I'm still in the fortress?"

Confusion rolled off the stranger in strong waves.

"Excuse me?" Helen asked.

"The fortress. Formerly known as Dawson's Manor. This is the library is it not?"

"Formerly known as?" Mrs. Dawson asked.

"It's been years, of course." The man moved to a bookcase, removed one of the titles, and dusted the edges of the old book. He clicked his tongue as if disappointed in the dirt. "Dust and light are a book's worst enemy," he informed them.

"Excuse me? But who the hell are you and how did you get here?" Helen stepped forward and her voice rose.

He sat the book down and removed the glasses from his nose. "I told you. I'm Giles, the keeper of the books. As for how I got here…well, you hold the answers to that. I was calmly studying, talking with a friend, and then suddenly I appeared here. I assume one of you shifted time on my behalf."

Amber's hand reached for the pendant on the chain around her neck and looked at Helen. Helen's necklace was hidden under her shirt, but she too held one of the time traveling stones.

"Did you summon him?" Amber asked Helen.

With Amber's words, Giles leveled his gaze once again to her.

Helen exchanged a look with Mrs. Dawson. "We must have."

"But you don't know who he is?"

"We were looking for a cure for you, Amber. I thought one of the books was going to fly off the shelf, not pop a man out of nowhere," Helen told her.

"Amber?" Giles asked.

"Aye."

The way the man watched her now softened. Some of the anxiety in the room eased.

He stepped in her direction and peered closer.

Amber hid under the hood of her cloak and stepped out of the man's reach. He stopped his advance as if sensing her distress.

Helen moved between the two of them. "Don't touch her."

Giles looked over Helen's shoulder. "I won't."

29

"Do you know who I am?" Amber asked.

"I'm almost afraid to ask. Can I see your face?"

Amber reached to her head and slowly removed her hood.

"You must be her."

"Must be who?"

"The woman Kincaid is searching for. Tell me, Amber…what is your surname?"

Amber searched out this man's thoughts, his feelings and didn't sense any harm could possibly come from his gentle soul. "MacCoinnich. Daughter of—"

"Lord Ian and Lady Lora," Giles said before he dropped to his knee and bowed his head. "My Lady."

Amber sighed. "That is not necessary in this century. Please rise."

He didn't rise right away and Helen shuffled her feet. "Don't see that every day."

It had been some time, but Amber was used to the gesture. "Please, Giles. 'Tis not necessary."

He stood and stepped closer. Once again, Helen intercepted. "Dude, I mean it. Don't touch her."

He lowered his eyes. "Forgive me. I never thought I'd meet any of the original family. I'm humbled…honored."

Amber pulled the hood of her cloak over her head to mute out the noise inside her head.

"You have us at a disadvantage, Mr. Giles. It appears you're comfortable in my library and have knowledge of Amber…but we know nothing of you." Mrs. Dawson indicated the sofa. "Perhaps we can get comfortable and you can tell us who you are. Where you're from."

"It's just Giles."

Amber settled into a chair to avoid sitting close to anyone in the room.

Giles sized up Mrs. Dawson. "Did you say this is your library?"

"You did say Dawson's Manor, didn't you?"

He nodded.

"I can't take credit for the naming of my home, but I am Mrs. Dawson. The library was the pride of my late husband, but it was created by the both of us."

Where Giles held himself back in reserve from Amber, he burst with enthusiasm at Mrs. Dawson's confession. "*The* Mrs. Dawson? Really?"

Mrs. Dawson caught the back of the sofa as she made her way to a chair. Giles was at her side in an instant, ready to assist her. Unlike Amber, Mrs. Dawson happily allowed him to help her. "I'm sure there are other Mrs. Dawson's out there, but I'm the only one here."

"How rich is this? Mrs. Dawson and Amber MacCoinnich both under one roof. How did I miss this in the books?" Giles shifted his gaze to Helen. "And who might you be?"

"No one, I assure you."

"Clearly you're someone. I didn't come here under my own power. I *assure* you, mine isn't that active."

Amber sensed Helen's worry about revealing information to the stranger and decided to lead the conversation instead of chase it.

"Giles?" Amber gained his attention. "Might we offer you refreshment while we sort out what transpired to bring you to us?"

"I'm good."

She turned her attention to Helen. "Can I trouble you for tea? And perhaps you can inform your husband of our guest?"

Helen's brow lifted. "Good idea. I'll be right back."

Amber calmly laced her fingers together and placed her hands in her lap.

"What year is it, exactly?" Giles asked as calmly as if he were discussing the weather.

"Two thousand and twelve," Mrs. Dawson informed him. "What year did you arrive from?"

"Twenty-two thirty-one."

"How is it possible that a man so far in the future has

31

any knowledge of me?" Amber asked.

When Giles smiled, his eyes crinkled at the corners like a lad half his age. "You're a legend, m'lady. If not for you and your family, none of us would exist. You're Druid royalty."

****

"Computer!" Kincaid shouted as he shielded himself. "Lockdown. I repeat. Lockdown!"

The computer responded, setting the alarm inside the fortress. The red strobe light flashed and the high-pitched cry of the alarm informed everyone on the compound of a breach in the security.

"Lockdown activated. Lockdown activated. This is not a drill." The computer calmly spoke in the speaker systems throughout the fortress.

Kincaid walked around the chair where Giles had been seated before he vanished. He felt the familiar zap in the air after a shift in time took place. Only Giles wasn't a traveler.

Which meant someone took him.

But who? And how?

Colleen rushed into the room, followed by Rory and Allen. All were battle-ready with weapons drawn.

Colleen assessed the room quickly, lowered her weapon. "What's going on?"

"Giles. He's gone."

Rory and Allen stiffened their spines and lowered the muzzles of their guns to the floor.

"Gone?"

"We were talking. Then the energy in the room shifted and he disappeared."

"Shifted?" Colleen asked.

"Disappeared?" Was Rory's question.

Kincaid met Rory's eyes. "He shifted in time."

Before Rory could utter a word, the room filled with half dozen other warriors.

"Giles isn't a traveler."

"Close your eyes. Smell the air," Kincaid told him. "Tell me that doesn't smell of time travel."

Rory didn't close his eyes, but the confusion around his eyes relaxed. "Holy hell."

"He's not marked," Colleen stated what everyone in the room already knew. Giles wasn't strong enough to carry the mark of a branded time traveling warrior.

"He shifted. I witnessed it with my own eyes."

Colleen twisted to address the men filling the room. "I need every traveler to gather those left behind. Rory, you and Allen congregate those here into the safe room. Colin, you and Owen spread throughout the compound with the others...inform everyone to gather and await further orders."

The men nodded and hurried from the library.

Kincaid rested his right hand on his sidearm, comfortable that it was close by. He was reminded he'd left no less than three back up weapons in his suite. *Sloppy! You're getting sloppy, Kincaid!* He scolded himself and moved about the room reaching beyond his shield to sense if the energy that shifted Giles was past or future.

Before he could narrow the energy, Colleen announced. "He's gone back."

Her gifts often scared him, and nothing scared him. "Agreed. But how?"

"Was he chanting? Reading from a book?" She moved around the room as if some bit of evidence would manifest. All the while, the strobe light blinked off and on in the room.

"Not chanting. He did possess a book. But when does Giles not have a book in his hand?" That was nothing new.

"What were you talking about?"

"The MacCoinnich's."

"The first family?"

"Yes. I asked him to research a portrait I noticed on our last journey. The paths led back to them."

From the hall, he heard several people moving quickly through the house and down the stairs.

Colleen closed her eyes and lifted her hands into the air. "The energy is strong and unlike any I've felt before."

"A strong blaze."

"No. A short, hot blaze. I don't think Giles has gone back far. Two…three hundred years at most."

How the hell does she know that? Even as the question filled his head, he knew better than to ask it. Colleen's gifts were greater than any. That was why she led them.

"Can you sense where he went?"

She hadn't yet opened her eyes. "Nowhere. He's…oh hells, he's still here. Right here."

"In the fortress?"

Colleen's lips drew into a thin line and a tiny bead of sweat rolled off her brow. "Not such a strong fortress. The bands aren't secure, which is why he easily slid through." Then, without warning, Colleen opened her eyes and shook her head. "It's gone."

So was Giles. But at least they knew he was still in the house. How difficult could searching back two or three hundred years be?

Chapter Five

Nervous anticipation ran like fire ants up and down Giles's spine. He was rooted into the seat he'd been offered and didn't dare move. Amber MacCoinnich, *in the flesh*, watched from beneath her hooded cloak. The lady was ill—that was plain to see from the ashen color of her skin to the dark circles beneath her eyes. Even still, she was more beautiful than Kincaid suggested. Giles had a million questions but didn't dare ask any.

The young woman who'd protected Amber from his touch had asked that they not begin to unravel how Giles had come to be in the twenty-first century until after her husband returned.

"How does my library change through the years?" Mrs. Dawson asked, obviously making small talk while waiting for the man of the house to arrive.

What surprised Giles was how few people were in the home now. Such little protection for the women was a grave mistake.

"The shelves surrounding the fireplace are the very same. The others have been remodeled and more are added to hold the growing collection. I believe that wall..." He pointed to the wall behind Amber, "is pushed back, making the room larger."

"And you're the librarian?"

Giles smiled into the thought. "I suppose you can call me that. I'm the fortress historian and am called upon often to search out a particular time or genealogy."

"How fascinating," Mrs. Dawson said. "I would think computers and those electronic book things would make these old books obsolete."

"They are. But some work shouldn't be translated

into a computer where anyone could hack and collect the data. A keeper of the books, that would be me, has been a part of this library since…well, since you."

Mrs. Dawson shook her head. "You're mistaken about that. I may own these books, but I have very little knowledge about most of them. I haven't even attempted to collect more since Mr. Dawson passed away."

Giles knew for a fact that the books never stopped growing in numbers. Many of the tomes were spread among the safe houses in the world, but their point of origin was right here in Dawson's Manor.

From the front of the house, he heard a heavy door slam against a wall, instantly bringing Giles to his feet.

Before he could move more than a foot, a massive man filled the doorway. His stony expression and sheer bulk made Giles's heart kick in his chest. Now *this* was a warrior. Giles stood no chance in battle against a man this size, and there was no telling if he held Druid blood.

"Simon, please," Amber whimpered. "This man means us no harm."

"Are you sure, lass?"

"Positive. He is from the future and is Druid. Now please, calm yourself so I might be able to hear what he has to say before I am forced to retreat. Your fear is unfounded."

"I don't *fear* him."

"No, you fear for us. You can see we are unharmed." Amber lifted a pale hand to her head.

Giles pushed past his comfort and extended a hand to the warrior. "I'm Giles," he told Simon. "Your wife and Mrs. Dawson somehow summoned me."

Simon hesitated, but then clasped Giles's hand. His strong grip was painful, as if to remind him he could snap him if necessary, not that this man needed to do anything other than walk in the room to prove that.

"Helen?" Simon addressed his wife. "What have you done?"

36

Giles backed into the couch and waited to hear what Helen had done.

Simon didn't sit. Instead, he took up the space beside his wife while she explained.

"Mrs. Dawson was searching inside a few books...looking for a cure for Amber. I attempted to find the right book with my gift. I sensed something by the windows, but found nothing. We requested help from the Ancients and Giles appeared."

"And you know a cure for Amber?" Simon asked.

"I don't know what is ailing the lady. But perhaps I can help. I do have extensive knowledge of the books in this library and many others. I'd be honored to help if I can."

He turned to look in Amber's direction. "What's making you sick, m'lady?"

She drew in a long-suffering breath. "My gift. I'm an empath. Since the day we destroyed Grainna, my powers have grown to the point of crippling my movement...my life. My mother foresaw my death in our time and sent me here to protect me. Only this is no better. Though I don't share my mother's ability to see the future, I know I don't have long in this world as I am."

"Don't say that," Helen scolded her.

Amber lifted her soulful gaze to Helen. "I'm not trying to frighten you. I'm stating a fact. I know my death is inevitable. I would have returned to my family to die at home, but their pain would be too great for me to bear as my last thoughts. Selfishly I must stay here where only the three of you will suffer the pain. For that I'm sorry."

Giles would have liked to offer reassurance, but all his books pointed to the fact Amber did die young.

Simon rested a hand on his wife's shoulder as he addressed Giles, "The Ancients brought you to us, so you must hold the answers."

"I've never heard of any Druid dying because of their gift. Quite the opposite. But then there has never been a

37

presence as dark as Grainna who needed to be defeated. Didn't it take your entire clan to destroy her?"

"Aye."

Giles stood and started to pace the room. "It's been told that when one Druid destroys another the surviving soul can absorb the powers of the other."

"Only if the Druid is dark. Amber isn't," Helen reminded them.

"My powers increased, but not the way Amber's did," Simon said.

Giles stared at Simon with renewed interest. "Which MacCoinnich are you?" Could he actually be in the presence of two original family members?

"My mother is Liz. Elizabeth MacCoinnich."

"You're Finlay's son?"

"Yes. Adoptive, but Fin is my father."

Giles scratched his head. "The books don't speak of an adopted son."

Simon shrugged. "I was born in this century to my mother. We both traveled back in time."

"The books aren't clear, but I always thought there were some connections made through time travel."

"While the refresher on the family tree is fascinating, can we get back to saving Amber's life?" Helen's voice cracked as she spoke. "The Ancients aren't known to drop arbitrary people into our laps without a purpose. You must know something useful."

"Right!" Giles crossed the room to the book he'd been studying when he'd slipped in time. "I was searching this book for references to you, Amber. There are some passages in here from your family's children, and their children."

"Why me?"

"Kincaid asked that I search for the name behind a portrait he noticed on one of his travels. He'd not seen it before."

"Kincaid?" Amber's soft voice asked.

38

"Yeah." Giles stopped flipping pages and straightened his shoulders. "Did you by chance sit for a painting? One with your hair down and without the robe you're wearing?"

"Aye. Last season. The portrait hangs on the wall in my parents' chambers."

"Seems I found the answer to Kincaid's question, but not to yours." Could the Ancients have brought him to this time because of his question and not to save Amber? Or was there more to learn from the old leather-bound pages?

"Let me help." Helen jumped up from her chair and placed her hands over the book. "Show me!" she whispered.

Without warning, the book opened, slamming the cover to the table, and the pages within flipped, paused, and started flipping again.

Giles spotted the page numbers as the book paused every few chapters before moving on. When the end of the book was reached, the book closed and slid across the table, catching Giles across his thighs.

They all stood perfectly still and said nothing. And then Mrs. Dawson chuckled. "I do believe that was a magical slap," she declared. "Seems you have some reading to do, Giles."

Giles lifted the book, felt the energy around it snap against his fingertips.

"I suppose you're right."

"I think I'll retire." Amber slowly walked to the door and offered him a smile. "Thank you in advance for searching for answers, Mr. Giles."

"I won't sleep until I've found a cure." He wouldn't.

Once her retreating footfalls were no longer heard, Simon turned his attention toward him. "How do you like your coffee?"

Coffee? Real coffee? Perhaps this century had its perks after all. "Black."

****

39

"Can we follow him?" Rory asked

"We could try, but we might be running into a trap. Whoever did this is powerful," Colin said.

They met in the basement safe room while Sybil and Mathew searched the compound looking for breaks in the wards they'd placed to protect those inside.

"But Colleen feels he hasn't left the house. How can we be falling into a trap if he's still inside these walls?"

"How did he shift time? He's not marked and he wasn't in any of the portals." Kincaid absently rubbed his left arm where his mark had been etched into his skin like a tattoo over a decade ago. Only warriors, and strong ones at that, were chosen to shift time. Kincaid's ability to take others with him made him more valuable than most.

"He was summoned," Colleen said with absolute conviction. "The path of energy sought him out."

"Are you sure, Lena?" Only Colin got away with calling his sister by her pet name.

She nodded once then directed her attention to Kincaid. "You were talking about the first family."

"Yes. And Giles was searching for information about the youngest daughter. He thinks hers was the portrait I saw on the wall of the Keep."

From the stairwell, Sybil and Mathew jogged down to join them.

"Well?"

"Everything is secure. There was a breach over the library when we arrived." Mathew glanced at Sybil.

"Did you mend it?"

Sybil shook her head. "We didn't need to. It mended itself."

Her announcement took everyone by surprise.

"I don't like this!" Colin shoved out of his chair. "Someone, or something, reached its hand into our fortress, snatched Giles, and covered its path? Who is that powerful?"

A name threatened to burst from Kincaid's lips, but

he kept it to himself. Grainna was long dead. "Can you trace Giles, Colleen? Narrow the timeframe?"

"I might. Then what? Do we send a team to retrieve him? We can't afford to lose warriors."

Kincaid shook his head. "No. You send me and me alone."

Rory huffed out a breath. "Don't be ridiculous."

"I'm not. I can keep anyone and everyone in this room from touching me, and I alone can bring Giles back without the aid of a portal. Can you do that, Rory?"

He and Rory had fought side by side for years. He understood the other man's concern, but no one in the room could boast Kincaid's unique ability to retrieve Giles. Bringing others would certainly open them up for loss, a loss Colleen pointed out they could ill afford.

"I hate to agree, but Kincaid is right. If Giles was removed to trap us, the play will be on them when we send our immortal," Colin said.

"He's not immortal," Rory reminded them. "Just cocky."

Kincaid felt a rare smile on his lips. "You're just jealous."

"Bloody ass." Rory's expression hardened but he didn't argue more.

"It's agreed then," Colin said. "Colleen will trace the flow of energy. Kincaid, you should rest until we have a lock on Giles. We'll go from lockdown to high alert and schedule more scouts on watch. Any objections?"

Kincaid systematically met the eyes of all the warriors; each one gave a nod, and lastly Rory grunted his approval.

Up in his room, Kincaid set out a fresh uniform and checked his weapons for charge. With everything set for a twenty second recovery, he stripped and forced himself to lie in bed. He stared at the ceiling and felt his natural defenses shield him. He pushed the unease of his pending solo journey from his mind and attempted to sleep.

When he closed his eyes, he saw her...the woman in the portrait. He tried to shake her image and found a dull pain settling behind his brow.

****

The women had all gone to bed, and Giles sat at the desk trying to make sense of what he read. Each passage indicated different people, different unions. None of them talked of powers or illness. The more he read the more frustrated he became.

Simon returned with another pot of coffee, which Giles couldn't help but accept. Though he knew at some point, the caffeine would probably leave him in a heap on the couch, who knew when he'd ever have the opportunity to drink the real stuff again in such quantities.

"Find anything?" Simon asked.

Giles pushed his fingers beneath his glasses and rubbed his tired eyes. "Nothing that makes any sense. It reads like a bible. This couple begot these children. These children begot these. I understood about the strong family bonds long before now. I see no reason this information is important or how it might help serve Amber."

"Is it a complete family tree?"

"Not hardly. There are generations with very little information. Missing links and names that changed with marriage. I even added an entry or two after I had learned of a branch that wasn't represented in the pages."

"From other books?"

"No, no...from the warriors. When they return, they sometimes have intel that helps fill in some of the pages."

"You've spoke of these warriors. Who are they?" As the hour grew late, Giles could hear the thick Scottish accent fill Simon's tongue. With Amber, it was simply there. With Simon, it was as if he was readapting to his new time and slipping in and out of the brogue.

"I'm not sure how much I should tell you. I'd hate to change the course of the future by saying something vital."

"A little late for that, don't you think? Besides, the

Ancients wouldn't have assisted you into this time if they didn't want you here."

"You really think the Ancients had a hand in this?"

"Who else?"

Giles couldn't imagine. "The Ancient power is so seldom talked about in my time. I've doubted it existed."

"Who do you think guide us then? The moon?"

"It's hard to believe in something you've never seen with your own eyes. So few people have any faith in a higher power in my time. Oh, they may say they do, but do they truly believe it? No."

Simon sat forward, leaned on his elbows, and lowered his voice. "The Ancients are real, second only to God. I have seen their power, witnessed them...as has Amber."

Giles swallowed and felt Simon's words soak into him. He shivered in the warm room.

"They brought you here, and I for one will learn everything I can from you. I have sworn to protect Amber and, so far, have only been able to stand by and watch her deteriorate toward a slow painful death. You may not see exactly what the Ancients want you to see because you're not looking hard enough...or because you don't believe they hold the answers. Lora would never have sent Amber to this time if the answer to her survival was anywhere else. I have to believe we will find a way to save her. She did not survive Grainna only to die now."

Simon's hard stare made the coffee sit like a stone in his gut.

"Now, let me ask you again. Who are these warriors and what is it they do?"

Chapter Six

Kincaid stood among his peers who all held expressions of doubt and concern. Unless they were traveling to retrieve another branded warrior, none of them had journeyed in time alone. Ever. Safety in numbers and all that...

He couldn't say for sure if any of those in the room held any blood relation, yet Kincaid considered each of them a brother...a sister. They were his family and had been since his father abandoned him. Leaving them was the only thing about the trip that bothered him.

What was he worried about? He'd find Giles, grab him, and bring him back.

"You have the path?" Kincaid asked Colleen. The blank expression on her face would have troubled him if he wasn't used to her stoic exterior.

"I have *a* path."

He peered closer.

She blinked twice.

What are you not telling me?

"I don't like this!" Rory said.

"We heard you the first time." Owen shoved the other man's shoulder as he spoke.

"Give me one good reason two of us can't go."

Colleen responded to Rory while never losing eye contact with Kincaid. "The loss of two warriors is twice as hard as the loss of one."

Kincaid swallowed. Not that he feared for his life. He didn't.

Colleen on the other hand, did. That was obvious.

The air in the room hung heavy, like a thick fog threatening the shore for weeks on end. Kincaid cut through it, met the eyes of his brothers, and ignored his rising heartbeat.

"Destiny is not something one can avoid," he said and, because he felt it deep in his soul, he told them, "I *will* see you again."

"Fuck!" Rory mumbled under his breath.

"Until then." Kincaid focused on Rory, met his green-eyed gaze. "Until then."

He turned toward Colleen and saw the blue aura surrounding her. From it, he saw one tiny strand. When he focused, he noticed it turn red, then white-hot. That was his path…his destiny.

"Are you ready?" she asked.

He nodded.

Then, as if he wasn't already uneasy with his solo journey, Colleen, who never smiled, offered a half-ass grin.

The energy of her power and his circled around him as he focused on the white strand that would lead him where he needed to be.

The lids of his eyes started to drift closed so he could remove everything except the single thought of his path, but then Colleen's rapt attention forced his eyes to hers. Beyond her, he saw a white light in the form of a woman. Her hair flowed down well past her hips, her soft glow welcomed him into her warmth. The woman opened her lips and spoke, but it was Colleen's voice he heard. "You cannot change who you are…but you can shape who you will be."

Before Kincaid could utter one syllable the world around him dropped away.

The familiar shift in time was a comfort. He remembered the first time, the exhilaration, the way the light flashed around him like a vortex, and the way the shift shoved his stomach up somewhere near his neck. He swallowed it down then and didn't even feel it now. The weightless feeling was nothing more than falling into a body of water after a high dive. No fear. No worries. He would land as he always did, alert and ready to battle or observe.

He felt the pull of his exit approaching and waited until the last second.

He jumped and found himself slammed back into the vortex, falling.

What the hell?

The ink in his arm sparked hot and he kept falling. Without thought, he attempted to jump again and ended up on his ass in the shift.

Instinctively, he shielded himself and waited. The journey wasn't letting him go. He knew he'd flown past Giles and his intended target, but he was powerless to stop.

The world stilled, briefly and the shore of a rocky cliff came into focus. There, he witnessed two teenage boys kicking water and a young woman lifting her heavy skirts, joining them in the fun.

Before he could smell the salt air, the world shifted again. He landed between the dark shadows of stone walls. There stood a clan...men and women alike. They held hands with one focus. The youngest, the young woman from the beach with her dark hair swept over her brow...her eyes shot like daggers across the room.

When Kincaid managed to look away, he lost his ability to breathe. The world dipped again.

On some level, he realized he was being shown a series of events, but he couldn't process any of them before he saw another scene.

He was in the Keep. Felt the familiar walls as if it were his own bedroom. The turret where he and his men had last been wrapped around him like a blanket. Only this time the blanket had a hood and he couldn't see past the folds of material.

Nausea built in the back of his throat in hot waves.

"Enough!" he yelled to anyone listening.

He slid faster than he'd ever before and slammed onto

the floor. Birds chirped in his head as the world came to a crashing halt.

"Oh, shit!"

Kincaid heard the shout through his fall, rolled onto his shoulder, and came up on the balls of his feet with his blaster in his hand.

Feet away sat a man with a primitive weapon pointed directly at him. To the man's right, a bottle tilted on its side. The smell of hops and barley filled the air.

"Who are you?" Kincaid demanded.

The man inched his finger toward the trigger of his weapon. "You just dropped into my living room. Who the fuck are you?"

He didn't release the man's attention. Flat screen TV, not a vid scan or halo projection. Not the tube type either. Leather chair, not the synthetic fabric of the twenty-second century. The air felt cool...artificially cold. *Wow, is that Freon?*

Kincaid had never been in this century, avoided it like a rampant case of Pox. Grainna lived in this century...at one point or another. For that, he felt his heart beat reach dangerous proportions.

He stood to his full height, felt his shield like the invisible armor that it was.

"Freeze, Mother Fucker."

Kincaid made nice, lowered his weapon, and lifted his hands. "I come in peace."

His adversary squared his shoulders and gave a curt laugh. "You've watched too much late night television."

Actually, he only watched the news. Which he had to admit was late at night. But he didn't think that was what the man was referring to.

"Who are you?" he asked again.

Kincaid narrowed his eyes. "Does it matter? I just dropped into your living room. Does that happen to you often?"

The man's jaw twitched and Kincaid grinned. His

ease of the situation told him he'd seen the like before.

"Damn Druids. Life was easier when I only had to deal with drug dealers and lowlifes."

The nausea that rolled in his gut, now settled and Kincaid released a rare laugh.

"It's not funny. Damn good thing my kids are with the ex. This would have put them on the therapy couch for years."

The man's weapon now pointed toward the ground.

Kincaid took a chance, lowered his shield far enough to extend a hand. "I'm Kincaid. From the future. I'm looking for a friend."

His unexpected host glared at his offered hand. "He's not here."

"I can see that. But you must know where he is, or I wouldn't have been brought to you."

The man released the cock of his gun, holstered it, and rolled his eyes. "Just when I thought life was going to get back to normal." He took Kincaid's hand, shook it hard once. "I'm Jake. Jake Nelson."

Through a hooded gaze, Kincaid observed Jake Nelson as he moved about his home, switching off his television set and snatching an old phone from a cradle. He punched in a series of numbers and held the devise up to his ear.

"Who are you calling?"

Jake held up his palm as he spoke into the phone. "Hello, Matilda."

Matilda?

"Don't you wish! No. I have a…visitor. Someone I think you should meet."

Jake paused again and huffed out a laugh. "No. His weapons look scary but for all I know they're toys."

Kincaid was half tempted to shoot the old TV into tiny pieces of dust to demonstrate the power of future firearms. He didn't. Seemed Jake was having a pointed conversation with someone who knew about Druids. From

Jake's relaxed state, so was he. "Hey! You're the one who moved across the country and told me to call you if anyone showed up. Someone showed up, Selma. So wipe the green shit off your face and get your skinny ass over here. I'm paid to put away crap from this time, not deal with nomads from the future."

I'm not a nomad. I have a cause...dammit!

"Drive your broom or twinkle your nose...or hey, take the bus, just get here." Jake hung up the phone and crossed his arms over his chest. "You know...you guys need to develop a warning bell or something. You're bound to give a guy a heart attack."

Kincaid was tempted to crack a smile. The man reminded him of Rory, even looked like him a little now that he thought about it. Same dark hair, same eyes.

"I would have knocked if I knew how," Kincaid told him. "I take it you've had visitors before."

"Round about. I've seen more shit in the last couple of years than I can explain." Jake nodded toward Kincaid's weapon. "That thing work?"

Impulsively, he moved the hip where he held his blaster away from the man. "It works."

"Fire projectiles?"

He shook his head. "Not bullets, if that's what you mean." Instead of elaborating, Kincaid glanced around the room trying to pinpoint the time in which he'd landed. "What year is it?"

Jake narrowed his eyes. "You don't know?"

Kincaid hesitated, unsure of how much to reveal. "Who has *visited* you in the past?"

"What year are you from?"

The two of them stared each other down...asking questions and not giving answers.

He lifted his own personal shield and prepared to wait the other man out.

****

Selma Mayfair twisted her fingers around the phone

49

receiver and cursed Jake Nelson...again. The man aggravated her from the top of her head to the very tip of her polished toes. At least he called her and not his colleagues at the police station. She'd have to give him that. Apparently, he was going to keep the oath he made to the MacCoinnich's. And the one he gave to his ex-partner, Todd, who was happily married and living in the sixteenth century with Myra and their bushel of kids.

Hitting speed dial, Selma waited through the rings until someone at Mrs. Dawson's picked up.

"Hello?"

"Hey, Helen...it's Selma."

"Hey there. How are you settling in?"

Selma had relocated to the west coast after Simon returned to the twenty-first century. She'd met Liz, Simon's mom, less than two years ago, and felt it was her responsibility to stay close to the only two MacCoinnichs living in her century. Before meeting Liz, Selma thought herself a witch, hence Jake's catty comments about flying brooms and green faces. Now she understood her heritage was deeply rooted in Druid blood. To those around her, she was still witchy Selma, which suited her fine. No one would think anything of her lighting candles and casting spells.

"I'm unpacked but the car is still in the shop. It really didn't like the long drive."

"Cars are picky sometimes."

"Listen, I just got a call from Jake. Seems someone *popped in* unexpectedly."

Helen sighed. "Popped in?"

"He wanted me to come over and check out his futuristically dressed visitor. I thought maybe Simon could come along."

"Friend or foe?"

"Hard to say. You know Jake. He's not exactly warm and friendly."

"I don't know, Selma. He's always been nice to me."

She snorted. "That makes one of us."

"Hold on…" Through the phone, Selma heard Helen tell Simon about Jake's visitor. When she got back on the line she said, "He's on his way now to pick you up."

"Good. I didn't want to go alone. How's Amber?"

"Not so good. We have to figure out something to shelter her. Every day she grows weaker. She hasn't even left her room today."

They talked for several minutes in joint misery over Amber's plight before hanging up. There wasn't anything they alone could do. It would take intervention from someone outside their circle, and they had a rather powerful circle.

Simon arrived within twenty minutes, idling his two-door Audi R8 in the drive.

Selma felt dwarfed at Simon's side. The man was built for the Highlands and barely fit behind the wheel of his fancy car. "What did Jake tell you?"

"Just that he had an unexpected guest. One from the future."

"Did Helen tell you about Giles?"

Selma shook her head. "Who's Giles?"

"A visitor from the future. We think he may be able to find something for Amber."

"Helen didn't say anything over the phone." The freeway was relatively free of traffic as they wove through the cars en route to Jake's place in the valley.

"She's convinced all telephone calls are monitored. Seems the government has stopped asking permission to tap calls, lately."

Selma would like to disagree, but she couldn't. Everything fell under the guise of national security, and the public didn't put up much of a fight as their liberties were slowly being stripped away…for their own good of course. Or so the elected officials told them.

"You think Giles and this visitor are linked?"

"Might be. No way to know for sure until we meet

this guy."

She grabbed hold of the dash as Simon took an off ramp at high speed.

Two blocks away from Jake's house, Simon pulled over and started to remove his shirt.

Selma tried not to stare while Simon instructed her about what he wanted her to do. "We need to find out if this guy is looking for Giles...for Amber...for me. We can't take any chances that we're bringing an enemy into the house. It doesn't make sense he'd end up at Jake's. Unless he can't control his time travel."

They both knew those who couldn't control their time travel couldn't be trusted.

"Giles told me about warriors from the future. Men and women...all Druid, who weave in and out of time to protect the family, our secrets. But there are others, too, who attempt to undo what these warriors protect." One of his shoes hit the floor followed by the other.

"More Grainnas out there?"

Simon's jaw tightened. "None as powerful. But it seems Giles and his people keep those who wish to be like her from gaining power."

"There's good and evil with every race. I guess it's too much to ask for all Druids to get along."

Simon reached for his jeans.

"Hey!" Selma shot a hand in the air. "What are you doing?"

He stopped his hand at his zipper and delivered a dimpled grin. "I'm going in with you, but you'll do all the talking. Ask this guy who he is, who his people are...why he's here. I'll determine if he's telling the truth."

Then, without removing his pants, Simon winked and shifted form. A small flash of light illuminated his body and before Selma could say abracadabra, a four legged fur ball climbed out of Simon's jeans and jumped in her lap with a loud meow.

Selma knew he was a shifter, but she'd never seen

him shift in person. "Wow!"

Cat-Simon meowed again.

Without thought, Selma gave his head a pat. "Can you understand me?"

A strange sense of crazy washed over her when Simon nodded and nudged her hand toward the door.

"Here goes nothing."

She stepped out of the car and lifted Simon into her arms. "I'll let you down when I get inside," she told him. "Cats don't follow people."

Simon meowed again when she rapped on Jake's door a few seconds later.

Jake flung open the door and met her eyes. She tried to ignore the skip of her heartbeat every time she saw the man. Didn't matter how good looking he was, he was an arrogant ass most of the time.

"'Bout time you got here. Who's this?" he asked looking at Simon.

"Every *witch* needs a cat," she said as she pushed past him and into the house.

Simon scratched her arm and she instantly let him go.

"So, where's this visitor?"

Chapter Seven

So this is the cop's Druid back up? Kincaid attempted a smile, knew it wasn't his strong point, and decided to drop the act.

He let his eyes travel over the petite woman who couldn't be much more than five feet five...he noted her spiky heels and decided she was closer to five feet two. Her curly red hair exploded from a clip and framed her freckled nose. Her green eyes and the hand on her hip told him she either had Irish or Scottish blood running thick in her veins.

"So you're future-boy?" She directed her sarcastic question his way, sweeping a glance over his frame, and dismissed him with a tiny shake of her head. "Must not be very powerful if you're carrying all that firepower on your hip."

She talked big, but he couldn't tell by just looking at her if she could back up her words with a set of powers of her own. He felt a tremor of power in the room, but with his shield up he couldn't tell how strong it was.

"It's never good to show all your cards," he told her.

The cat she brought in circled her feet for a few seconds before disappearing behind the couch.

"Well, future-boy...who are you and why are you here?"

Jake stood beside her, his arms crossed over his chest.

"I'm Kincaid. I'm here searching for a friend."

"Who?"

His first instinct was to hold his tongue. He did and the room grew silent.

"Not going to tell me?"

"I have no idea if I can trust you," he stated the

obvious.

"And we don't know if we can trust you. The time travelers I've met all knew when and where they were going. They didn't end up in a random location."

She had him there. "What's your name, Irish?"

"Half Irish, half Scot."

Beside her Jake huffed out a laugh. "And half witch."

She rolled her eyes. "Selma Mayfair."

"Selma?" The name tickled his memory and then he realized why. "A direct descendant of Elizabeth and Finlay."

The snarky expression fell from her face. Obviously, she had no knowledge of her very distant heritage. Lucky for him, Giles traced several names down and Selma was used in every generation for centuries.

The cat circled his legs and snarled at the barrier of his shield.

"My parents aren't Liz and Fin."

"I didn't say they were. I said descendant. But since you've used Elizabeth and Finlay's familiar names, I assume you know who I'm talking about."

The cat bumped up against him again. Instead of letting the cat bring attention to his shield, he allowed the feline to move closer. The small lift of his protection brought on a wave of power that stole his breath.

"Listen, Kincaid...you need to start trusting me here. Start talking. Who are you looking for?"

He shifted on the balls of his feet and felt a snap in the air. *Was that Selma?*

"Before I tell you anything, I need to know what you know about Liz and Fin."

Jake took a step forward. "Listen, asshole...you came to us—"

The other man didn't finish his sentence before the space inside his shield expanded and sparked. Within a blink of an eye, the cat at his feet shifted and Kincaid found his neck in the tight grip of a very large, very naked warrior. His angry eyes and set jaw told Kincaid he'd have no problem snapping him in two.

Jesus...a shifter. That's rare.

"Elizabeth is my mother, Finlay my father...now answer the lass. Who are you looking for?"

Kincaid stared into the eyes of a MacCoinnich. A man he was sworn to protect. "Giles," he choked out.

The grip on his throat eased.

"Who is this Giles to you?"

"He's a librarian." If the man holding him was anyone other than a MacCoinnich, Kincaid would have him at arm's length. Instead of engaging a fight, he calmly answered this man's questions. "He's a friend."

"*What* are you?"

The question would have sounded odd to an outsider, but to Kincaid it was about rank. "I'm a warrior. A branded warrior."

The hand holding him eased now, but it hadn't slid away from his neck.

"One last question, Kincaid. What were you and Giles speaking of when he disappeared?"

He narrowed his eyes, stared directly into those watching him. "We were talking about a portrait of a woman."

The hand at his neck fell away. With the connection broken, Kincaid's shield shot up. Not that he worried this man would harm him now. Still, he'd take no chances.

"I take it his story checks out?" Jake said behind them.

"Ah, Simon?" Selma said. "Much as I like the peep show, I think it's kinda creepy that I'm no longer guessing what you wear under your kilt."

Jake grunted. "You don't *have* to look."

"Like you'd divert your eyes if a hot chick was standing here naked. Such a hypocrite."

"You're Simon MacCoinnich?" Kincaid asked.

"Aye."

From behind him, Jake handed Simon a throw from his sofa. He wrapped it around his waist.

"And you know where Giles is?"

"Aye."

This was going to be easier than he originally thought. "Then you can take me to him and we'll return to our time."

Simon looked between the couple standing behind them and back. "No."

"Excuse me?" The hair in Kincaid's neck stood up.

"I'll take you to Giles, but he will not return until a cure has been found."

"A cure for what?"

Simon didn't smile, didn't reveal any emotion at all. "To save the life of the woman in the portrait."

The hair on Kincaid's arms joined that of his neck. "She's here?"

"Aye. Amber's here. Come." Simon started for the door wearing a blanket.

"Wait," Selma stopped him. "How am I going to get home? Your car only seats two."

Simon glanced at Jake.

Jake grunted. "Fine. And Kincaid...if you walk around like that in two thousand and twelve you're going to get hauled in to the nearest police station."

Kincaid glanced at the strap on his hip holding his blaster, noted the long blade on his back and another side arm on his leg.

Jake stepped forward, lifted his hand. "I can hold them for you."

He stood back. "I don't think so."

Jake shrugged. "Can't blame me for trying. Where are your clothes, Simon? You walk out like that and people will think I'm having a damn orgy in here or something."

Selma laughed.

He pointed an accusing finger her way. "Enough from you."

Five minutes later Kincaid climbed into a gas powered vehicle and sped through a vaguely familiar town.

The airway was free of traffic, but the ground was car to car. Simon maneuvered through the city, shifting between other cars. "Looks different to you?"

"More than you can imagine."

Simon huffed a laugh. "I grew up in the sixteenth century. I can imagine a lot."

Kincaid watched the other man's profile. "Why are you here? In this century?"

"Two reasons. My wife and Amber."

"Is Amber really dying?"

"Yes. Faster every day."

"What from?" His insides grew cold as he spoke.

"Her gift. She's empathic." Simon spared him a glance then returned his eyes to the road. "She'll sense us before we reach the city limit. That shield you use...can you cloak your thoughts, feelings?"

"I can."

"Good. Do so. She doesn't need to feel anything from you. With Giles in the house she's been driven to her bedroom."

"Why is she so sensitive? The empaths I've met—"

"None of the empaths you've met did battle with Grainna. Amber has and, without a strong filter, she's unable to cope with the growing power."

Kincaid thought of the haunted eyes in the portrait he'd seen. Now he understood the emotion behind the expression. It was as if the woman had given up all hope. That would certainly kill her...sooner than later.

They exited a highway and the familiar landscape sharpened. "We're going to the fortress."

"It's only a house. A big house, but a house."

They rounded what would eventually be the opening to the compound. There weren't any walls, no protection. "Who lives in these homes?"

Simon glanced to his right, then left. "Neighbors."

"You haven't obtained the properties, yet?"

"What do you mean?"

Damn...when had Dawson's Manner expanded? He thought it was before the turn of the century. Apparently not. "All of this," he said, waving his hand around, "is part of the compound in the future. Beyond the walls of the fortress is a barrier of wards protecting all who live within."

"Like I said. It's just a house. Only a few of us live there. It's hard enough for Amber with neighbors a few blocks away."

No wonder Simon was so careful. He was virtually alone in his quest to keep those in the fortress safe. "The future isn't bright, Simon. All these homes need to be obtained and walls need to go up. This should be one of your main priorities."

"Should you be telling me this?"

"If not me, who? I'm not the only Druid who can travel in time."

"You're talking about the others...the ones Giles warned me about."

Worry shivered up Kincaid's spine. "Lethal bastards who will search a trail of energy to find you and your family. Change the path of time as you know it."

"Change time?"

Kincaid ran a hand through his hair. "Yes. Some caught word of Grainna and want to stop her from ever being destroyed. Others simply want your power to enhance their own. With only two of you in this time...you're vulnerable."

"Grainna is dead."

"But what if any part of her journey to death was altered? I'm a warrior, Simon. I have fought by your ancestors' sides my whole life. They haven't known we were there, but we've stopped the others from changing time more than once."

"You've been to MacCoinnich Keep?"

"Many times. After your time and in my own time."

"It's still there now?"

Kincaid wanted to laugh, but didn't. "Of course it's still there. Cloaked and hidden from the eyes of many, but it's very much still standing."

Simon shook his head. "Then why weren't we sent there to live? Why here?"

"That I don't know."

Simon gripped the steering wheel hard. "Now's a good time to hide your thoughts. Amber doesn't need to worry about what's going on in your head."

"And who will cloak your thoughts?"

When Simon didn't answer, Kincaid knew he couldn't, and that Amber would suffer the knowledge and worry of her cousin.

****

The soup Helen had brought Amber earlier was now stone cold and untouched.

Downstairs she felt Helen and Mrs. Dawson's pain. They knew it was nearly time for her to leave this world. Even though Simon was far away, she felt him inside her, too. His anger rose with the thought of her life washing away like a tide and removing all evidence of her existence.

Amber clutched the edges of the sink in an effort to hold herself upright. In the mirror, a reflection stared back at her. The dark circles under her eyes and distinctive cheekbones were a living testament of her failing health. The heat billowing inside Amber's head grew to an impossible girth. Her fevered skin should have left her flushed. Instead, she was sheet-white and appeared to have been drained of all her life-blood. In the center of her chest, her heartbeat sped too fast, making her gasp for air. Around her neck was a sacred stone centered in a necklace that could take her back to her family. In a moment of weakness, she scraped a razor against her finger and placed it on the stone. She didn't want to die here. She wanted her mother and father at her side.

A lone tear fell as she placed her bleeding finger on her necklace and closed her eyes. Maybe she wouldn't make the trip. At least she'd know her parents could place her next to her ancestors and mourn her properly.

They would survive. They always did.

A shuddering breath left her burning lungs and she began her chant. "In this day and in this hour…"

Light glazed the back of her eyes and the bathroom started to spin.

Her last thought before her body hit the floor was, *'Tis over.*

****

At least there's a gate around the main house. Kincaid couldn't believe the lack of security for the Manor. He felt no magical wards protecting the house, the property. *How can this be?*

Simon pressed a button and killed the engine.

Kincaid stepped from the car and stared up at the familiar fortress. The landscape had changed, and the house itself wasn't as large as in his time. Yet it still felt like home.

The front door of the home hit the wall and a petite woman ran down the stairs, ignoring him, and franticly screamed at Simon.

Tears ran down her face as Simon caught her. "What is it, lass?"

"It's Amber. She collapsed. I can't wake her, Simon…I can't wake her."

Simon ran toward the house, Kincaid followed. His stomach turned stone-cold. Were they too late? The walls of the home shot past him as he took the stairs three at a time, keeping pace with MacCoinnich. They spiraled up, turned down a hall, and ended up at his bedroom door. Or it was his bedroom in the future.

Simon skidded to a halt and entered the room at a

slower pace.

Kincaid took in the scene slowly. An old woman sat in a chair on the opposite side of the bed from where Simon knelt. The woman who'd informed Simon of Amber's state hugged the banister of the bed and cried. The only familiar face in the room was Giles. Kincaid met his eyes and he nodded to the woman lying on the bed.

Dressed in a nightgown he'd only seen several hundred years back in time, Amber MacCoinnich had the complexion of Sleeping Beauty and a slow pace of breathing that couldn't sustain her for much longer. The long dark hair framed her head and fell past her waist. Even under the sunken eyes and drawn features, her beauty was unmatchable.

Simon touched the side of her forehead, which had a trickling of blood. "What happened?" he asked.

"I heard a noise and ran in. She was in the bathroom on the floor."

Simon lifted her thin hand and placed his lips to the back of it. "Don't leave us, Amber. We'll find a cure."

Kincaid wasn't sure they could find a cure fast enough. For some reason, the thought of this woman dying before he could see the color of her eyes made him ill. He nodded toward Giles and indicated the hall.

Giles stepped around the woman at the foot of the bed and started toward the door.

"You're not going anywhere, Kincaid," Simon demanded.

MacCoinnich didn't need to spend these last hours with his family worrying about him. Kincaid said the only thing he could to put the man at ease. "I will see this through, Simon. You have my word."

Content with that, Simon turned back to the bed.

"Am I glad to see you," Giles said once they were out of earshot of the others.

"What do you know?" Kincaid asked.

"Is that the woman from the portrait?"

"Yes."

"Well, it's safe to say something forced me here to find her. They're desperate to save her life."

"I can see that."

"Do you know who she is?"

Kincaid tasted her name on his lips again. "Amber MacCoinnich. Youngest daughter of Ian and Lora."

Giles lowered his voice. "All the books say she died young. We might just be witnessing her death."

That didn't feel right. "Or we're here to help find a cure."

"I've looked, Kincaid. There isn't a way to remove her gift. It's part of her." Giles swiped his glasses from his face and pinched the bridge of his nose.

"Then I'll go home, gather a healer, and bring them back to buy us time."

"That won't work. Her brother Cian is a healer. More powerful than any you and I have seen, and he wasn't able to help. The only thing that has brought her any solace is the cloak the family charmed for her. It acts as a buffer but according to Helen, it's growing weaker."

"A cloak is her shield?"

"A filter really. Mutes but doesn't stop everything from penetrating completely."

He blinked several times, feeling the answer...or at least a temporary reprieve... was close.

"What are you thinking?" Giles asked.

Every Druid had some ability to read the intentions of others. Though to be honest, Kincaid had never worked hard to peer into others' minds. To do so would mean he'd have to open himself, lower his shield, and allow someone in.

He said nothing and stared at the door leading to his room. The wooden barrier was easily breached...a swift kick and someone could walk right in.

"I hate that I can't see a thing inside your head, Kincaid. Something is working for you," Giles said.

He stepped back over the threshold and motioned for Simon to follow.

"I have an idea," he said when they moved to the second floor landing.

"What?" Simon asked.

Instead of answering, Kincaid decided to demonstrate. "What is Giles thinking about?"

Simon stared at Giles. "He's worried, as we all are."

"No. What's he *really* thinking?"

Simon winced and closed his eyes. "That her death is inevitable."

Right. "Now, what am I thinking?"

This time Simon stared with thinly veiled hatred sparking from his eyes. "Nothing. I...what's the point, Kincaid? Amber is dying. We don't have time for games."

Kincaid lowered his shield and stepped closer to the man. He expanded his shield and surrounded the other warrior. "Now, what am I thinking?"

His right eye twitched as Simon peered close and tickled the edges of Kincaid's brain. "You can shield her."

"I can try. The fix will be temporary and I have to be close to her. But maybe it will give Giles time to find a cure."

The twitch in his brain expanded as Simon searched for more answers. Not liking the sensation, Kincaid narrowed his shield and shut the man out.

"What are the risks?"

"For Amber? Nothing worse than her immediate death if it doesn't work."

Funny how Simon didn't bother asking what the risk to him was. There wasn't any guarantee the noise inside Amber's head wouldn't transfer to him, destroying them both.

Chapter Eight

Simon consoled his wife while Kincaid moved around to the far side of the bed. He removed the sword strapped to his back and set it beside the table.

"What's he doing?" Helen asked.

"Trying to help."

A fish swimming in a round bowl would have had nothing on all the eyes in the room watching him.

He eased his frame to the edge of the bed and felt his weight dip into the mattress. The closer he moved to Amber, the higher his heart rate soared. In times of flight, he'd expand his shield and suck travelers with him into a vortex of time. This was different.

The tight grip on his shield loosened in small degrees. Not because he feared what would happen to him, but his fear of what it might do to her.

Okay Amber MacCoinnich...I'm going to invade your space for a little while. He sighed and expanded the shield again. If he looked hard enough, he could see a shimmering blue light expand from his body and pulsate out as he moved the barrier between him and the world. As the tip of Amber's finger breached his circle, he felt a tug and noticed the blue rim grip hold of her hand and pull. A small tremor of fear surged over him when he tried to pull back his shield just to see if he could, only to find it unyielding.

Kincaid concentrated on her hand, thought he saw one of her fingers twitch. He placed a hand next to hers and she moved again.

Energy rushed over him and the light of his shield sparked.

Everyone in the room gasped.

When Kincaid let go, the shield he liked to call his own, poured over Amber and molded itself to her frame. It hugged her like a robe, nothing like Kincaid had ever seen before.

Amber's chest rose and fell in a heavy sigh. When her finger lifted, Kincaid reached out and touched her. The molded shield expanded with his touch and bubbled them both inside.

His heart gave a massive kick in his chest as the unconscious emotions of the woman at his side slid into him. He released an unmanly moan as his head filled with pain. Her pain. Bracing a hand to her side to keep from crushing her, he closed his eyes and attempted to absorb the impact, deflect it...survive it.

His eyeballs were on fire and the flesh on his bones felt as if someone was dripping acid and eating away all rational thought.

How did she survive this?

"Kincaid?" Dread filled Giles's voice.

He shook his head. "I'm—" he swallowed down bile, felt a wave pass only to return.

"What's happening?"

Inside Amber's head, he heard her respond to the distress of Helen's voice.

"Shh!"

"Is she okay?" Helen franticly asked.

His gut rolled as if he'd been hit with a spiked medieval hammer.

"For God's sake, woman, shut up," Kincaid ordered.

As those in the room held their collective breath. The pain slowly eased. He tightened the shield around them and attempted to thicken the barrier. The slow process left him breathless with sweat pooling on his brow.

He opened his eyes and noticed Amber's hand tighten around his. She hadn't woken, but he could feel her. Her soft breath washed over his skin with every exhale, her heart stopped its uneven rhythm and found a comfortable pace.

When Kincaid looked to the others in the room, he noted that the sun had started to set, casting long shadows in the room.

"She's resting now," he told them.

"Is she okay?" Helen asked.

He felt a kick in his head. It was as if the words triggered something inside of Amber and made her panic.

"She is for now. She needs to rest and heal. Maybe by morning I'll be able to let go of her hand."

Giles offered a small smile. "How do *you* feel?"

"Better than ever," he lied.

Giles shook his head. "I'll return to the library. Can I get you anything?"

The old woman pulled herself to her feet and spoke for the first time. "Come, Helen…let's prepare something to eat for our guest. Have something here for Amber when she wakes."

The woman's soothing voice brought a blanket over Amber and filled Kincaid with warmth.

Kincaid offered the woman a smile and was greeted with one in return. He realized then he didn't know her name.

As if she read his mind she said, "I'm Mrs. Dawson."

That would make sense, as the Manor was named after the original owner. "A pleasure."

Mrs. Dawson limped from the room with the use of a cane and followed Helen out.

Simon stood to follow the others. He hesitated at the door and stared down at the both of them. "Let me know when she wakes."

"I will."

"The pain inside her…was it…"

Kincaid shook his head. "I don't know how she survived it."

Simon swallowed. "I'm one floor down."

"I'll call out if we need you."

He gave a swift nod and closed the door behind him.

Alone with Amber, he stared at her porcelain features and felt a smile on his lips. "You look better in person," he whispered. *Even close to death.*

He moved slowly, arranging her hand on his leg while he attempted to pull his fingers from hers. It didn't work. He lifted one booted foot to their joined hands and tugged it off, kicking it to the floor before reaching for the other. Once he managed to take off his boots, he stood while holding her hand and removed the weapon on his hip, set it on the nightstand.

Having a beautiful woman beside him in bed was never a hardship, but an unconscious one he couldn't let go of proved more awkward than any encounter he'd ever had.

As he moved around the bed, he felt her anxiety rise. It was as if she worried he would leave and the full force of the pain would return. Kincaid maneuvered himself with his back against the headboard. The bed wasn't large enough for him to lay there and not touch more than her hand. Their clasped hands had two choices. They could lay on his thigh or her chest.

He rested them against her first, felt the swell of her breast, and groaned.

Not a good choice.

He rested their hands on his thigh. That was marginally better.

"Well, Amber MacCoinnich...when you wake up try not to freak out too hard." He looked down at her innocent face. "Something tells me you've never had a man in your bed."

The thought made him smile and inch closer. He would reflect on why the thought empowered him later, for now he'd just try to thicken the barrier around them and sift through the jumbled pain inside her head and rid her of it.

After an hour inside her head, he felt the emotions of

those closest to them swimming on a thin surface, but those from outside the walls of the house were gone. The blue barrier around them was so thick he doubted a bolt of lightning could penetrate it.

At some point, Helen slipped into the room and set a tray of food by the bed. Kincaid felt her concern and he did his best to shield the emotions from the sleeping woman on his side. Before Helen could say a thing, he brought a finger to his lips. "Shh."

Helen blinked a few times and quietly left the room.

He clicked off the light and slid down in the bed. He rolled to his side and switched hands. He rested his arm over Amber's waist, realizing again how thin she was. Too thin.

Kincaid closed his eyes on the pillow beside her and felt her push against him to get closer.

He continued to sift through her thoughts until his brain reached its own limit and needed to rest.

Somewhere in the night, he woke long enough to realize Amber shifted in her sleep. She had his arm grasped to her side and had rolled over, offering him her backside.

Without a doubt, when she woke and realized she was spooning with a stranger, she'd freak. But right now, Kincaid didn't care. He ignored his rising hormones, calling himself all kinds of names for being turned on by a woman who was near-death, and he forced himself to go back to sleep.

****

If Amber knew death would be this warm, this welcoming, she would have let herself go long before now.

The cloud she floated on surrounded her, blocked out all the pain, and left her strangely hungry. Even that was a welcome relief. She'd not felt the need to eat in so long she'd forgotten the feeling. Sleep overshadowed everything, however. The ability to rest without interruption was heaven. Maybe that's what her reward was for such a burdened life. Sleep and hunger, the things she couldn't enjoy in her failing body.

Her last thought before leaving her body was that she died before returning home. Without the crushing pain clouding her thoughts, she was thankful her time came before plaguing her family with her death. This way they might think she lived a good long life.

She snuggled into her cloud and drifted off to sleep again.

Then her stomach rumbled, loud and unrelenting.

The cloud moved behind her and grasped her hip.

That can't be right.

Amber forced her eyes open, fearful the pain would return. Her room was before her just as it had been when she was alive. The sun reached its morning rays into her room and asked her to wake.

The unfamiliar feeling of being alone made her close her eyes again. The pain in her head wasn't there. The voices of others...gone. A deep voice, one she'd never heard before, chanted one word. Sleep.

Her head started to follow the soft chant and then the bed dipped behind her.

Amber's eyes sprung open, and she slowly turned her head.

Behind her...no, pressed up against her with his arm draped over her clasping her tightly was a dark stranger.

Oh, God. Panic, always close to the surface, bubbled inside her.

The stranger opened his eyes, his piercing gaze met hers, and Amber screamed.

She scrambled to the other side of the bed only to find herself trapped by the large man's iron-grip.

"Calm down."

She kicked, yelled, and pushed against him as he pinned her to the bed, his body unwilling to let her go. Amber pulled in the energy of the room and added heat to her hands as she shoved.

The man cursed and clasped her hands to prevent her from burning more of his skin. "Dammit, Amber hold still."

The door to the room flew open. Amber twisted on the bed, saw Simon, and yelled for him to help her.

"What's going on?" Simon asked but made no effort to remove the man who crushed her to the bed.

"She woke up."

Amber attempted more kicks, found her legs pinned beneath her captor. "Get him off me," she pleaded with Simon. Why was he not helping her? Her foot connected with the man's shin.

He rolled on top of her, full on now and pinned her hands above her head. "Enough!" he yelled at her.

Stunned, she stopped moving. No one…and she meant no one, ever yelled at her.

Her chest rose and fell with his. They both panted and stared into each other's eyes. He was angry, that she knew by the fierce look on his face and perhaps the small steam that seemed to be bouncing off him. Blue steam that rolled off him like an aura.

"Talk to her, Simon. Tell her what's going on."

"Amber, listen to me, lass."

"Get him off of me, Simon."

Simon knelt down by the bed but still didn't push the stranger away.

She struggled again only to feel the man's knee slip between hers. Panic crawled up her throat and she squeezed her eyes shut.

"He's here to help, Amber. He's holding the emotions of others away. Can't you feel it?"

Amber heard Helen gasp.

She looked toward the door to find Helen and Giles standing there. Amber hadn't felt them coming. Deep inside she reached for the emotions of the others in the room and only felt one. The man holding her down.

"Don't look for trouble. It's taken hours to thicken the

barrier. If you push against it, it might not hold," the stranger told her.

"How do you know I'm pushing?"

"Because we're linked."

"Linked?"

He nodded, his breath swept hot over her. "Don't panic." He winced as if her worry wounded him.

He lowered one of her hands in his and brought it up to her eyes. "Do you see the light?"

Blue light glistened.

"What is it?"

"My shield. It's keeping out everyone's thoughts but ours."

"He speaks the truth, lass," Simon assured her.

Amber stared into the dark brown eyes of the stranger in her bed. She forced her breaths to slow down and took him in. He wore a small amount of hair on his face in a way that flattered his strong jaw without hiding it. His broad shoulders and thick arms reminded her of the men of her time. Even though he was draped over her like a thick blanket, he wasn't hurting her. It was as if he was holding himself above her without placing all his weight. It was strangely comforting…like the dream of being folded in a cloud. A strong, heavily muscled cloud that smelled of spice and man.

No smile reached his lips, but she noticed his eyes spark with mischief. Then, without any warning she knew on a deep level he felt every curve of her body and was keenly aware of the minimal clothing she wore.

When her cheeks warmed, the man holding her smiled. The effect devastated her. She'd never felt desire for a man before and was mortified the man holding her was aware of her thoughts.

"I'm going to move off of you now, Amber. Don't run away."

"Why?"

He lifted their clasped hands again. "Because I don't

know if I can keep everything out if you let go."

"Truly?" Her palm in his warmed.

He lifted an eyebrow. "One thing at a time."

He shifted his weight, rolled to the side, but kept one hand in hers at all times.

She used her free hand to pull down her nightgown that had inched up in her struggles, and pushed the majority of her body as far away from the man in her bed as possible.

"How are you feeling?" Helen asked.

"Confused."

"That's to be expected. Waking up next to a strange man in your bed has to be a first for you."

"Waking up next to *any* man is a first." She lifted her chin and stared at the man holding her hand. "Who are you?"

"The name's Kincaid."

Her eyes narrowed as another name popped in her head. "Your name is Gavin."

From the door, Giles chuckled. "You're quite right, m'lady. It is Gavin but no one dares call him that. Gavin Kincaid prefers the use of his last name only."

"Is that so?"

She tried to read the man's mind but found it difficult.

"I go by Kincaid." The smirk on his face unsettled her and made her want to challenge him. After all, he'd slept next to her, yelled at her, and forcefully restrained her before she even knew his name.

"Well, *Gavin*..." The smirk on his face grew when she used his given name. "How is it you came to be in my bed?"

Before he could explain himself, Simon and Helen told the story as to how Gavin Kincaid had searched for Giles and ended up traveling to their time. Helen launched into finding Amber near death on the bathroom floor, how they needed to do something, and quickly, if Amber was going to survive.

While the tale was told, the hand holding hers grew warm. A shiver ran up her arm as if Gavin ran a hand along her skin. Was that a result of his thoughts about her, or her own wishes? How much of her thoughts could he read? And why was it so difficult to read his clearly?

"You have questions." He told her, interrupting Helen's story.

"Can you read my thoughts?"

"Not word for word."

That's a relief.

"But I sense your feelings stronger than you'd like." There his smirk was again.

She tugged at her hand but he didn't let her go.

"I wouldn't if I were you." He gripped her fingers.

"I don't want you in my head."

"Do you want the thousands who were in there before, instead of me? Am I that distasteful to you, *Lady* MacCoinnich?"

"I feel your advantage over me, *Gavin* Kincaid." *And I don't like it!*

His eyes fell down her lithe frame. "The mouse holds an advantage over you."

Giles cleared his throat. "Show some respect, Kincaid. She is a MacCoinnich."

"Respect runs both ways, Giles. This MacCoinnich would be *dead* if I hadn't intervened. Seems all she wants to do is run away and break every effort I've made to keep her alive."

Amber huffed an exasperated breath. "Sleeping next to a woman is a hardship for you, *Gavin*?"

He leaned forward, much too close for her comfort and lowered his voice. "The women I sleep next to don't try and run away when they wake, *m'lady*...quite the opposite."

Beside them, Simon heard the exchange and lunged toward Kincaid.

Amber felt, more than saw, the blue shield around

74

them expand and Simon bounced off the force field and hit the floor. His contact with the shield brought a wave of pain over her, an instant reminder of the crushing agony she'd been in only yesterday.

The hand in hers squeezed.

Simon took to his feet and approached again.

"Stop!" Gavin ordered.

"Please, Simon...don't."

"Apologize to the lady!" Simon demanded.

The words didn't come quickly, but Amber knew Gavin wasn't happy with his actions. She had baited him, and needed to carry some of the blame for Simon's need to protect her. "My apologies, Amber."

Chapter Nine

Anyone else using his first name as freely as Amber did would normally be the recipient of a clear cut down. But every time his name tumbled from her soft, pink lips, one of the links to his soul opened and let her in a little deeper. Not even his lovers knew his name, nor would they have cared to ask.

Names aside, the two of them needed to find some peace until it could be determined if the strength of his shield could surround them both without them touching. The woman holding his hand was stronger than anyone in the room could possibly know. The pain inside of her had the power of an F-5 tornado and was just as destructive. No wonder it had nearly killed her. All that strength would fall like dust in the wind when she realized touching him constantly meant a lack of privacy while bathing…and any number of other activities.

The thought left him smiling, but he knew her reaction wouldn't be favorable.

"How long are we stuck like this?" Amber lifted her hand.

"I can attempt to break away, keep the shield around us both."

"Can you do that?"

"Shielding us from the physical, yes. From the mental anguish inside of you? That I don't know. It's taken half the night to remove the chatter in there." He glanced at the top of her head. "I never let you go."

"You don't think it's going to work…letting go and keeping my gift restricted?"

"More curse than gift."

Her gaze fell to the floor. "My curse to bear, not

yours."

Where had the spunk gone from her voice?

"So you want to give up? Have me let go so you can die in agony?" His words were meant to be harsh and they met his mark.

"I don't want to give up. I haven't even had a chance to live."

"Stop it! Both of you. Don't talk about dying!" Helen yelled at both of them. "No one is going to die. Not today. This," she waved a finger between the both of them. "This is temporary. Giles will find a way to save you, Amber. A way for you to move on with your life without holding someone's hand and without your gift strangling you." Helen had her hands on her hips now as she glared at him. "And you. You'll behave, hold her hand, and remember she's not some floozy you can talk to like you may have other women in the past."

"I'm not a child," Amber told Helen.

"No. But we both know you're as innocent as they come. Ian would never let a man near you let alone sleep in the same bed." She pointed a finger at Kincaid now. "You need to think about that...and not in a sleazy guy way either. Amber is someone's daughter, someone's sister and those someones will have no problem hunting you down, shield or not, and take you out if you so much as harm a hair on her head."

Simon laid a hand on his hysterical wife's shoulder. "I don't think you need to threaten the man, lass. He understands."

Helen shrugged his hand away and placed it on her abdomen.

"Helen?" Amber's soothing voice, deep with her Scottish accent, washed over him. "I appreciate your passionate plea. I'm sorry I've caused you stress. Rest assured I'm not ready to give up. Gavin and I will figure out a way to cohabit the same space until something more permanent can be figured out."

"No more talk of dying!"

Amber smiled and tilted her head to the side. "No more talk of dying."

The room grew silent for a few minutes and then Amber spoke again. "Giles…have you slept?"

Kincaid noticed the fatigue behind his friend's eyes.

"I can sleep later."

"You can sleep now," Amber told him. "We need you sharp. It wouldn't bode well to have you skim over something important in one of your books because you're exhausted. Helen…when was the last time you and the baby ate?"

Kincaid glanced at the other woman's hand resting over her stomach and grinned. Now he understood the emotional outburst. Pregnant woman were the most hormonal and pregnant Druids were even more so.

"We could eat," Helen said.

"Simon, why don't you take your wife down to the kitchen and feed her. I know I'm hungry and am looking forward to leaving this room."

Simon glanced between Kincaid and Amber.

"We'll be down shortly," Kincaid assured him.

Once they were alone, he turned toward her. "You did that really well."

"Did what?"

"Deescalated the situation, put everyone to a task, and took the focus off of you."

"My mother had five children, and a husband with a temper that matched his ability to strike anyone with lightning. When the grandchildren started coming, the Keep was a volatile brewing pot of emotions and hormones. My mother faced each argument with a calm strength that made all of us try to please her."

"She never lost control?"

"Of course. But never when it really counted. Not that I saw in any account."

"It's a rare quality to have people bend to your will

78

without brute strength or manipulation."

"I don't have much in the way of physical strength, I'm afraid."

It dawned on him then, that her life of seclusion probably limited her ability to do much of anything. "How old are you?" The age in the depths of her eyes exceeded her years, but her innocence said she wasn't old enough to buy a bottle of wine in this century.

"Nearly thirty."

Not as young as he thought. "How long have you been isolated?"

"I've avoided others for nearly ten years. The last few have kept me apart from my family more times than not."

"No wonder Helen's worried about you."

"I've been a burden to them for too long, Gavin. Simon and Helen deserve a good life, not one plagued with me pulling them down. Helen doesn't often leave the house so she can be here for me. Simon is crazed trying to find a cure. The only person in the house that doesn't worry about me continually is Mrs. Dawson."

"Why is that?"

"I don't know. I've never been able to read her completely and didn't think on it for long with so many other emotions in my head." She closed her eyes, drew in a big breath. "Now my head is blissfully silent. I feel you there, but nothing is weighing on me."

Her confession pleased him.

"But it's temporary. Sooner or later we will have to let go." She opened her eyes. "When we do, the others can't know about it. Their worry will make the attempt worse."

How could she think of others, their emotions, when her own were so fragile one lift of his little finger and her world would crash in. The cauldron of pain, voices, and distress inside her the moment he'd touched her the first time made him physically ill. The thought of that touching her again...no. "I don't think you're ready for me to let go." He knew if he released her now, the walls around her would crumble, and the pain would slam into her.

"I don't believe I am either. Which places us in a very precarious situation."

"Is that so?"

She lifted her chin, a move he noted on her more than once when it seemed she was trying to show courage she didn't have. "Aye. You see I have need of the bathroom and I refuse to walk around in a nightgown any longer. While you may have intimate knowledge of a woman's body, I'm painfully naive about a man's." The color in Amber's cheeks blossomed as she spoke.

A grin played on his lips but he didn't let it show. "I've fought among men in your time. Some throw off their kilts in battle to save the plaid."

"Some do. But I've only seen such things from afar. Or my nephews, but...well..."

"Amber?" He said her name softly, repeated it until she looked directly at him.

Embarrassment filled her eyes.

"I'll close my eyes."

She smiled then, and the effect hit him in the gut and spread heat lower. This was the look he wanted to see from her the moment he'd noticed her portrait on the wall of MacCoinnich Keep. The haunting expression in that painting dissipated with a smile...one that reached her eyes.

"I'll close my eyes, too." The relief in her voice was comical.

"I'm not shy, m'lady. Look all you want. Consider me a live human anatomy lesson."

Her eyes grew wider. When he laughed, she grinned.

"You're teasing me."

He winked. "Maybe a little."

They scooted off the bed together and walked around the room while she gathered a change of clothing. She passed over her multitude of dresses and skirts and chose a pair of jeans and a pull over shirt to change into. Using the bathroom proved a little difficult as they both held a foot or ankle while the other used the facilities.

As he promised, Kincaid kept his eyes shut while she dressed and, although he'd given her permission to look, she turned her face away and squeezed her eyes closed when his own needs called.

"I have never shared a bathroom with a man."

"They don't have bathrooms in your time," he reminded her.

"Don't be so sure. Lizzy, Simon's mother, was determined to have water piped in. There's a hidden closet in each wing with a primitive toilet."

She picked up a brush and attempted to pull it through her hair. "This is difficult with one hand," she told him.

He came up behind her and lifted her shirt until the skin of her waist was exposed. He placed his palm against her and freed her hand. Amber smiled at him in the mirror and quickly brushed her hair before pulling the bulk of it back in a tie.

He tucked her hand in the crook of his arm when they left the bedroom for the first time. All the while Kincaid felt a smile, a grin...or full-on happiness swimming inside of him. He couldn't help but wonder if those were Amber's emotions or his. Because he couldn't remember a time in his life when he felt this at ease.

****

Selma shoved her hand into the bag of chips, flipped the channel on the TV, and plopped her feet up on Jake's coffee table. She checked the time on the clock ticking on the mantel of his fireplace and knew he'd be home soon. He'd probably grumble about her letting herself in, but he'd get over it. She took great pleasure in pushing Jake's buttons. The man was too uptight for his own good. He'd have an early heart attack at this rate. Selma made it a personal goal to get the man to lighten up and take himself less seriously.

Besides, she didn't have any friends in LA and she didn't want to eat dinner alone again. She could have made her way to Mrs. Dawson's home, but with Amber's health in such a dire state, she didn't think that option was the best.

The sound of Jake's car pulling into the driveway prompted her to turn up the mindless show she was watching, and dig into the bag again.

As expected, Jake stepped around the corner with his service side arm pointed toward her, saw her and dropped the muzzle of the gun to the floor. "What the…"

Unaffected, she placed both hands in the air and pulled a breathy voice from deep within her and said, "Please don't shoot, officer."

He growled and holstered his gun. "Breaking into a cop's house isn't smart, Matilda."

His pet name was growing on her.

"I didn't break in."

"Oh, I don't remember giving you a key." He stepped around the coffee table, grabbed the remote, and switched the set off.

She waved a chip in his direction as she spoke. "I have my witchy ways. No need to break anything to get in here." She popped the chip in her mouth and made more noise than necessary before swallowing it.

He tugged off his belt that held all his cop toys and laid it on the table. "You know, I think I liked it better when you lived a thousand miles away." There was no heat in his words.

"Your life was boring before you met me."

"I'm a cop. My life is never boring."

"Predictable then."

She knew his friendship pool was shallow and that Todd, his partner who now lived several hundred years back in time, was his best friend, almost like a brother.

He spread his legs in a typical officer pose and crossed his arms over his chest. "What are you doing here,

Selma?"

She swept her feet from the coffee table, tossed the bag of chips in their place, and started toward the kitchen. "I thought I'd disturb your boring, predictable evening and convince you to join me for dinner."

He followed her into his kitchen. "Why would we do that? We don't like each other, remember?"

"Call it an exercise in patience...or better yet, we can attempt to remove the stick you have up your ass. Compromise is good for you."

"Compromise is important when two people give a rat-shit about each other. We don't fall into that category. And I don't have a stick up my ass."

She opened up his nearly empty refrigerator and poked her head inside. "Yes you do. Geez, Jake, your cardiologist must love you." She removed a brown box with leftover pizza and tossed it on the counter.

"Hey, that's still good."

She opened the lid, grabbed a rock-hard slice of pepperoni and sausage, and tapped it against the counter with a solid thud. "I've had week old bagels that were fresher than this." She dug back into the science experiment Jake called a refrigerator and took out two beers. "Open these," she told him as she thrust them in his direction. "I'll figure out if there's anything salvageable in here."

Jake grabbed the beer before they dropped to the floor. "You know how to cook?"

She found a head of lettuce that looked workable and a couple of potatoes. "And I don't even need my cauldron." In the freezer she found a couple of chicken breasts...*I can work with this.*

Jake leaned a hip against the counter and twisted off the caps on the beer. He handed one to her and tilted his back for a drink.

She watched him out of the corner of her eye as he grew used to having her in his space. He might not be smiling, but that stick was beginning to wiggle free of his anus. "Pots and pans?"

He pointed his beer to the right of the oven.

She found what she needed and placed it on the stove.

Jake pushed away from the counter, taking his beer with him. "I'm going to shower. Try not to burn my house down."

His snarky comment put a smile on her face.

Chapter Ten

It's just a hand!

Amber flexed her fingers in Gavin's without letting go. He stood over her by at least eight inches and took up more than half his side of the stairway as they descended into the main floors of the Manor. The space felt bigger somehow. Maybe the lack of voices in her head added to the space as they past the many rooms of the house en route to the kitchen, but the world was different.

The smile on Amber's face was difficult to shake and she couldn't remember another time where she wanted to close her eyes and simply listen to the bones of the house creek and settle.

"Everything feels new to you," Gavin said before they rounded the final hall to the back of the house.

"'Tis hard to describe. Every step down was met with pain before." She glanced up the stairs. "Now they are just steps. The pain... it was—"

"You don't need to describe it. I felt it the moment I took your hand. You're a strong woman, Amber MacCoinnich."

Her smile fell. "I had given up."

Gavin squeezed her hand. "I know that, too."

The kitchen buzzed with Helen moving around the space and cooking for what looked like a small army.

"I didn't know what you wanted so I made a little of everything. It's nearly noon, and eggs didn't feel right. I have soup and sandwiches...salad." The smell of bacon made Amber's stomach growl.

She was half way through her chicken and bacon sandwich when Mrs. Dawson made it into the kitchen.

"There you are, lass," Simon greeted the oldest

member of the house by pulling out a chair for her and kissing her cheek.

Mrs. Dawson, the big flirt, blushed and smiled while accepting a cup of tea from Helen.

"I'm surprised we didn't see you when Amber woke up. Surely you heard her."

Mrs. Dawson grinned at Gavin and Amber with a wink. "Amber was bound to be upset waking next to a stranger, but she's smart, and would realize fighting was useless. No need for me to rise before nature intended."

"Does wisdom always come with age?" Gavin asked.

Mrs. Dawson pointed a wrinkled finger in Gavin's direction. "Are you saying I'm old, Mr. Kincaid."

For a moment no one said anything and then Mrs. Dawson started to laugh. "You are too easy," she told them.

Giles joined them several hours later, the lines on his face had smoothed over with the sleep he'd managed. He told them he was ready to tackle the library. All the while Gavin held her hand or rested his hand intimately on her waist when she needed all ten fingers. There really was no room for embarrassment, and Amber refused to allow the way she was raised to cloud her judgment now. It's just a hand, she told herself. A hand that sometimes gripped her waist with warm fingers and sent unfamiliar shivers up her spine, but...only a hand.

At one point, she felt Helen's eyes on her, her worry pushed through Gavin's barrier. Instead of calling Helen on her thoughts, she turned to her temporary twin. "Gavin? Would you mind terribly if we took a walk?"

"Outside?"

With the sun on her face and the wind in her hair...how long had that been? "Preferably."

"There are no wards protecting the property."

"And no need for such during this time. Please." For the first time since she'd arrived in this century, she didn't need to wear the cape over her shoulders, and the thought of the elements on her skin made her smile. The worry of the neighbors emotions overshadowing her own wasn't a concern...she only had to hear the birds in the trees and smell the fragrance of the flowers.

Gavin exchanged glances with Simon. "Fine, but we need to retrieve my weapons from your room."

"Don't leave the property," Simon warned them. "Jake wasn't kidding when he said the neighbors will report you if you walk around obviously armed."

"Protecting her with one hand will prove difficult without weapons."

Simon nodded his approval and Gavin and Amber retrieved his weapons before they stepped outside.

"Tell me, how does this change in the future?" Amber asked as they left the house.

He looked around, offered a half smile. "The fortress expands well beyond the boundaries you see now. Adjacent properties, in all directions, are purchased and a wall is built around everything."

"Like MacCoinnich Keep?"

"I suppose you could compare the two, but the Keep is much larger."

"I would think so."

"Over time, more Druids come to reside here. More families fill the homes around the compound."

"Why?"

"For protection. For survival."

"Is the future so bleak?"

"Compared to life in the sixteenth century...no. I suppose you're better equipped to handle the coming changes than many. It's those who live solitary lives in this time without any survival skills at all who fall first."

"Will there be another war?"

They walked to the edge of the cobblestone driveway and started around the grassed in perimeter of the property. A small hillside sat on the North end of the land, offering some barrier of the neighbors on the other side. Much of the secluded land sat in the back of the house where Mrs. Dawson had constructed a flower garden and over two acres of lawn. Several stone benches gave those in the garden a place to sit and watch the natural wildlife frolic in the sanctuary provided.

"More of a complete collapse of society. The economy survives for a little longer, but when it finally collapses and people aren't able to feed their families, neighbors turn against neighbors. The cities have it hardest. Those who live out here, and beyond manage to survive if they can protect what's theirs. The government of this country starts to unravel and they search for power that will help them gain control of the people."

Without Gavin voicing his meaning, Amber knew he meant magical power. Anyone abusing their power sickened her. "Which means we never stop hiding who we are."

He shook his head and lifted her hand, helping her around a small pond in the corner of Mrs. Dawson's yard. "We band together, become stronger. Fortresses like this one become cities of themselves. Wells are dug for water, gardens are planted and livestock is gathered. Food can be obtained outside the walls, but we don't depend on it."

"Sounds like home." She tugged him over to a bench and sat to enjoy the fair weather. Gavin kept a constant eye on the world around him. "What about the Others?"

"With the world in a constant power struggle, the population becomes susceptible to dictator. Many humans try, and some succeed for short periods of time. Imagine how far a powerful Druid could reach and control if—"

"I don't have to imagine. Grainna controlled a small army and affected everyone, Druid or not, before she was destroyed."

"I suppose you don't."

"The Others are Druid?"

"Yes. Collecting power, using theirs for personal gain."

She thought on this for a time and released a long-suffering sigh. "Who is your leader?"

His eyes pinched together in thought. "There isn't one power, or one Laird controlling anything. We work as a collective. All of us wish to survive and strive for a better life for our children."

Amber paused. "Do you have children?" A wife? She glanced at their joined hands.

Gavin shook his head. "That's not in my plan."

Part of her was relieved. The other part held a sliver of sorrow. "Doesn't everyone want to find someone to share their life with?"

"I'm a warrior, Amber. I've traveled in time more often than you. There's always a possibility I won't return. I won't put another person through the anguish of not knowing what happened if I don't return."

The sadness in his voice told her there was more to his explanation than he offered, but he didn't elaborate, and Amber wasn't about to probe his thoughts for their deeper meaning.

"I suppose that's fair. Sad, but fair."

"This from the woman who was ready to die before being educated on the male anatomy."

Heat rushed to her face but she refused to let him see her squirm. He was teasing her again, probably in an effort to make her more comfortable at his side. "I didn't want to die."

"You were giving up."

She wanted to deny him, couldn't. "A quick noble death is better than a slow useless death." Amber noticed a bird land on a limb of a nearby tree. It cocked its head to the side as if it listened to them.

"I understand the need to die in battle versus wasting away in a small, dark room."

"For years now, I wondered why I was spared... Why couldn't I have perished when Grainna was destroyed instead of being forced to live the way I have?"

Gavin placed a second hand over hers. "It wasn't your time. And we will find a way to keep you from a slow, painful death."

She wanted to believe him. "And if we can't, you must not blame yourself for letting go."

He squeezed her hand. "I'm not letting go."

Maybe not now...but sooner or later, you'll have to.

A fluttering in the tree caught her attention again. In it sat a large black crow.

The breath in her lungs caught and chills ran up her arms. Crows were a common bird in this part of California, but she never did like seeing them. The omen they represented, the memory of Grainna taking the shape of a crow to fly among a flock to spy on her family sat firmly in Amber's memory.

"What is it?"

She told herself the bird wasn't watching them, but when she moved closer to Gavin's side, the bird's head turned toward him. As a child, she could tell if Druid thoughts were present in any animal around her. With the impaction of so many emotions inside of her, she hadn't concentrated on an animal in years. Amber pushed against Gavin's shield, reaching for the animal.

"What are you doing?"

"That bird...it's watching us."

Gavin laughed. "It's just a crow." He stomped his foot intending to scare the bird off.

It didn't budge.

The smile on Gavin's face fell.

Amber pushed against the shield again.

"Stop doing that, Amber. It's just a bird." But even as the words left Gavin's lips, she knew he worried the bird was something more.

He stood and brought him with her.

The bird watched them.

"Let's go inside."

Before they could step in that direction the crow took

flight, aiming in their direction.

Gavin shoved her behind him, removed one of his weapons, and started to fire.

Inside Amber's head started to scream. Laughter, chaos…pain blinded her. She hit the ground grabbing her head with both hands.

****

The sound of laughter filled Kincaid's head moments before the bird blew into chunks of feathers and blood and hit the ground. Several crows appeared from out of nowhere and flew away into the sky. More laughter assaulted his ears. He took aim at the other crows and noticed that both of his hands clasped to his gun.

He lowered his weapon and swiveled around.

Amber sat curled in a ball at his feet.

He'd let her go. *How could I have let her go?*

Kincaid placed a hand on her face and sat on the ground beside her. "Amber?"

She whimpered and snuggled into him.

He closed his eyes and heard the noise filling her, felt the pain threaten to take hold and not let go. He gathered her in his arms, reached under her shirt to maximize their contact. The places they touched sparked and brought wave after wave of pleasure. Like dipping in cool water on a hot day. "I've got you."

He closed his eyes, pulled power from the world around him and added layers to his shield. He dropped his lips to the top of her forehead and tried to calm the noise inside. "I'm sorry," he whispered and kissed her head.

She crawled into his warmth and the pain slowly eased. In his arms, her limbs loosened around him, reaching for skin. Seemed the barrier of clothing was too dense to feel the full power of his ability to shield her. One tiny hand wrapped around his neck, the other held his bare arm.

They sat entangled in each other's arms while the world calmed around them.

CATHERINE BYBEE

The sweet scent of her skin, her hair, mixed with the realization that tears slid from her eyes.

He kissed her temple and ran the pad of his thumb over her cheek to remove her tears. He knew the pain was getting better, even if worry that it would come back filled every inch of her.

Her eyes fluttered open and looked up into his. His breath mixed with hers and caught in his chest. The need to keep her safe mixed with a heavy dose of desire and not in a sleazy guy way as Helen had so eloquently put it. But a need to taste Amber's tears on her full lips and drive all the pain, all the anguish, away.

Her eyes slid to his lips and she caught her lower lip in her teeth.

Kincaid would probably curse himself later, but tasting her wasn't something he was willing to wait to do any longer.

He ran his thumb over her bottom lip, releasing it from her teeth and he leaned in and placed his lips on hers.

Amber didn't gasp in shock or push him away. No, the fingers caressing his neck kneaded his flesh and she moaned. The tiny sound vibrated through his body and every inch of his skin sang for more. He tilted her head back farther, parting her lips. He reminded himself he was kissing a woman who'd probably never been kissed before. The tip of his tongue licked her bottom lip, letting her get used to the sensation and intimacy.

Shy at first, she opened for him, let him explore, and then matched his actions. Some kisses were more innocent than others. Their kiss went no further, even though Kincaid would have liked nothing more than to touch more of her, taste more of her. This seductive kiss was dangerous enough, but it did seem to be driving away the shadows in her head. So he kept kissing her as his erection strained against his tight pants. She hadn't noticed...or if she did, it wasn't bothering her enough to pull back.

Breathless, she broke away and stared into his eyes.

Innocent doe eyes blinked and brought him into focus. He loved that he'd brought out the fullness in her lips with his own and could only imagine what she'd look like after he'd made love to her.

He shook the thought from his head, knowing she could read him if she tried hard enough.

"Do you feel better?"

"I do."

He looked around them, noticed a space free of unwanted birds. "We should go inside."

Her gaze fluttered to the sky. She shivered and wiggled off his lap.

Chapter Eleven

Millions of women throughout time had been kissed, but Amber couldn't help question if every kiss felt as earth shattering as the one she'd shared with Gavin. The heat of his shield wrapped around her, pulling her closer to the man holding her, and his body welcomed hers like a lost member of a family. In Gavin's arms, Amber felt like a woman for the first time in her twenty-nine years.

At least if I die now, I'll go to my grave with some knowledge of passion. She thought she'd never have an opportunity to experience anything so intimate. The thought of dying wiggled in right behind the elation of her first kiss. If it wasn't for Gavin letting her go, she wouldn't have collapsed and he wouldn't have needed to cradle her the way he had.

Amber knew protecting her might be a two-handed job. What would happen next time?

We can't hold hands forever.

Gavin hesitated on the steps into Mrs. Dawson's home and turned to her. "You're not going to die."

"Perhaps not today."

Not happy with her response, Gavin pulled her alongside him into the house. Once inside he yelled. "Giles!"

The door to the library was open and the librarian ran from the room. "What's wrong?"

"The perimeter has been breached."

Alarm filled Giles's face. "Computer!" he called. "Oh, damn…that won't work. What do we do?"

"Gather Simon, Helen, and Mrs. Dawson and meet me in the safe room." Gavin paused half way down the hall. "Wait…does Mrs. Dawson have a safe room yet?"

"The iron vault in the basement?" Amber asked.

"Perfect."

Moments later, the six of them packed into the twenty by twelve foot room with the vault door closed. Amber sensed Gavin's irritated state as he glanced around the small room. "This is not going to work for long."

"What isn't going to work? And why are we down here?" Simon asked.

Gavin toed one of the boxes and dust plumed into the air. "When was the last time these provisions were rotated?"

Mrs. Dawson sat in one of the three chairs in the room. "That would be back when Mr. Dawson was alive, I'm afraid. I didn't see a need after he passed."

"Well, there's a need now. The property has been breached."

"What does that mean?" Helen asked.

"Before we discuss this we need to secure this room."

"The room is solid, Mr. Kincaid," Mrs. Dawson told him.

He offered a patient smile and said, "Not from entry, but from ears. Giles?"

Giles nodded and patted down his pockets. "Oh, right!"

Gavin reached to his leg, pulled up his pant leg, and retrieved a knife. He handed it to Giles who made a tiny cut on his finger. He walked around the room, placing a print on every corner.

Amber and the others watched in fascination as the stoic librarian prepared the room for something.

"Ready," Giles told them.

Gavin then lifted his free hand in the air and sparked a flame to each drop of blood. He squeezed her hand. "I'm going to have to expand my shield to the others. Or at least try. If the pain is too great I'll pull back."

Amber stiffened her spine and gave a single nod.

Gavin turned to the others. "For Amber's sake, try

95

and clear your minds."

The blue light shielding Amber and Gavin pulsated and grew. In an effort to ease her growing anxiety, Amber closed her eyes and concentrated on the warmth of the hand holding hers.

She felt Giles first, then the hazy presence of Mrs. Dawson.

I hope this works, was the thought in Giles's head.

Helen and Simon entered the circle at the same time. Concern from Simon threatened to swallow her. Helen was chanting the words. *Think of nothing, think of nothing.*

"Amber?" Gavin's soft voice had her opening her eyes.

"I'm all right."

He leaned close to her ear. "You're a terrible liar."

A dull ache punctured her brain and started to swell. "Just hurry."

Gavin wasted little time. "From this moment forward, inside this room, the protective arms of our ancestors, our brothers, and sisters shall filter out unwanted ears, unwanted eyes. As I bid it, make it so...give us a sign to let us know."

The small flames glowing from Giles's blood expanded, and then burned out completely.

Amber slumped against Gavin and the protective shield around the others returned to just the two of them.

He led her to a chair and sat her down.

She cursed the weakness inside her, hated the effort her body needed for a simple spell. Without the others in the shield, the pain instantly eased to a dull ache.

"Better?" Gavin kissed the edges of her fingers.

"Aye."

"Protective wards are sealing in the conversations in this room. I suggest if anything truly dire needs to be discussed, it happens in here."

"How do we know if the wards are holding?" Simon asked.

"Place your hand over the edges of the room." Gavin instructed.

Simon moved to the corner, waved a hand in the air, and drew it back shaking it as if it stung.

"Simple enough? It will take more of us to place wards over the manor and property. With so few of us here, I'm not sure how successful we'll be. Though two of you are MacCoinnich's, I assume you'll both be more successful than the rest of us."

"You do this in the future?" Helen asked.

"More like maintain. Wards are piled upon over the years making them stronger with each generation."

"What happened that prompted this?" Simon asked.

Gavin glanced at Amber then the others. "We noticed a crow watching us. When it didn't scare away easily, we both knew it was more than an omen. Before I destroyed it I heard it laughing."

Amber hadn't been sure if that had been in her imagination or not. She shivered, liking it better when she thought it was all in her head.

"Breaching this compound is as easy as flying over or walking into it. We need to set wards and monitor—"

"Wait...the crow was laughing? How's that possible?" Helen asked.

"We heard the laughter in our heads," Amber told her.

"But I thought the shield was protecting you from that kind of thing."

Disgust rolled through Gavin and hit Amber in her chest. "It wasn't your fault," she told him.

He shook his head. "I let you go. I didn't have to destroy the crow. It wouldn't have been able to hurt us."

"Your instincts told you to shoot."

"You let Amber go?" Simon asked.

"For a few seconds."

"I take it that didn't work out very well," Helen said.

"The pain was instant and debilitating," Gavin told

them.

"Let's not lose focus here," Amber redirected them. "A crow, quite possibly guided by a Druid, was feet away from us today. That hasn't happened since…"

"Since Scotland…since Grainna." Simon's words made those in the room pause.

"Controlling animals was one of her gifts?" Gavin asked.

"She could shift, like Simon. But her *gifts,* as you call them, were too many to count."

"Grainna is dead." Simon started to pace the small room.

"That doesn't mean there can't be others out there like her," Mrs. Dawson, who had kept silent, reminded him. "I may not have read all the books in my library, but there are several tales about evil like hers that have existed since before she entered this world. Let's not forget about Helen's previous employer."

"A Druid?" Giles asked.

Helen nodded. "He and his brother…and yes, they were evil to the core. But they too are dead."

"There are always more to take their place. We can only hope none become as powerful as Grainna." Gavin squeezed Amber's hand while he spoke.

"The crow couldn't have been a shifter. It must have been controlled by someone who could talk to animals."

"How can you be sure, Simon?" Mrs. Dawson asked.

"When a shifter is injured, they can only hold the shift for a short time. You said you destroyed the crow."

"I did," Gavin said.

"Well, whoever decided to invade the sanctuary of your home picked the wrong one. Simon is the most powerful shifter ever known." Giles said.

"We don't know if that's true," Simon said.

Giles shook his head. "Oh, I'm sure. It's well documented. *First son of Finlay MacCoinnich soars the skies, and swims the oceans, surpassed by none other.*

Other books state similar themes. Shifters themselves are rare."

"I'm sure there are others." Simon clearly didn't like the praise.

"I remember everything I read, Simon. You're a rare duck…pun intended. Talking to animals, bending their will…that sort of thing is much more common among Druids than your gift."

"I could do that as a child."

"And now someone is watching us. We need to trace the power and find its source."

"How do you suggest we do that, Kincaid?" Simon asked.

Gavin turned to stare at Helen. "Do you find objects, people, with your gift?"

"I have, but I don't know if I can follow power."

"Have you ever tried?" Giles asked.

Helen shook her head.

It looked like she'd have her chance.

****

Giles walked beside Kincaid and Amber as they moved about the library securing wards. At one point, Kincaid stopped beside Amber, removed the band she had holding her hair back, and secured their wrists together with it. "To keep you from slipping away again," he told her.

Amber smiled and for the first time since Giles had known Kincaid, the man's face softened. The binding holding them together triggered a thought hovering in his mind. A possible solution, though he knew it wouldn't be the favored solution.

Once the room was as secure as it could be, Giles returned to the table in the center of the room covered in books. "Kincaid, Lady Amber… I'd like to show you what I've found so far," he told them before they could follow Simon and the others out.

"Something hopeful?" Amber asked.

"Something interesting. I'm not sure how hopeful."

Once they were seated, Giles swiveled several leather-bound books around so they could see the passages he'd found. "These books are not in this library in the future, which is why they stood out to me. This one," he tapped on the one closest to him, "was the one I was reading when Helen and Mrs. Dawson summoned me. Inside it speaks of your parents, Lady Amber. About their strong bond and ability to lead armies. Of course, it doesn't say your mother led any, but my guess is she raised strong sons who fought alongside their father. Most books of this time don't outright give women their due share of praise."

"We understand how history works, Giles. And we already knew the MacCoinnich's raised a strong family, both for the times and in their Druid abilities. What about this book struck you as unique?"

Right! Moving on. "You see, before you arrived, Kincaid, Helen attempted to search for more information inside the book. Power beyond us flipped pages inside, stopping often, and continued on."

"Power beyond us?" Kincaid asked.

Amber sat forward. "You mean the Ancients?"

Giles exchanged glances with Kincaid. Neither of them had a strong faith in Ancient power, but he hadn't seen such a strong reaction out of a simple request before.

"That's what Helen said. Anyway, last night I read the pages where the book stopped. It talked about generations of MacCoinnich's and other strong Druid families."

"A lesson about the family tree?" Kincaid asked.

"At first, that's what I thought it was, but this afternoon I found these other books and attempted to cross reference the information to see if there was something linking them together. What I found was each of the couples both came from Druid families. Both had Druid blood."

"That can't be rare," Amber said.

"Actually, as the years move on from your time, it does become rare. As each century passes without guidance, some Druids never even know of their heritage. And in this time, we know many Druids think of themselves as witches, or that they're crazy."

"Selma thought herself a witch until she met Lizzy," Amber reminded them.

"Exactly. It appears after the millennium more Druid connections occurred. Maybe because of the time travel brought on by your family...or awareness on a more secret level. Who knows, maybe Kincaid and I being in this time as we are, was predetermined to set the course for the future. It's hard to say."

"The books led you to learn about the strong gene pool between Druids. How does that help us?" Kincaid's voice was all business and no smile met his lips.

Giles dropped his gaze to their joined hands sitting on the table. "Amber, tell me, were your parents bonded? Had they exchanged Druid wedding vows?"

"Aye. As are Tara and Duncan."

"I'm assuming, only by what I've seen of course, that Helen and Simon are not bonded." Giles refused to meet Kincaid's stare, knowing the man would probably follow his line of questions.

"No. Nor are Lizzy and Fin."

Kincaid turned to Amber. "Why not?"

Amber shrugged. "When we were battling Grainna, there was too much uncertainty about the outcome. I don't believe my brother, Fin, wanted to risk Lizzy's life. Then there was always the question about how time travel would affect the couple if they were separated for any amount of time since bounded couples share part of their souls."

Giles pinched his eyes together. "You mean to say your family believed the other partner would perish if they traveled separately in time?"

"Is that not true?" Amber asked, her eyes wide with

question.

Kincaid released breath. "No, Amber. It's not true. It's only when the soul has left this world, this plain, that the surviving mate yearns for the other. Yes, most die within a short time when that happens, but not when one travels in time."

Amber brought a hand to her neck and played with the necklace she wore.

"The bound couples in the books I've read about often outlived their unbound cousins. Which is why in our time," Giles waved a hand between him and Kincaid, "when couples are married, Druid wedding vows are *always* exchanged. It has made us, as a race, and the couples stronger. You know each Druid has a unique power, some more than one. Bound couples, with enough practice, can use their mate's power as well."

"I've never seen my mother create lightning as my father can."

"She probably hasn't been encouraged to try. The power is never as strong, but it does happen. The more powerful the couple, the more powerful the bond."

Giles sat back and let the information soak into the two Druids in front of him.

"Your mother had the gift of premonition, is that right?"

"Aye."

"She told you to live here."

"Aye. If I were to survive I had to come with Simon to this time to live my life."

"Did she say anything else?"

Amber's eyes fluttered several time, her face lost all color, not that it held much.

"She did."

Giles held his breath and Kincaid started to squirm. The man never squirmed.

Amber stared directly at Kincaid. "She said a Druid awaited me in the future, and that this warrior would be the balm that saves me."

Chapter Twelve

It's not me. I'm no one's balm.

Yet as Kincaid stared at his hand already bound to Amber's, he knew how wrong he was. No one in his time had the ability to shield others. Some had the ability to shield themselves, but only for short periods of time and not beyond their own life force.

It's what made him valuable to the team.

It's what made him valuable to Amber.

It's what was keeping her alive.

A massive wave of sorrow vibrated between the two of them as Giles's words soaked in.

Bonding with anyone wasn't his plan. If this was the only solution Giles was going to find in his books... "Keep searching for answers," he told him.

"Of course." Giles wouldn't look at him.

Kincaid stood and Amber followed.

"Before you leave." Giles stopped them. "Kincaid, were your parents bonded?"

"My father raised me. My mother was not Druid."

Giles scratched his head. "That's right. I seem to remember that. And your grandparents?"

"My father spoke of a mother. I didn't know my grandparents."

"It's safe to say they weren't bonded either?"

"One can assume."

"Yet your powers are stronger than most." Seemed Giles was thinking aloud.

"Your point?"

"No point. An observation. Perhaps another answer is in your lineage."

Was he suggesting another man for Amber?

Kincaid swallowed hard, not liking the taste of that on his tongue. "I'm an only child."

Giles turned pages in his book, already moving to the next option. "Right. A cousin perhaps…"

"What are you suggesting, Giles?" Amber asked. "That I bond with just anyone because of their gift?"

"If that's the answer—"

Amber pushed her chin into the air. "My father didn't arrange a marriage for me, and I'm not about to let a man I hardly know make that decision on my behalf."

"Of course not. I'm not suggesting… But if the answer lies in bonding—"

"Keep looking," Kincaid said again.

Giles offered a single nod and returned to his books.

Half way down the hall to the kitchen, Amber pulled him to a stop. "Let's keep the information Giles gave us to ourselves for now. The others will worry."

"I agree. We need to weigh our options before bringing anyone else into the discussion."

Amber shook her head. "I'm not sure any discussion needs to occur. This is neither their problem nor their choice."

No, it's ours.

"Nay, Gavin. The problem is not yours either. 'Tis mine and mine alone."

"Did you read my mind?"

She hesitated. "I-I suppose I must have. It wasn't intentional."

Unsure of how he felt about her being inside his head, he offered, "You don't need to make any decision tonight."

She studied the floor below her feet. "No, I don't. But we both know this…" she squeezed her tied hand in his… "cannot last too long."

His jaw set and his back teeth started to pulse with the unintended pressure. His need to see her smile made him repeat her words. "Is holding my hand such a hardship, m'lady?"

There it was...a slight lift of her lips. "There are times you annoy me, Gavin Kincaid, but nay, holding your hand is no hardship."

"It was my kiss then?"

His heart lifted when she smiled full on and her cheeks turned an adorable shade of rose. "Is it polite to talk about kissing?"

"I suppose it depends on what time you're from."

"In my time, women would talk to each other about such things...but never a woman to a man."

"You know this from experience?"

Her dark eyes sparked when they finally met his. "I have not held another man's hand in years...not even my father's. I have no *experience,* as you say."

Kincaid lifted their joined hands, kissed the edge of her fingers.

She tugged but he wouldn't let her go. Not again. "Tsk, tsk...I'm teasing."

Her spark simmered into a quaint smile. Anyone else and he would swear the look was practiced and devious. But Amber had no way of honing the sort of womanly wiles that could sway a man with a look.

"We have time, Amber. Plenty of time to consider what needs to happen."

"I want to believe you."

"Then do."

She closed her eyes for a moment, the mirth on her face slid away. "When I was a child, before Grainna, I could sometime sense things before they happened. A small portion of my mother's gift lived inside of me."

Kincaid held perfectly still, too wired into her next words to move.

"I've not felt her gift for years. Until you took hold of my hand."

"W-what did you see?" *Do I really want to know?*

"The picture wasn't, still isn't clear." Her eyes

squeezed shut tight as if that would bring her visions into focus. "There's pain, uncertainty...and darkness. Something is coming. I don't know if I'll be here for it, but it's coming."

"Darkness?"

With her eyes still closed, she tilted her head; her long hair drifted to the side of her body and made him want to push it back.

"Encircling the darkness there's a blinding light that sparks around it. The light beyond sings, calling to me." She opened her eyes suddenly and stared directly at him. "That is what I see. What I feel is urgency. This time you speak of that we have, may be in theory only. In reality...I think not."

Kincaid blew out a long breath. "Do we have tonight?"

"My feeling and visions have no timeline."

Is that better?

"We should dine, Gavin. Think on what Giles has learned and make no assumptions."

The need to act...to do something, itched on the surface of his skin like ants crawling over ones' feet with the need to be brushed off. "We need to plan."

"Plan for what? Darkness?" Her shoulders folded in with a small laugh. "No need for that. Darkness will come regardless. We need to remember our convictions, what we stand for, and move from there." She nodded toward the kitchen. "Let's sup. Fuel the body, and the soul and mind will follow."

"Are you repeating your mother's words?"

Amber shook her head. "Nay...my father's."

Later that night, with Giles's words running through his head and Amber's small frame lying perfectly still next to his, Gavin held her hand and stared at the familiar ceiling above his head. Neither of them spoke, both of them lost in their own thoughts.

Every few minutes, he'd hear her voice in his head.

Amber's thoughts, her worry, skidded across his mind like a fly buzzing by.

Her desire for her mother's council was most apparent. When she shifted her weight on the bed, he felt her unease over sharing the space with a man.

On a completely caveman level, Kincaid enjoyed the fact she'd never shared her bed with anyone. In his time, he avoided virgins like the red plague. Not hard to do when most women were rid of their virginity before they were allowed to drive. He could say he avoided innocents...women who didn't guard their heart and didn't understand the underlying risk of being with him.

Amber might be innocent, in a virginal sense, but she wasn't naive to the dangers of life.

If the truth were told, she could probably teach him a thing or two about the risk of living.

Who would willingly move through time, some five to six hundred years in the future, to live? Who could say they had come against the greatest evil ever known and survived...and she had been what, a teenager?

"I was twelve...nearly thirteen," Amber's soft voice said beside him.

Content with the fact he could feel her inside his head, he released a sigh. "Was it awful?"

"I was little more than a child. I'd been told all my life that my brothers, Duncan and Fin, needed to travel beyond our time to prevent Grainna from regaining her power. I was told of her threat, but didn't truly understand it until I saw it myself."

He turned on his side and watched her as the light of the moon shone in from the windows. Her gaze was fixed on something above her.

"She followed Fin and Lizzy back to our time as an old woman. It wasn't long before her curse was broken and every day was a fight for survival. I'd been told all my life to use my gifts only when necessary. To hide them." She smiled, taking Kincaid by surprise. "Then Lizzy confronted all of us. Told us to work together, pull our energy together to fight Grainna. Can you imagine my excitement when I, a mere child, was encouraged to help battle evil?"

"It made you feel worthy."

"Aye. Worthy and needed. I worked harder...searching other's thoughts, the intentions of the animals around us. Anything. I'd sit in my room at night and spark fire from my fingers so often my fingertips were black." She laughed. The memory fresh in her mind filled him with warmth. "I realized the thought of Grainna coming back into her power truly terrified my father." She twisted in the bed and looked at him. "My father is never frightened. Worried, maybe...but frightened? Nay. Never."

"He understood the risk."

"He did. More than any of us. The evil she spread before we defeated her was a black soupy fog that darkened so many families, so many lives."

"Yours most of all."

"Cian lost a young woman caught in the fist of Grainna. He never did recover completely. His pain gripped me more than anyone's. It was his pain I felt knife through me once we destroyed Grainna. It was as if I couldn't breathe. Everyone else celebrated her demise and I slowly started to feel all the pain she left in her wake."

Kincaid swallowed.

"Before she died, when I saw her for the first time, I thought, my God, she's beautiful. How could someone so lovely be so evil? Then she looked at me as if she read every thought and I closed my eyes to the beauty I saw and focused only on the evil I felt. The evil the others around me witnessed. She scratched inside my head, trying to sway me. I felt her crawling in my mind like a worm in mud."

He scooted closer.

"I suppose one could say that was the moment I grew

up. That was when I put my childhood behind me."

"You were too young."

"We had no choice. It took all of us to defeat her. How old were you when you first went into battle?"

"That's different?"

"Why? Because you're a man?"

"That...and I was raised as a warrior."

She tucked her free hand under her cheek and rolled onto her side. "You're not unlike the men in my time. Eager for blood and battle at a young age."

"I've never been bloodthirsty."

"I would hope not. Avoid battle, but if you can't...come out the victor."

"Your father's words again?"

"Aye."

Amber seemed to forget she was in bed with a man and curled beside him with a smile on her face as they talked. When was the last time he chatted with a woman in his bed?

"He's a legend you know."

"My father?"

He nodded. "Ian...your brothers."

She grinned. "My father would scoff at that. Duncan, too. Fin, however, would love the title."

"Vain?"

She gave her head a small shake. "Proud."

"What about Cian?"

Her smile fell. "He would say the cost was too dear for the title." She paused, lost in her thoughts he couldn't read. "What does history tell of the women?"

"Your mother is considered the matriarch. Your sister, Myra...she's talked about often, and Tara and Lizzy are as well, but not like the men. My guess is men edited the books in time and didn't give the women their due."

"I would say not. Lizzy led all of us many times. She had little faith in her own abilities, but knew together we'd be stronger. My father and Fin wanted nothing to do with

110

involving the women in battle."

Kincaid couldn't completely relate. Women had always been a part of the team in his time. He knew of some men wanting to keep their women safe, which was probably why Kincaid opted to avoid involving his heart in his affairs. However, the women were often stronger in their Druid abilities and sometimes more levelheaded. Their usefulness on the team was unprecedented. Yet the women didn't accompany them on many missions located in Amber's time for obvious reasons. They did try to go undetected. If a woman were brandishing a sword, she'd be a target or very memorable.

"I miss them," Amber said pulling him from his thoughts. "I want to see them again…"

He heard her next thought in his head. *Before I die.*

Her words cut deep.

****

Selma walked barefoot, with a cup of steaming hot coffee in her hand, through her two-bedroom apartment that housed her small office. She'd left Jake close to midnight. He'd fallen asleep in his recliner with the remote on the arm of the chair. Though the stick didn't completely wiggle free of his sphincter during their dinner, he did manage to crack a smile or two in her presence. For a reason she couldn't even explain, she wanted to see the man let go of his tight grip of control. Every once in a while, when he was snarking at her, she'd notice a brief smile, a flicker of mirth behind his eyes.

Had he always been so rigid? Did he laugh with his children…with his ex-wife?

Selma fired up her computer and checked her inbox for orders. Her online business for all things Wiccan had been profitable for several years. It helped that the books she'd written still sold…well, the first one anyway. The second one edged too close to the truth about Druids and straddled the religious fence, which made many readers uneasy. Thankfully, when she'd written it she didn't know

111

CATHERINE BYBEE

she was Druid. She truly thought she was a witch. Still, between what she'd learned in her life, and what seemed to be inside her from her ancestors, Selma realized who she was.

She wouldn't be writing any more books. The first one, Sixth Sense, hit all the bestseller lists and landed her a few talk show spots several years ago. She'd been famous for a short time and ate it up. Now the only people who recognized her would have to follow her website and check out her "about me" page.

She printed out a half dozen invoices, flagged a back-order, and noticed a repeat customer's name toward the bottom of her inbox.

He called himself Norman Rockwell, which made her laugh the first time she'd seen it. He always ordered her love potion, and he did so every week. The mixture of herbs would only work if the recipient cared for the giver. Or so Selma believed. The last package she sent to Norman she added a small charm...asking the Ancients to give the man peace with whoever the potion was meant for. Based on how frequently he purchased her love potion, it seemed the woman he was attempting to snag wasn't interested.

Selma opened the order, full on expecting to see another need for her love potion.

That's not what she found.

The order form was blank. Looked like Norman Rockwell wasn't in the buying mood. He was however in a ranting mood.

Under the "special instructions" box her customer filled the space with hate.

YOU FUCKING BITCH. THE POTION WAS FOR ME AND HER, NOT HER AND HER FUCKING EX. YOU KNOW WHAT YOU DID. I KNOW WHAT YOU DID. I KNOW WHER...

The box didn't leave more room for him to write, cutting him off.

112

Her hand trembled as it moved over the mouse to delete the email. She hesitated and decided to keep it in her inbox. Over the years, people had asked for refunds, said her "shit" didn't work. This kind of hate mail didn't happen...not to her anyway.

Probably because most, if not all, of her "shit" did work. That would be the by-product of being the real deal.

Obviously this love potion worked...just not for the man giving it.

She glanced at the address she'd been sending the package to. It was a P.O. Box in Bullhead City, Nevada. Not more than a six-hour drive.

The P.O. Box she shipped her orders from was several blocks from her apartment, giving her some space from disgruntled customers. The precaution had been an afterthought when she moved to California. Now, she was happy for it.

She shook Mr. Rockwell from her head and moved on to the next order. When her morning ritual was complete and the coffee in her cup hit bottom, she moved to her supply closet and hand-packed and mixed the herbs for her orders.

When she was finished, she filled her bags for the post office and started from her office. The monitor on her desk clicked onto a screen saver, reminding her she'd left it on.

With her hands full, she concentrated on the mechanics of her computer, willing it to power down.

Nearly as quickly as she thought of turning it off, it did.

The smile on her lips spread. Using her mind, her gift, to control the electronics around her never got old. She even managed to unlock simple mechanical structures...like the front door of a certain police officer's house.

It was early, and the post office was quiet.

"Hey, Paul," she greeted the postmaster behind the

desk by name.

"Hi, Selma. Lots of orders today?"

"A few." She hoisted the bags onto the counter and handed them over one at a time.

"Does any of this really work?"

"Of course it does," she said with a grin.

Paul was in his mid-fifties, and his belly stuck out a little more than nature intended. Seemed like he enjoyed his job and always greeted her with a smile.

"My wife went on your website. Said you sell tea and crystals."

She placed another box on the counter and waited for him to weigh it and add the price to her list. "Crystals hold energy. And tea or, more precisely, herbs can ease the mind and soul into accepting the truth."

"Sounds like mumbo-jumbo to me. No offence."

"None taken." She'd learned long ago to disregard the general disbelief from the public.

"I went to a palm reader once at the county fair. Do you read palms?"

"No." She didn't need to look at a palm to have a feeling of the people around her.

"The woman told me I needed to stop smoking or I'd get ill." He paused with his hand on the package. "I didn't tell her I smoked. Spooky how she knew."

Selma stifled a laugh and placed her hand over his. "From the looks of the yellow around your fingers, I'd say you smoke two packs a day." She released his hand. "Guess you didn't believe her."

He stared at his hand as if it were a foreign object. "You think that's how she figured it out?"

She shrugged and folded up her now empty bag.

Paul gave her a total, which she paid with her credit card. "It's hard to quit. Try damn near every year."

When he handed her the receipt to sign, she brushed her finger over his and planted the seed for him to ignore his nicotine cravings. There were no guarantees, of course.

But she liked Paul and didn't want to see the man suffer with cancer.

"Every cigarette you don't smoke is a victory," she told him.

"That's what my wife says."

"Smart woman."

She tucked her bag under her arm. "See you tomorrow, Paul."

He waved and as she turned to leave, she smacked into the man standing behind her in line.

"Excuse me."

"Sorry," he said. His voice was small even though the hand he'd held out to keep her from falling gripped her elbow.

She looked up to see the man's face, and he released her and stepped back. Her body shuddered as unease crawled over her skin. His dark eyes didn't meet hers as he moved around her, dismissing her as quickly as he'd entered her space.

When she stepped out into the hot California sun, she shivered. The thought of her morning email had her looking over her shoulder.

"Paranoid much?" she asked herself.

Yet instead of driving home, she detoured toward Mrs. Dawson's.

Safety in numbers and all that.

Chapter Thirteen

Helen met her at the door with a bottle of Tums in her hand.

"Oh, boy…that's not a good sign." Selma pushed her way inside and wrapped an arm around her new friend's shoulders.

"I'm told it's a sign of a full head of hair." They walked down the hall and into Mrs. Dawson's parlor, or living room as most people called it.

"Blonde like you or brown hair like Simon's?"

"Has to take after his father. There's no way a blonde would come out with a full head of hair."

"It's a boy? Are you sure?" Selma sat beside Helen with a huge smile on her face.

"Amber told us last week."

Selma glanced at the ceiling, envisioning the room above where Amber usually hid. "How is she?"

Helen heaved a sigh. "So much better with Kincaid here."

"Future-Boy?"

"Excuse me?"

"The guy who showed up at Jake's? The guy from the future?"

Helen laughed now, getting the joke. "Right. Yeah…" Helen launched into an explanation of what had occurred since Kincaid had shown up.

"So let me get this right. Amber…little miss virginal and innocent has to hold Future-Boy's hand twenty-four-seven to keep the voices out of her head?" Selma couldn't imagine.

"Yeah."

The thought sunk in. "How is *that* working out?"

"I-I don't really know. It's not like I can pull her aside and ask what she's thinking... or how he's behaving."

"Is he being cool about it? I can't imagine what he's thinking."

"He's probably thinking he's stuck. He let her go for a moment yesterday and she was instantly ill." Helen lowered her voice and placed a hand over Selma's. "Between you and me...I think he's the guy Lora told her about."

"The one who saves her?"

"Has to be. She's different around him. She smiles. Can carry on a conversation."

Selma couldn't remember being in the woman's presence for more than an hour in the past. "The emotional pull of others is gone?"

"Dormant, I think. Certainly tolerable. What her gift should be, if you ask me. Simon told me she was like this years ago. Before Grainna."

"That's wonderful."

Helen's sigh told Selma her friend wasn't so sure. "What?"

"I'm worried. Something happened yesterday, right before Kincaid let her go that makes me think something awful is going to happen very soon."

Her own forbearing of the day's events sent shivers over her. "What happened?"

"Amber and Kincaid were outside walking. A crow watched them and freaked Amber out."

"Crows are often mistaken as a bad omen. That doesn't mean anything."

Helen shook her head. "No. This crow wasn't alone and was controlled by someone. A Druid. They were watching them. Kincaid told us that in the future this house is filled with Druids in order to fight off Others."

"Others...what others?"

"Druids not leading noble lives. People who found

out about us. Oh, I don't know. It sounds like this house is a fortress for those inside. He suggested we start to build that stronghold now. This morning, he encouraged Simon to acquire the funds to buy out the neighbors' properties."

"Seriously?"

Helen nodded. "In his time, the fortress is four times as large. The property anyway. The house changes, but it's the walls around the place that extend to damn near the interstate."

"That's five miles away."

"I know."

Selma sat back...paused. "Makes sense."

"Does it?"

"Yeah...if Amber wasn't surrounded by the neighbors maybe she wouldn't be having such a hard time."

Helen frowned. "I hadn't thought of that."

"None of us did. With the recession and the prices of houses dropping like crazy, now would be the perfect time to buy. Maybe the buffer will help in the future."

Selma thought for a while then asked, "So who controlled the crows?"

"We have no idea," Helen told her. "It seriously bugged Kincaid. And I don't think that guy bugs easily."

"He's a big man with big weapons."

"And a huge power. His shield is stronger than a vault in Fort Knox."

"Really?" Selma asked.

"Yeah."

They sat there for a few minutes, both staring away from each other and not speaking.

Helen snapped her head toward her and held her stomach at the same time. "Why are you here?"

"Do I need a reason?"

"No...but you're not here by accident."

The problem with having her world filled with Druids was the realization that secrets were impossible to keep. "I feel like someone is watching me. I'm being paranoid." Selma told her about the email, about the post office. "Paranoid. The guy in the post office didn't look at me twice."

"Never disregard your sixth sense."

Funny, the quote was one Selma has used in her book. "I know. Which is why I'm here I guess. I'd have bothered Jake, but he's at work."

Helen lifted her eyebrows a few times. "Jake, huh?"

They talked about him, his stoic disposition, and general "assholiness".

"You can always stay here," Helen told her. "I'm sure Mrs. Dawson wouldn't mind."

"I couldn't."

Helen shook her head. "Maybe when Amber was plagued with all our feelings you needed to stay away…but not anymore."

"The guy in the email is just ticked his girl hooked up with someone else and I'm just being paranoid. I know it."

"I don't know, Selma. There's a reason you're here, and I don't think it's paranoia."

Selma painted on a smile and pretended to blow off the feeling of being watched.

****

Hours later, after visiting with Amber, Future-Boy, and his friend, Giles, Selma returned home and worked her way into her evening routine. She popped her dinner into the microwave and tossed a salad while she watched the evening news.

"…the scene was out of a Hollywood macabre script," the reporter said. "Although the police aren't reporting details of the crime scene, it's safe to say the blood-bath reported by the neighbor had ritual written all over it."

Selma lowered the salad dressing in her hand and willed the volume of the TV to increase.

Police activity outside an apartment building filled

the screen. The coroner pushed a gurney past the camera, and a second one followed.

Selma blinked and turned back to her dinner.

"This kind of horror hasn't affected Bullhead City in years."

Her gaze snapped back to the screen.

"The ties to Southern California stem from the male victim. Victor Morales was a veteran of the Army once based at Camp Pendleton. His friends say he'd recently re-united with his high school sweetheart, and the two planned to marry. Instead of their families celebrating their union, they will be planning their funerals."

Liquid dripped down her arm, and Selma noticed the dressing emptying from the bottle.

Her sixth sense raced up her spine, edging toward terror. The news switched to the weather as if the people in the previous story meant nothing.

Selma dropped the empty blue cheese dressing bottle, snatched her purse from the counter, and ran out of her apartment.

Aware of everyone, everything around her, she managed to shove into the driver's seat of her car and turn the key.

Without direction, she found herself in front of Jake's home standing at the front door with salad dressing sticking to her fingers. She kept looking behind her as noise from inside Jake's home caught her attention.

She knocked, ready to use her gift to shimmy the lock on the door and let herself in.

The doorknob wiggled, bringing relief.

She opened her mouth to tell him he took long enough, and immediately shut it when an adorable blue-eyed girl opened the door.

Selma blinked, backed up, and looked at the address on the door.

No, it's the right place.

"Hi," the girl said with a dimpled smile.

"Hi."

"Kelsey, don't open the door," Jake's voice yelled from the back of the house.

"Too late, Daddy."

So this was Jake's daughter…

Before Selma could wiggle her mind around that, another girl made her way to Kelsey's side.

Identical twins?

How was it Selma didn't know that? Jake's daughters were twins?

"Sophie!"

"Too late." Selma said for the girls.

Jake appeared behind his daughters with a spatula in his hand and frustration on his brow.

"Who are you?" the one wearing green, Sophie if Selma could tell by the names called out, surmised.

"I'm Selma."

"Daddy's girlfriend?"

Selma met Jake's gaze.

She started to shake her head when Jake broke out in a rare smile. "That's right, Kelsey. This is Selma…my g-girlfriend."

He nearly choked on the title while he waved Selma inside.

****

Giles ran a hand through his hair before letting it fall to the stubble on his chin. He hadn't slept and couldn't imagine doing so now.

"There's nothing more. Nothing!"

Kincaid glared at him from across the table. Giles knew nasty words sat on the tip of the man's tongue, but with a woman at his side, he said nothing.

"Keep looking."

"Where?" He motioned toward the walls of the library. "I've searched. Books have flown off the shelves and there isn't anything more. Only one word is repeated."

Amber said nothing and stared at their hands.

"Bonding," Giles said in a shout. "That is the answer. It's everywhere."

"There has to be another answer."

"Does there? I think not."

Kincaid gripped the edge of the table.

"I know it's not the answer you want. But it is what it is. Amber must bond with someone…someone with your ability to protect her. Even then she would need to learn to use her mate's gift to survive."

Kincaid stood. The chair behind him skidded across the floor.

Amber tensed.

"Please, Gavin…Giles can only report what he has found. The fault does not lie with him. He is only the messenger."

Thankful for her kind words, Giles bowed his head. "I'm sorry there isn't another path."

He noticed the force behind her smile. "You have been a blessing, Giles. Please…go and find your dinner…a bed. I see the exhaustion in your eyes."

Instead of leaving the room, Giles knelt beside her, ignoring the man towering over him. "Forgive me for not finding the answer you seek."

She reached toward him, didn't touch, and graced him with a smile. "You have not disappointed me," she told him.

Beside him, Kincaid growled.

Without being dismissed, Giles found his feet and left the room.

Outside the library, he leaned against the wall and shamelessly eavesdropped.

"Calm yourself, Gavin."

"He's not looking hard enough."

Giles winced with his friend's words.

"Do you truly believe that?"

There was a sigh, and again the sound of a chair skirting across the floor.

Giles squeezed his eyes shut.

"There has to be another answer."

"If there's not?" Amber's voice was so low Giles could hardly hear it.

After a long pause, he heard his long-time friend's response.

"Then we bond."

Amber, who seldom smiled let alone expressed any form of humor, laughed.

His friend wouldn't take her humor in good form.

"Bonding is not something you wish in your life, Gavin. I've been inside your head...I know this."

"We have no choice," he argued.

Giles started to leave his perch, annoyed at his own lack of respect for the private conversation.

"There is always a choice. 'Tis what separates us from animals...from slaves."

The conversation stilled and stopped Gavin in his tracks.

"There is no need to make a decision tonight," he heard Amber say.

"You're right," Kincaid said much too quickly. "Tomorrow is soon enough."

The sound of chairs scraping across the floor motivated his feet.

In the sitting room off the kitchen, he found Mrs. Dawson staring out the window and rocking in a chair.

"There's a plate of food in the microwave," she told him.

"You shouldn't have."

"I didn't. Amber suggested it."

He worked his way in the kitchen and managed to power up the old-fashioned food warmer. The amount of power it took to run one of these things was asinine.

"Where are Helen and Simon?" he asked as he filled a glass with tap water.

"They retired."

Giles noted the darkness out the window.

What time is it anyway?

The time on the clock on the stove flashed eleven thirty-three.

"Do you know how to use the coffee maker?" she asked.

The request caught him off guard. He glanced at the machine. "I think so."

Mrs. Dawson turned her head toward his. "It's going to be a long night, Mr. Giles. I suggest you brew a pot."

Chapter Fourteen

"Grainna's name was used, and Kincaid called the woman Amber."

"Amber? Are you sure?" Raine asked.

Mouse rubbed his hands together, obviously happy to deliver good news for a change.

"What century was this again?"

"Twenty-first."

How did I miss that? "Describe the woman."

"Petite, almost sickly. Her skin was pale, as if she didn't spend time in the sun. Dark brown eyes and long dark brown hair."

"How long?"

"It was pulled back. But longer than the way most women wore it in the twenty-first century."

"She was Druid?"

"Yes. Powerful. She knew I was in the crow the moment it landed by her side. Kincaid didn't believe her at first."

Raine tilted her head to the side and met Mouse's eyes. "You exposed yourself?"

Mouse trembled, as he should.

"I needed to get close to hear them. Kincaid's shield surrounded both of them. I had no choice." Mouse's words ran into each other. "I released the bird before he destroyed it."

"Then what?"

"I don't know. I was too far away to witness anything. The fortress is nothing but a large home with a small perimeter in that time. Easily breached if we should go in and take it over."

"If Amber is the Amber MacCoinnich you describe,

infiltrating the fortress will call her family down on us. You don't think her father would leave her in a century so far from his own without a visitation plan, do you?"

Mouse swallowed. "No."

"We wait...we watch. Go back, find out the name of every occupant in the house, everyone who enters and leaves. Who are they...where do they reside in that time? Are any of them warriors or is Kincaid alone? I want art, Mouse...bring pictures, voice recordings if you can get them."

He lowered his head and started to back out of the room.

"Oh, and Mouse...?"

"Yes, ma'am."

"Don't get caught."

****

Kincaid felt her intent even though she worked hard to shield it from him. The stronger he enclosed them, the more united they became.

She wanted to bathe, but wasn't willing to talk to him about it. She didn't want to leave this world unclean.

That thought drifted in his head.

He pretended he hadn't heard her while he scrambled for a way to keep her tied to him.

Bonding.

Was it his destiny to bond with a MacCoinnich? With Amber? Was she to one day bear his children? Children he never imagined having. He'd kissed her, once, and thought about repeating it every hour since. Bonding wasn't something a Druid committed to based on one kiss.

He led her up the stairs, away from the drifting voices coming from the kitchen where he assumed Giles sat talking to Mrs. Dawson.

Inside her room, he closed the door with a soft click. The bed brought his focus, while Amber stared toward the bathroom. Her cheeks flushed and he reached behind him and shifted the lock on the door.

"Come," he said as he tugged her toward the bathroom.

With his free hand, he turned on the water in the deep claw tub and poured what looked like bubbles into the bath. Kincaid saw Amber's gaze search the room for privacy.

Only he didn't want her hiding…and he didn't want to hide. Bonding wasn't in his plan, as Amber had pointed out. But the thought of abandoning her to die without his shield wasn't something he could live with. She was a MacCoinnich for God's sake. The family he'd sworn to protect at all cost.

Even his own life.

However long or short that was.

Perhaps if he could keep her by his side for a little longer another solution would evolve.

"I can sit beside the basin while you bathe," Amber offered.

"You could." He unraveled the binding holding their hands together and lifted one of her hands to his neck.

She watched, fascinated, until he undid the belt that held his weapons and let it drop to the floor.

Her eyes fluttered shut when he reached for the clasp of his pants. She caught her lower lip in her teeth when he kicked his pants free and squeezed her eyes shut even tighter.

He kept his boxers on and lowered her hand to grip his waist while he pulled his shirt over his head. He paused then to watch her holding him.

"Do you trust me, Amber?"

He knew she did, could feel it inside her before she answered his question.

"I must."

Yes. You must. He placed her hand on his chest and lifted her other to hold his arm. Her touch was timid, unsure, and more arousing than he anticipated. He watched the play of emotions wash over her face before he reached

127

for the buttons of the shirt she wore.

Fingernails dug into his skin. "What are you doing?"

"It's hard to bathe in clothes."

"But…"

"You said you trusted me."

Her alabaster skin came into view one button at a time. The front clasp of her bra held her pert breasts from his gaze. The need to touch her, taste her rose like hunger. Yet he didn't want to scare her, or take anything not willingly offered.

His goal was to bathe her, both of them, and only give what she wanted.

He left her shirt open and reached for the button of her Capri pants. That got her to open her eyes. Before her gaze fluttered to his, she looked at her hand against his chest then nudged her thumb over the outline of the muscle she held. The touch made his stomach quiver and heat surge lower.

You're beautiful. Her thoughts filled his head and made him smile.

"You heard that."

"I did."

Her dark eyes found his and her hand kept moving, exploring. "Are you trying to seduce me?"

"I'm trying to bathe you. But if seduction is what you want…"

She tilted her head to the side and he felt her swimming inside his head. "I don't even know what seduction feels like, Gavin Kincaid, as you well know."

The tips of his fingers slid over her hip, half touching the skin above her pants, half sliding to the skin under her clothing. Her eyes opened wider with the contact.

"Then let's start with soap and water and see what happens."

Her grin was infectious. "Lizzy told me a man will say anything to get a woman naked."

"Did she?"

"Aye, and Tara agreed."

He inched his fingers to the small of her back and stepped closer. "Your sisters-in-law are wise women. I don't think, however, they could have foreseen this situation quite as clearly as the one they describe."

"I don't think anyone could have imagined us at this point." Amber placed the hand resting on her hip up to her shoulder, and then wiggled free of her shirt. Her brave front was thin, but she continued to remove her clothing while he held her.

"Should I close my eyes?" he asked.

"Do you want to?"

His gaze slowly traveled the soft planes of her body, the dips, and curves. His mouth went dry. "No." He wanted to feast on the view she offered.

She paused. "I don't know if I'm ready for you to feast on anything."

"You're poking in my head again."

She lowered her eyes.

He brought his finger under her chin and raised her gaze to his. "Look harder and see my intentions, Amber. Yes, I want to touch you, taste you. You're a stunning woman I'm about to bathe with—something I've never done with a woman I haven't been intimate with. But for you, I will keep my hands where you want them. That I promise." With any luck, she'd want them everywhere.

"Isn't that hard for a man?"

"Impossible."

"Painful?"

"Sometimes." *With you…most certainly.*

She kicked her pants free and reached for the clasp of her bra. Her fingers trembled and the clasp fell away. The pink rosy tips of her breasts stole his breath.

Sweet Jesus what was he doing?

He went rock hard in an instant. The loose material of his boxers left little to the imagination. Maybe he should have chosen cold water.

He helped the straps from her shoulders and tried to focus on the tiny freckles on her left shoulder.

The overwhelming feeling of embarrassment radiated from the woman standing in front of him. "You have nothing to hide, Amber. You're beautiful."

"I'm too thin," she told him.

A woman was never happy with her own body. "Nothing that some food and exercise outdoors won't help."

The sound of the tub filling up brought his attention behind them. He stopped the flow of water and quickly shed his boxers.

"Oh, my," she whispered at his side.

Her hand started to slide away and he clasped it tight. "Don't get shy on me now, Amber. We're nearly there."

"Aye, but you're…"

"Aroused? Yes. Like I said, you're beautiful, and a man's body will respond to that beauty. My brain can't stop it, but I don't have to act on it." He lifted her then, placed her feet inside the tub. "You can remove your underwear under the suds. That way I can't see."

"But when we get out…"

"I'll close my eyes if you like."

She shook her head. "I'm such a child." She surprised him by bending down and removing her panties. "I'm tired of being a child."

Amber turned away from him, held his hand, and slid into the warm depths of the tub with a sigh.

With his back teeth grinding together and a tight grip on his emotions, he slid in behind her and sandwiched her between his legs.

Their skin touched everywhere in the small tub. The warm water was a pleasure to sink into, but the warm woman…now she was perfection. Only he couldn't exactly touch her…not yet.

He released her hand and settled his back against the tub. The bubbles in the water couldn't hide the soft texture of her hip against his leg, or the length of her lean neck as she brushed her hair in front of her.

Amber leaned forward, removed a bar of soap from a dish and a washcloth before scrubbing the two together. She was trying so hard to be brave, but he could feel the frightened girl under the sensual woman.

"Talk to me, Gavin. Your silence is killing me."

He leaned forward then, removed the washcloth from her hand, and slowly washed the space between her delicate shoulder blades. "The first time I made love to a woman I was scared to death," he told her.

She gasped, and graced him with a look over her shoulder. "Do I truly want to hear this?"

"You're naked in a bathtub with a near stranger. Arguably the most embarrassing position you've ever been in, in your life...I think it's only fair to share mine with you."

She blinked and a small amount of moisture filled her eyes before she turned around.

"She was much older than I was," he continued.

"How much older?"

Kincaid smiled and continued running the washcloth over her skin. "My best friend's step-mother."

Amber gasped, twisted again, a glimpse of her full breast made his mouth water. "Tell me you're joking."

"Why? It's the truth."

"Your best friend?"

He nodded. "At the time, anyway." He twisted her around and continued washing her. "Mrs. Robbins wasn't a mother in any way."

"She should be horse-whipped for seducing a young man."

"I wasn't that young. Besides, I knew what I was doing. So did she."

Kincaid watched the lucky bar of soap as it traveled up her arm and disappeared down the delicate skin between her breasts. His erection pushed between them

131

and it took every effort not to shift his hips closer.

"What possessed Mrs. Robbins to seduce you?"

"I was young...innocent, but unlike Mr. Robbins, I was moldable. I think she liked the challenge of teaching me what I'd only heard about from my friends." He dipped the washcloth below the waterline to scrub her lower spine. His thumb brushed over a small knot on her back and Amber moaned. He abandoned the cloth and worked the area of her discomfort with his fingertips.

"Did she teach you that?"

He pressed harder and was rewarded with a sigh. "That was someone entirely different. No, Mrs. Robbins taught me I had a lot to learn about women."

"That's right, you said it was embarrassing. What happened?"

The memory flooded his mind. "How much do you know about sex?"

She stiffened with his question but he refused to acknowledge the shift in her body. "I understand the mechanics of it," she finally said. "Lizzy told me it hurts the first time, but Myra told me it wasn't bad. Does it hurt a man?"

"Ah, no."

"I didn't think so."

Damn she was innocent in so many ways. "No, there wasn't any pain with Mrs. Robbins. She didn't even laugh when she barely touched me and I went off like a blast from a gun."

Amber actually giggled. "That's a bad thing...right?"

Her laughter kept him talking while he removed the band in her hair and tossed it to the side of the tub. "I was mortified. Mrs. Robbins didn't look twice and in no time showed me how to please her."

Amber tilted her head back when he filled his cupped hands with water and started to wash her hair. "Did you love her?"

It was his turn to laugh. "Mrs. Robbins wanted to be

loved by many. Hard to grow attached to a woman like her. Besides, she was much older than me."

"But you cared for her."

He did…in a small way. He forgot for a moment who he was talking to and said the first thing that came to his mind. "It's hard to not care a little for the first woman who gives you a blow job."

Amber laughed. "A what?"

Kincaid squeezed his eyes shut and tried to throw the image of Mrs. Robbins bent over his cock from his mind.

"No!"

He opened his eyes to find Amber watching him with stunned silence. He knew she'd read his mind and didn't try to hide it. "I guess your sisters didn't tell you about that."

"Truly?"

He shifted her again, and went about washing her hair with renewed vigor. "There is more to a sexual relationship between a man and a woman than intercourse." Mrs. Robbins taught him that…thoroughly.

"In my time, a woman's innocence is only to be given to her husband. Yet no man ever comes to his marital bed innocent. Seemed to me it wasn't fair."

"Which is why in time all that changes. I suppose Liz and Tara told you that."

"Aye, they did. Yet Liz reminded me often how a woman carries the burden of a night of pleasure while a man will often leave her to it."

He lathered the shampoo in her hair and messaged her scalp. "Preventing pregnancy was a woman's burden, as you call it, until about fifty years from now."

"Oh? What changes?"

"Male birth control."

"You mean the plastic thing that goes over…well, you know."

His "you know" was pressed against her back as she finally relaxed against him.

133

"Condoms... yes, there are those. But I'm talking about medicine similar to what a twenty-first century woman might use."

"I wondered if they might have invented something like that. When Liz told me about it, I thought she was jesting. Then I thought...if the physicians of this time could come up with a solution for a woman, they must be able to come up with something for a man."

"They did. The government funded the research as a way of controlling the population. For years, they added the steroid as a part of a routine physical for young teens. Once word got out that doctors were giving the drug to unaware patients, there was a huge revolution. After a decade the drug was re-introduced as a way for a man to never be accused of fathering a child that wasn't his."

"What about disease? Is that not a concern in your time?"

"We have a pill for everything."

"Oh..." she leaned her head back and closed her eyes as he rinsed the soap from her hair. "I guess your Mrs. Robbins didn't worry about anything then."

No, she didn't.

With the suds washed free, Kincaid leaned against the back of the tub and shifted one leg to lie over Amber's. At the same time, he nudged her back until she rested against his chest. Her hand fell to his leg, and he felt the timid stroke of her fingers.

"Thank you," she whispered.

"For what?"

Her eyes were closed, her lashes lay on her cheeks, and her skin smelled of the jasmine soap. The whole package warmed him in a way Mrs. Robbins never could.

"For this moment. Your shield has brought me more peace than I ever thought I'd have in my life. And you shared your most innocent moment to ease my discomfort."

He leaned his head back and smiled. "You're

welcome."

The words in her head filled his. *I can now die a happy woman.*

His eyes shot open, his jaw clenched. He searched her thoughts and found them cut off.

The image of a stream filled his mind. Instead of working past it, he envisioned it to keep Amber from his feelings. How can she think of dying? What could he do to distract her and keep her thinking of tomorrow?

Kincaid traced her arm with his index finger and enjoyed the small tremor it sent over her skin. Maybe a distraction would be the best medicine.

Though his body had relaxed against hers, it wasn't unaware that a desirable woman was tucked between his legs.

He walked his fingers up her arm and noticed her gaze drift to his touch. He stilled his hand and tilted his lips to the top of her head. The image of the stream shifted, and he knew it was something she'd placed in her head to keep him out of her mind. When he touched her, she couldn't concentrate and keep him away.

It wasn't fair, he knew, but he kept touching her and wiggled deeper into her thoughts.

Perhaps it was time for Amber to learn there was more to a sexual relationship than intercourse.

Though intercourse sounded damn good to him right about now.

Chapter Fifteen

The memory of the stream close to MacCoinnich Keep kept Gavin on the very edge of her thoughts. Oh, he knocked and peeked behind the closed door, but she only allowed a shadow of her thoughts to sift through. It was amazing, really, how quickly she'd learned to filter the information he silently heard from her. It was a blessing to be using her birthright, instead of it killing her. She'd forgotten so much about life in the past decade.

I can now die a happy woman. On one level, the thought saddened her, on another, she was thankful. She wasn't going to die in a puddle of tears without any redeeming memories of the past ten years.

Gavin drew in a breath behind her, and she thought harder about her home...about the Highlands and the endless green hills and streams she'd left behind.

The edge of Gavin's fingers traced her arm and caught her attention.

He'd been a gentleman while he attended to her hair...a naked and aroused man, but certainly in more control than she'd thought possible.

"You have the most beautiful skin," he told her. "Soft, silky."

She felt his desire through her gift, but didn't open her mind for him to hear her thoughts. For if he knew how wonderful every inch of his skin touching hers felt, he might use that information to his advantage.

Maybe his advantage wasn't a bad option.

After all, this was most likely the last night of her life. She wasn't about to force Gavin into a bond, and the longer they held hands, the more he'd feel obligated to keep her. His convictions toward her family had deep roots, roots she saw when they spoke. Bonding, however, was an eternal commitment, and perhaps someone else was meant for him in his life. Someone who wasn't as broken as she was.

"Is that a practiced line, Gavin Kincaid?"

His chest rumbled next to her back, making her smile. She felt his breath against the lobe of her ear and trembled.

"That depends," he whispered.

She closed her eyes and asked, "Depends on what?"

"If it's working."

Oh, it's working. She felt, but didn't acknowledge his hand that rested on her hip in the water.

"Tell me...how would I know if it's working?" She wasn't sure who was teasing whom, but she enjoyed the game.

He cleared his throat, and his hand at her hip pulled her tighter against him. "Well...the words make you ask yourself if my touch..." he ran his hand with a feather-light touch along her neck, "makes your insides warm or cold. If the words make my touch feel cold...then you know it's a line. If it makes you warm, makes you picture other places my hand can go...what it might do...then you know it's not practiced, but sincere."

Her throat went dry. "Where else can your touch go?"

His lips met the lobe of her ear in a gentle caress.

Her entire core clenched—her jaw, her stomach—lower in a place she knew was meant to react, but she'd never felt it respond before.

"Where do you want it to go, Amber?"

The sound of his lips saying her name made her smile. Though the thought of the stream by MacCoinnich Keep was running in the back of her head, the desire to let Gavin deep inside her made the grip on her thoughts slip.

"You're the teacher here, Mr. Kincaid," she used a formal name to play off his experience with Mrs. Robbins. "Why don't you show me?"

With a voice so low she had to strain to hear it, he

asked, "Are you sure?"

Words escaped her. His hands hesitated, as if asking permission before dipping into the food on a table. The urgency inside him was huge and under a thin layer of control.

He wanted her.

Though she couldn't name what she wanted, she knew she didn't want him to leave her like this...wet, warm, and incomplete.

Amber nodded.

The relief inside him made her smile.

Gavin's lips slid below her ear as his tongue showed her what a simple touch could do. While her mind sucked in the feeling of his lips on her, his hand under the water reached up and took the weight of her breast. The pad of his thumb ran over her, bringing her nipple to pert attention and making everything inside her respond with need.

Need for what she couldn't describe...but she wanted. Oh, she wanted.

"I probably shouldn't enjoy that."

He chuckled. "Why not?"

"I-I was taught—"

Gavin lifted her lips to his and cut her words off.

It didn't matter what she'd been taught. Her life was never going to be what her parents predicted. This— now—was all she need concern herself with.

Gavin's tongue stroked her bottom lip as he shifted in the cooling water to kiss her more thoroughly. His touch rippled over her skin, making her quiver. Thoughts of her troubles vanished under his kiss.

He shifted her on his leg until she was pressed fully against him and her hand rested on his chest. His body, pressed against hers, held its own armor, its own safety, and she wanted more...so much more.

Air cooled her damp skin at the same time Gavin ran his warm, hand up her back. He angled his head and kissed her deeper.

Mrs. Robbins did a fine job of teaching him to keep her warm. And his kiss...good Lord she couldn't breathe and didn't want to come up for air.

When his hand ran the length of her body, from breast to knee, she was possessed with a desire to touch him...all of him. Unsure of the liberties he was permitting her, she moved her hand slowly over his chest and low on his stomach.

My brave girl. The words were his, and they swam in her head.

Her lips slid away from his as he kissed her neck.

"You make me brave," she told him.

The stream she thought of now filled her...only she hadn't put it there...the image came from him. She wanted to ask him why he cloaked his thoughts. To do so would bring attention to the fact that she did the same to him.

His fingers ran up her knee on the inside of the thigh. "How brave do you want to be, Amber?"

"I know you won't hurt me," she whispered.

His eyes met hers as his hand slowly inched closer to the pulsating need resting within the apex of her thighs.

The stream in her head switched off and one thought penetrated all others. *Tell me to stop and I will.*

On the edge of sanity, she leaned toward him and initiated a kiss of her own.

Don't stop.

A deep sigh escaped his lips, and he kissed her with more hunger, more urgency, yet his hand moved slowly until she felt his fingers brush against the tangle of hair at her core. The intimacy was nearly too much until he brushed against her. She jerked against him and not away.

"Oh..."

"Shh," he moved closer, searching, until he found the place in her she hardly knew was there. "I've got you," he murmured.

Her eyes closed, her head rolled back on his arm.

139

Instantly his lips were on her neck, his kiss marking her. All the while, his fingers danced against her so slowly it made her crazy.

She felt her legs opening to him, wanting him.

He passed over the intense bundle of nerves so gently she gasped. He touched her again and her fingernails dug into his arms.

"Have you never touched yourself?" he asked in a hoarse whisper.

Her head fell to the side and quickly back. "Nay...I-I..." She'd tried, more than once, but the noise in her head never left her alone to complete the task. But not now...oh, not now.

"Shh...let me show you, my innocent."

She couldn't stop him if she'd wanted to. His hand moved over her with intent, fingers dipping just enough to make her want more while others passed over her and made her push against him. Her breath came in short waves as her lips sat against his neck. She was pliant in his arms and completely exposed to anything Gavin wanted.

Yet it seemed all Gavin wanted was to give her pleasure.

Everywhere he touched sent waves of bliss over her. There had never been a time in her life when she felt as unguarded as she did now, without a worry or concern from the world outside. It was only her and Gavin and, with only the two of them, the world sang.

His fingers took on a rhythm, rocking against her while he whispered in her ear, telling her to relax and just feel.

When her limbs melted, obeying his words, her insides focused on one place with intensity more potent than magic could ever reach. Of its own volition, her body reached for some unknown place, found it, and shattered into a million sparkling pieces.

She called out Gavin's name, heard the water in the tub splash against the tile on the floor, and couldn't bring herself to worry that a man, who was not her husband, had his fingers deep inside her.

****

"Girlfriend?" Selma hissed under her breath as he stood aside for her to walk in.

"Zip it, Matilda. You owe me."

She didn't...not really, but this was too fun an opportunity to pass up. The driving force that brought her to his door was buried for a later discussion. Love potions and the heebie-jeebies dancing over her skin would have to wait until the twins weren't staring at the two of them.

Jake pushed her into the kitchen where something on the stove was doing its best to send up smoke signals to the neighbors. "Oh, damn..." Jake jumped to the stove and removed the smoking pan. The black bread inside resembled some kind of a sandwich...or so Selma thought.

"That's a quarter in the swear jar, Dad," Kelsey said as she perched up to the kitchen counter.

"A swear jar?" Selma asked.

"Yeah, Daddy cusses—"

"A lot," Sophie finished her sister's sentence.

"I'm not that bad," Jake defended himself as he tossed the ruined meal in the garbage can.

Kelsey rolled her eyes and shook her head.

Sophie picked up a mason jar that sat on the counter and shook it. From the sound of the change ringing inside, the girls had quite the college fund going.

Selma took the jar from Sophie's hand and glanced at the writing on the homemade wrapper. Dad's F-Bombs = $1.00, everything else .25 cents. After glancing inside the jar and noted several green bills in the mix, Selma caught her lower lip in her teeth to keep from laughing out loud. *Priceless!*

"And that's only been a week."

"Yeah, and we're not here all the time," Kelsey told her. "He says he puts money in when we're not here, but I don't think he does."

"Hey!" Jake scolded. "*He's* right here...and I do."

Sophie sat taller and called him out. "Then why doesn't your girlfriend know about the jar, Dad?"

Selma cocked her head to the side and waited to see what bullshit was going to spew from his lips now. "Yeah, why doesn't your *girlfriend* know about it?" she asked.

His blue eyes found hers, and she noticed a slight smile on his lips. "Because I don't want to scare my *girlfriend* off by showing her all my faults."

The girls seemed to buy his answer while the two of them stared at each other.

Selma pushed away from the counter and grabbed the spatula from his hand. "I already know about your inability to cook."

"I'm not *that* bad."

Selma glanced into the waste container. "Oh, yeah? What's that supposed to be?"

"It's a grilled cheese sandwich."

"His specialty," Kelsey boasted.

"Just not today, eh?"

"If I didn't have to stop to answer the door, it would have been fine."

Somehow, she doubted that. "Ah, huh."

"It would."

"Are you guys fighting?" Kelsey asked. "Mom says Dad will never get married again because he only knows how to fight and not communicate."

"We're not fighting!" Jake twisted around and grabbed two more pieces of bread, mumbling under his breath. "Damn woman."

"That's another quarter, Dad." Sophie's ears were tuned into her dad's mouth.

"It's okay, Daddy," Kelsey said. "John can't cook either."

Something had gotten up Jake's ass, and Selma didn't have the heart to expose it with the girls in the room. She moved to his side and helped him butter the bread to cook another sandwich. "Who's John?" she asked, making conversation.

"That's Mom's fiancé."

Jake's hand hesitated as he grabbed the cheese.

So that's the problem. Jake's ex is moving on. That explains her elevation to girlfriend status.

"Yeah, they just got engaged last week. Kelsey and I get to be in the wedding."

"I'll bet that will be fun." Selma removed the knife from Jake's hand and let her hand linger on his.

He pulled away after a moment and turned to grab a beer from the frig. "Want one?" he asked.

"No, I'm good."

Without too much effort, Selma had the sandwiches on plates, cut up a lone apple from the fruit bowl, and poured them milk that had miraculously appeared in the fridge since the day before. The girls chatted while Jake brooded. They wanted to catch Selma up on their lives in the time it took to eat one meal. Kudos to them, Selma knew a heck of a lot more than before she walked in the door.

Jake took them to the park every Saturday he had them. Sometimes to play baseball, sometimes to play basketball. Every once in a while, Sophie would convince him to go ice skating. Listening to Jake's escapades on a bladed boot was worth the drive over.

Jake smiled. Once the conversations swayed from his ex, Kelsey crawled into his lap and the man lit up like a tree at Christmas. He clearly adored his children...and they doted on him.

The stick that had been so firmly up his butt wasn't there when he was with his kids.

It made Selma sad to know he couldn't find peace when they weren't around.

As the hour grew late, he shooed the kids off to brush their teeth and get ready for bed.

Selma cleaned up the kitchen...or in this case, tossed

143

the paper plates in the trash and cleaned the one pan. One of the girls ran around the corner, dressed in a nightgown. "Good night, Selma." Her small arms wrapped around Selma's waist, and she hugged her back.

"G'night…" Oh, damn, now that the girls had changed clothes, she couldn't tell which one she was.

"Kelsey."

"G'night, Kelsey." The girl let go and disappeared down the hall.

"They're adorable," she told Jake once he made it back to the living room.

He picked up a forgotten sweater on the floor and parked his butt in *his* chair.

"They're good kids," he said on a heavy sigh.

She could read his sigh and the language his body amplified as he took his time folding the small sweater.

"How often do they stay over?"

"Every other weekend…I get a mid-week visit and a month in the summer." From his tone, it wasn't enough.

"Doesn't seem fair…"

"It's best for them. Lindsey, my ex, lives in a good school district. The girls need stability. My job doesn't always offer that."

Still not fair. "They need their dad."

He stopped fiddling with the sweater and stared at the wall. "Looks like they're getting another one of those."

Wow! This was not the snarky man she'd grown to enjoy tossing barbs with.

"Back up the boat. This John guy might be the new squeeze, but these girls get one dad. Seems to me even they know that."

He shrugged, not agreeing, not disagreeing.

She changed the subject. "Do you really make 'em play ball all the time?"

"They like it."

The spark in his words made her continue her line of questioning. "Next you'll take them to target practice."

144

"Nothing wrong with a girl knowing how to aim and shoot."

Selma smiled. "I'm a girl and I've never been shown how to shoot a gun."

He snapped his eyes to hers. "That's a shame. It's a sick fucking world out there."

She waved a finger in the air. "That's a buck in the swear jar, buddy."

He laughed then... a full laugh Selma wasn't sure she'd ever heard from him before. The sound filled something inside her and made her want to hear it again.

"Sophie works that jar better than a Denny's waitress works tips. I swear her first car is going to be a fu...freaking Ferrari when she's sixteen."

"With the way you cuss, you're probably right."

"Yeah..." He stared at his hands. "I'm relieved she's getting married again."

Selma didn't remember asking.

"The alimony was killing me."

"I bet."

He sighed.

"Have you met John?"

He nodded, didn't meet her gaze. "Yeah. Nice enough guy...for a pencil pusher."

"Not a man's man?"

Jake smirked. "Desk jockey at some pharmaceutical company. Pitches new drugs or something like that."

"Polar opposite of a cop."

He shrugged, clearly lost in his own thoughts. "She couldn't handle being a cop's wife. Damn, we fought all the time. After the girls were born it was better...for about a year. Then it just sucked all the time. We couldn't find our rhythm again."

Selma felt her heart melt a little for the man who was clearly unhappy.

"Todd and I would hang. He'd tell me what an ass I was. He was like a brother to me."

145

She studied her hands, picking at the polish on her nails. She knew he and Todd were close. Poor Jake lost his wife and his kids, at least full time, and then his best friend. No wonder he fought everything Druid, everything Selma stood for.

"Love is more than a rhythm. More than routine," she told him.

"Maybe, but when you have kids you're supposed to suck it up...make it work."

Selma had a relatively picture perfect childhood. Her family was close, and her parents were still married. They, however, loved each other. They didn't have to *work* to make it work, or if they did, it wasn't apparent to any of the family.

"Your ex didn't want to work on it?"

He shook his head and didn't elaborate.

"I want what's right for them," he said nodding toward the hall where his daughters slept.

"You're doing the best you can, Jake. Cut yourself some slack."

He huffed out a laugh. "So, you're a witch and a psychologist?"

"Nope, just a witch."

He looked at her now, and something in his eyes shifted, looking deeper. "So what brought you here tonight anyway?"

She blinked a few times and tried to figure out a way to tell him her concerns without adding a burden to his already busy world..

"Daddy?" one of the girls called from the other room."

Jake offered a half-smile as he pushed off the couch. "Hold that thought."

He disappeared and when he didn't come back, she tiptoed into the room that housed the girls. It looked like they'd all climbed into the same bed and Jake had fallen asleep with a book in his lap...the girls snoozed right along with him.

Selma let herself out, realizing for the first time that Jake had a huge soft side...one he reserved for his girls.

Chapter Sixteen

Amber couldn't bring herself to be embarrassed. Gavin clearly knew what he was doing, knew her body better than she did.

He pulled her from the cooling water and carefully dried her with a ready towel.

Without covering himself with clothing of any kind, he lifted her into the bed in the other room and tucked her into his side. He didn't reach for her, nor did he take any more liberties with her.

"You're a gifted teacher, Gavin."

He stroked her damp hair as he spoke. "You're a beautiful student."

"I feel the need to thank you."

She heard his soft laugh. "My pleasure."

"Oh?" She twisted to see his face. "I don't believe you took your pleasure at all."

"One thing at a time."

We're running out of time.

"Would bonding with me be so awful?" he asked once she settled again.

She thought of the stream, hoped he couldn't read her thoughts. "We don't know if bonding will make your shield hold me without a physical link." He was whole and didn't need her ending his life if their bond wasn't strong enough. The danger for Gavin was too great for her to risk it.

"We don't know it won't either."

"'Tis not something we can try for a short time. If it doesn't work, we cannot undo it. You know this."

"We should try."

His hand squeezed around her, holding her tight, and

pulled her closer.

She couldn't. "Tomorrow will be here soon enough," she told him. Hoping her delay would pacify him.

She felt part of him relax with her words. Amber took his unspoken words as acceptance and closed her eyes...pretending to sleep.

Gavin fought exhaustion for several hours until finally he slept. His breathing became steady, and the stream she'd place in his head drifted to his own dreams. They weren't clear to her, but she knew they were a sign his conscious self was deaf to the world.

She closed her eyes and lowered her own barriers to feel him. Like all warriors, he was deeply convicted...and in Gavin's case, dedicated to seeing her safe, dedicated to a higher purpose than his own life, his own desires. A glimpse of hope touched her heart. Desire for her outside his need to protect her was there, but it wasn't enough to convince her that they needed to bond. Though she knew before she searched his feelings he couldn't possibly want to be bound to a woman he hardly knew, she couldn't help but wish for a different outcome.

An underlying desire for him to act rose to the surface of his dreams. He slept now from need, not desire. He wanted to stay alert to keep her at his side...to protect her. That thought brought tears to her eyes.

Sleep, she told him in her head.

He sighed deeply, and she repeated herself many times until most of his thoughts were a jumbled mess of dreams, none of it making sense, none of it meaning anything.

She rolled over onto her back, putting space between them but not letting him go.

Gavin didn't stir.

At the foot of the bed lay the cloak she'd worn nonstop before Gavin appeared in her life. With her foot, she removed the garment and caught it with her free hand.

Sleep, my love. Sleep.

He did.

She inched farther away from his warm frame and her pulse shot higher. The painful memory of the moment he let her go swam in her head, made her stomach turn.

Amber knew what was coming, and prayed to anyone listening that some of the impact would dissipate so she could leave him long enough…long enough to make her own choice for once in her God-forsaken life.

She'd only ever been a burden to those she cared for and wouldn't let Gavin take her on for eternity because of his sworn oath.

With the bulk of the cloak wrapped around her, she moved to the edge of the small bed, all the while encouraging Gavin to sleep through their temporary link.

Only their fingers touched as she stared down at his sleeping form. He was the most beautiful man she'd ever met, and she would be eternally thankful for him. She hoped, prayed rather, he'd know she appreciated all he'd given her. *I can't ask any more of you.*

Amber placed her arm at her mouth to stifle the pain she knew was coming…

Then she let Gavin go.

****

The image in his dream was so beautiful, majestic to the point his eyes hurt when he looked at her. She floated like an angel, with open arms as she coaxed him from sleep with the voice of a choir. Wake, Gavin…wake.

Only an equally calming voice told him to sleep. Amber. She told him to sleep and her drug was so much more potent. He needed to listen.

His dream switched, and the angel was bound, unable to speak. Only her eyes spoke, and they told him he had to act…act now.

His limbs ached as he rolled in his sleep. The bed squeaked, reminding him he wasn't in the century of his birth. No, he was tucked next to Amber…

He reached for her.

Gavin's eyes shot open while he sprang from the bed.

"Amber?" he said her name under his breath, at first…didn't see her…couldn't feel her.

"Amber?" This time he yelled. Every cell in his body woke, and every light in the room turned on. "Amber?"

He jumped from the bed, rushed to the bathroom.

She wasn't there.

The door to the room burst open. Simon stood there, much in the same state Kincaid was…naked and on alert.

"She's not here." Gavin's words filled the small room.

Simon spun in a circle and in a blink, shifted into a wolf.

He sniffed the air and bounded from the room.

Gavin ran after the wolf, up the stairs leading toward the attic. Behind him he heard others coming and only hesitated long enough to kick in the locked door to the attic and follow Simon through.

Amber was there, under a cloak, unmoving.

No. No…

Gavin grasped his head and fell on her. "No, dammit…this is not how we die."

She didn't move, her frame was cold and part of him bled.

"No!" He shoved the cloak from her head and stared on her pale face, her blue lips. "No."

"No!" The scream came from behind him. Helen he thought, followed by the sound of a struggle. "Do something. Someone do something!"

Gavin stroked Amber's still face and closed his eyes.

This isn't right. This can't be…

A tear fell.

He couldn't feel her breathing and knew he was too late.

His destiny was lying in a cold heap on the floor in a dirty attic, and he could do nothing.

Amber was his destiny…

This isn't going to happen!

Gavin grasped the bottom of the cloak covering his woman and bit at the edges until he managed to rip a strip of fabric away. With it, he grasped her cold hand, forced back desperation, and bound them together.

"From the North, to the South, in the East or in the West. Where you go I'll follow, your light will shine my way…"

Behind him, he heard those who gathered talking, but didn't comprehend what they said.

"It's my love I give you, past my dying day." The air charged with a current swirling around him, he felt the power of his bond even if the woman he was bonding himself to wasn't aware. "Where two hearts beat, there is now but one." He pulled the tie over their hands tighter. "This tie that binds us together shall never…ever…be undone."

His world exploded and pain swallowed him into a vortex that stole his breath and everything went dark.

****

Blinding light emitted from the couple right before Kincaid crumbled over Amber's still form. Simon fell on them first, his fingers moving to Amber's neck, and then to Kincaid's.

"Are they…"

"Nay. Their hearts still beat," Simon told them.

Giles released a deep sigh of relief. Maybe his friend wasn't too late. He'd heard the shout from the kitchen and scrambled up the stairs two at a time, only to see a wolf bound from Amber's room and up the final flight to the attic of Dawson's manor. When he witnessed his friend bending over Amber, he thought to pull him back, let him know there was nothing he could do, but then Kincaid started to chant. Giles attempted to move forward to stop his friend, but couldn't move his feet.

Simon nudged Kincaid, but he didn't wake. It was clear his shield wasn't elevated in his current state, but who knew how long that would last. "We should move them," Giles suggested, surprised he could step toward the couple now, when he couldn't a moment before.

Giles nearly buckled under his friend's weight as Simon followed behind him with Amber.

They placed their still bodies on the bed, Kincaid's hand in Amber's, and covered them.

"Why aren't they waking up?" Helen asked between sniffles.

Simon grabbed a throw from the end of the bed and wrapped it around his waist.

"Maybe we should call a doctor," she suggested.

"And tell them what, exactly?" Giles asked. "Drugs aren't going to fix them."

"Well, we have to *do* something. Standing here watching them breathe isn't doing anything!" Helen voiced all of their frustrations.

Simon moved to her side and laid a hand on her shoulder.

She moved into him, buried her head in his shoulder. "We have to do something."

Mrs. Dawson, who'd been silent, moved into the room as old women do...slowly and intently, in a way that had everyone parting the way. "Giles, m'dear, will you kindly gather the candles in the library. Helen, if you can help him, I'm sure we'll have enough."

"You have an idea?"

"I can only do what it is we understand. We'll ask the Ancients for their guidance, for their protection while these two souls fight their way back."

"Back from where?"

Mrs. Dawson narrowed her eyes to Helen. "From death."

Her words grounded everyone in the room.

Giles and Helen gathered handfuls of candles from the library and returned to the third floor room.

Simon stood beside Amber, his hand on her forehead.

Helen placed the candles around the room, and Simon lit them with a wave of his hand.

"Now what?" Giles had been a part of a few group effort protection spells, but never with anyone as powerful as Simon.

Simon grasped Amber's limp hand and offered his other to his wife. Helen lifted a hand to Mrs. Dawson. Giles completed the loop by grasping Mrs. Dawson's and taking Kincaid's.

"Just listen, and believe we can make a difference," Simon told them.

Before Simon opened his mouth, the flames rose, bringing heat to the room.

"In this day and in the hour, we ask the Ancients for their power. Surround these two with each other's protection. Draw from us for their resurrection."

In Giles's hand, Kincaid's began to shudder and heat, making holding him nearly impossible.

"If the Ancients will it so, give us a sign and let us know."

The words no sooner left Simon's lips than Giles's hand turned red-hot, forcing him to let go. When he moved to grasp his friend again, he found he couldn't. He opened his mouth to apologize but found Simon in much the same state. The warrior shook his hand and blew on his palm.

"It worked." Giles shouldn't have been surprised, but he was.

Mrs. Dawson patted his back and offered a smile. "It's time I found a bed. Wake me if anything happens."

"Yes, ma'am," Giles said as he lent a hand to help her down the stairs. "Did you see this happening?" he asked her once they were half way down the first stairwell.

"No. Not this." She took another step, limping her old bones down. "I just knew none of us would sleep well this night."

"So it wasn't a premonition?"

"Not in the way you're thinking. More of a global

feeling."

At the first landing, she paused to catch her breath.

"What is your global feeling now?"

Mrs. Dawson patted his hand, sent him a placating smile. "Asking me to predict the future, Mr. Giles?"

He lowered his gaze. "Asking if they're going to make it?"

She released a short laugh. "There is wisdom that comes with age, I think," she said nearly to herself. "Amber is arguably from the strongest line of Druids known...Kincaid...well, I don't know his parentage, but Lora did tell me Amber's savior would be a very powerful man. Do you believe our Kincaid is that man?"

A warm feeling washed over him. "Yes. Kincaid is one of the strongest within our band of warriors. Never wavering. If anyone can save Amber, it's him."

Mrs. Dawson's wrinkled face squished together in thought. "Then we have to believe they are meant to be...the question is if he acted in time."

That very thought had run through Giles's mind repeatedly since he uncovered the need for Amber to bond in order to survive. With Kincaid's reluctance to step up, he constantly worried the man would wait too long, and look what happened. They were both comatose, Kincaid bonded to Amber and Amber had been close to knocking on death's door.

"I can't help but wonder why I've not seen any of this happening in the books. I've read so many tomes and none of them talk of Amber and Kincaid specifically."

"That might be because Kincaid was too late..."

Giles cringed.

"Or, more relevant to your direct concern, I like to think the reason is the Ancients have hidden this brief moment in time to allow Kincaid and Amber the free will to decide for themselves what path they should take. No one, no matter what time they are from, wants to think their life is predetermined down to their mate." A coy smile spread over Mrs. Dawson's face. "I'd like to think the fact we found the two of them nearly naked means some of their free will has spoken already."

Giles's shoulders started to fold in slowly until he laughed. "I didn't realize that. I was too focused on the fact Amber wasn't moving...and Kincaid was bonding to someone who'd already passed."

Mrs. Dawson hummed out a sigh. "Not everything is as it seems. Had Amber truly passed, he couldn't have bonded with her. 'Where two hearts beat, there is now but one', the verse speaks for itself."

"Of course."

Mrs. Dawson started down the second flight of stairs and Giles moved to help her again.

"So they are both alive?."

"And healing..."

"But if Kincaid was too late?"

Mrs. Dawson hesitated. "Then the reason the books don't speak of them is because they don't exist in your future."

Yet, even as the words left the wise woman's mouth, he couldn't help but think somewhere...somehow...even that information would have been written somewhere...by someone.

"I hate the not knowing."

She paused, met his gaze. "Then think of Amber's mother. Lora sent her daughter here to survive. This was her only chance, and now that Kincaid is bonded to her, she must live."

Giles felt his jaw grow tight. "But what of Kincaid? He can perish and Amber not be affected. She would carry his gift, his protection...and he could die."

One-sided bonds didn't last. If there was one thing written in time, it was the fact that when one bonded with an unwilling partner, the bonded one followed their love until the end, which often came too soon, and the other moved through life more powerful, but slightly incomplete. If Amber lived, and Kincaid died, she would fulfill her mother's premonition.

Giles helped Mrs. Dawson to her room, offered to fetch her water...something...

She waved him off, and he fled back to the upper story of the mansion

Helen had pulled a chair next to Amber's side of the bed while Simon paced.

"I can stay. There is no reason for all of us to stand in wait," Giles told them.

They both turned on him. Simon spoke first. "Do you think you're the only one invested in the two of them?"

Simon's short tone had Giles pushing his glasses up on his nose, standing taller. "No. I'm thinking of your wife...your unborn child."

Simon shifted his eyes to Helen and his fierce expression softened. "Mayhap you should find your bed."

Helen rolled her eyes. "Oh, please, I'm not going anywhere. Bring a cot in here, a bed, whatever. I'm not leaving this room until they wake up."

"Lass?"

Helen shot a hand in the air. "Don't lass me. Amber is *our* responsibility." Tears leaked from her eyes. "If she dies, we need to tell everyone what happened. We can't do that if we don't see it."

Giles stared at the still couple on the small bed. He couldn't help but believe Amber would live. It was Kincaid he worried about.

Chapter Seventeen

This isn't right. This can't be...

Gavin's voice penetrated Amber's dreams. Only she shouldn't be dreaming. She should be passing over.

She tried to open her eyes, but found them too heavy. Her limbs were equally difficult to move, and she found herself lying in a state as if waiting for something.

I'm sorry, Gavin, she told him in her head. *I couldn't let you sacrifice your life for mine.*

Instead of any vocal response, she heard Gavin repeating the same thing over and over... *This isn't right. This can't be...*

He couldn't hear her, she realized. Unable to do anything but hear his plea, Amber felt the weight in her heart grow heavier.

This isn't going to happen.

A tremor surged up Amber's hand as Gavin's words changed. The power of the northern winds rushed up her frame and lifted her arm. Pinpricks of sensation circled her wrist, and she heard Gavin's words through the soupy fog of death.

With each sacred word of the Druid wedding vows he uttered, she felt her heavy heart begin to pick up its pace. Part of her wanted to ward him off, tell him he was too late...she was already leaving. But he continued and the branding of his hand to hers loosened the weight holding her down. Yet when she tried to open her eyes again, she saw nothing but scalding light.

She searched for Gavin, his voice, anything...but there was nothing.

He was there, she could sense him, but there was no voice to accompany his presence in her mind.

She felt Helen, Simon, Giles, and Mrs. Dawson nearby, but couldn't hear their words.

Silence, something she prayed for more times than she could remember, met her world of white nothing.

Minutes ticked by…maybe hours…still nothing.

Gavin…where are you?

Nothing.

The familiar cloud of panic threatened to choke her. The need to find Gavin, to help him find her, pulled her thoughts inward.

Then she heard him… *This is not how we die.* His voice was weak…fading.

Nay.

Amber pushed against the shield holding her down, opened her mind, and pictured it exploding.

She shot up in bed, her eyes opened, and she gasped for breath.

"Amber!" Helen was at her side in the time it took to take another breath.

The feel of Helen's hand holding hers, felt unfamiliar. Giles stepped into the room from the hall.

"You're awake."

Gavin needs me. "Aye." Her eyes traveled to the man beside her. "Gavin!" She pulled from Helen's grip and placed both hands on his still body. "Gavin?"

"He hasn't woken up."

Amber shot Helen a confused look. "What do you mean?"

"He found you…in the attic."

Amber looked at their hands, noticed a torn cloth in his fist. "Oh, God. H-he… It wasn't a dream?"

Giles moved to Gavin's side. "Not a dream. He bonded to you."

"Why?" she asked in a whisper.

"To save you."

Simon moved into the room, pushed past Helen, and laid a hand on Amber's shoulder.

159

She looked over at a man who was as close to her as a brother. "Why isn't he awake?"

"I don't know, lass. He's grown more pale while you were clearly coming back to us."

"How long have we been like this?"

Helen lifted two fingers. "Two days."

Two days?

Gavin, can you hear me?

Bonded couples could talk to each other with their minds, but there was nothing getting into his head from hers. "Gavin," she said aloud.

"We've called both your names. It didn't seem to help," Helen told her.

This isn't how we die. Gavin's words penetrated her mind.

Gavin?

He couldn't hear her. But she heard him.

...we die.

Gavin drew in a deep breath and then didn't follow it with another.

Amber chilled. "Nay." He was slipping. She could feel it.

She pulled his hand close to her and wrapped the tie around them. "From the North..."

Simon pushed on her shoulder. "Stop! Think of what you're doing."

The weight of Gavin's shield hovered over her. She pushed it against Simon's hand and he was thrown to the floor. "I know what I'm doing."

"From the North, to the South, in the East or in the West. Where you go I'll follow, your light will shine my way. It's my love I give you, past my dying day. Where two hearts beat, there is now but one. This tie that binds us together shall never be undone." She closed her eyes and rolled her head back as the force of her vow rose from her and into him. *Now breathe!*

He did...a long gasping breath.

Can you hear me, Gavin?

His eyes fluttered but did not open.

The next breath that entered his lungs was one she coaxed from him...and then another. *Don't die...I don't even know you yet.* The words in her head hit a deep abyss, until finally she heard his voice.

It wasn't our time to die.

Tears sprang to her eyes. *Nay. This world isn't finished with us.*

I need to sleep, Amber...just a little longer.

She gripped his hand. "He needs to sleep," she said for the others in the room.

Those in the room sat in silence.

Amber closed her eyes and willed Gavin to breath...one breath, two...

"Ah, Amber?" Giles asked.

"Yes?"

"Uhm...do you realize you're both hovering above the bed?"

She looked below them, realized a foot separated them from the mattress. "'Tis Gavin's shield."

"I've known Gavin for a dozen years. Never seen that before."

She concentrated on lowering their bodies, felt the air beneath her give slightly. The blue aura around them thinned, and she felt the sheets under her. Amber uncoiled their joined hands and moved to push Gavin's hair from his face. She noticed then, that they broke contact and the outside world didn't rush in. She lifted both hands before her eyes and studied them. "We're not touching."

"Oh, my God, Amber," Helen uttered.

"You're cured?" Simon asked.

"I-I don't feel anything beyond our thoughts. Is Mrs. Dawson home?" Laughter teased close to the surface because of the sheer fact she needed to ask about the mistress of the house.

"She is."

"Seems the books were right. Bonding was the answer," Giles said.

Amber met Giles's gaze. *Yes, but was the price too much to pay?*

****

Selma varied her routine, didn't leave the house at the exact same time and never went to the post office when she didn't expect a line. It sucked, since lines weren't fun to wait in…but it beat walking in empty parking lots with the spider-crawling sensation that had hooked its way up her spine and wasn't letting go. She'd visited Dawson Manor once since Amber and Kincaid had fallen into their comatose state, and when she drove home that night, she felt the eyes of someone watching her. That someone was powerful.

Selma realized then she didn't need to bring trouble on those in Mrs. Dawson's home…not until they were all whole again and could defend themselves.

The walls of her apartment were becoming much like a prison. And it was ticking her off. There hadn't been any more emails or requests from her lover-boy. In the wake of his unwelcome email and the news coverage, which she realized now probably wasn't her guy, everything had been painfully silent. She wasn't sure what was worse…knowledge or nothing?

Nothing. Nothing was definitely worse.

After thirty minutes of watching a reality show featuring up and coming, or wanna-be singers, Selma switched off the set with her mind and pushed herself off her couch. "What is wrong with you?" she asked herself. "You're Druid, for crying out loud. Protect yourself!"

Yes, she could manipulate mechanical switches, lights, televisions, her computer, even the microwave when needed, with her mind. But her real gift was what she shipped to the world. It was what had made her believe she was a witch to begin with.

She left her living room, switching off the light as she

passed with her mind. She graced her storage room with the same light show and found her box of charms. A variety of crystals, bits of amber, and even more precious stones lay in a velvet casement. She thought of her friend and picked a large dark amber stone originating from somewhere in Europe. She gathered several herbs and moved into her kitchen.

She'd never once gathered this many powerful elements in a protection spell. *I'm probably overdoing it.*

The thought of the people in her life surfaced, and she returned to her room to gather a few more stones.

"Go big or go home."

She rubbed her hands together and willed the candles in the room to light. They were already surrounding her. It was her safe room. If anyone came after her here, they would find an unrelenting ward, briefly impenetrable, allowing her time to call for help.

She lifted a candle and dripped the wax inside a pestle. A dash of Juniper flaked on the hot wax, which she let burn before adding the bits of amber.

"For protection," she mumbled. She added a small amount of betony and a dash of agrimony. "To ward off evil. Keep the wearer of this gem from harm. And finally...for wisdom." She added acacia. "So the wearer might know evil is upon them and respond quickly."

She circled her hands over the smoke and flame and added one more charm...her Druid gift. "If the Ancients will it so, charm these gems and keep the wearer whole."

The flame in the stone bowl grew hot and then blew out.

Selma moved about the room, blew out her candles, and willed the lights in the room on. While the stones cooled, she assembled the bits of jewelry that would house the charmed stones.

If someone was watching her, they might come after those around her...and that wasn't something she could live with. If no one was watching her...then the jewelry would simply be a nice gift and perhaps keep unwanted attention away. It was a win/win in her book… and hers was the only book that counted right now.

She was placing the last stone in the jewelry when her phone rang. Helen's happy voice met her ears.

"Someone sounds excited."

"Amber woke up and bonded to Kincaid."

Selma's hands fell and she stared across the room. "Bonded?"

"Yes. Oh, my God, Selma, you should have seen it. The room glowed in this bright blue sparkly light—"

"Sounds like an animated film."

"I'm serious. Sparks…pixy dust…call it what you want, the room freaking glowed."

"How did Kincaid respond?"

"He hasn't regained consciousness."

Selma rubbed her tired eyes. "Wait, he's still out?"

"Out cold. Amber said he needs to rest. We all finally left their room. Well…Amber kicked us out."

"Wait." Selma shook her head, not able to picture what Helen was saying. "Amber kicked you out? Soft and moldable Amber told you to leave?"

Helen's giggle brought a lift to Selma's lips. "Yeah…she said we all needed to stop staring at the two of them and go."

"Wow." Selma couldn't picture it.

"And another thing…"

"What?"

"The voices, the emotions…they aren't there anymore."

The ache in Selma's jaw from her smile started to fade. "What do you mean?"

"Amber's gift…it's like it's not there."

"How's that possible?"

"I don't know. Maybe Kincaid's gift is sheltering her. She's not holding his hand every second of the day and she couldn't even tell if Mrs. Dawson was in the house."

"How can that be?"

Helen blew out a breath. "I don't know. Giles is in the library searching for answers. He's never heard of any Druid losing a power, or even a power weakening once they bonded. Maybe once Kincaid wakes we'll know what's happening with him."

"Could he have sucked her power inside him?"

"We don't know. Amber certainly seems to have control of his power. She damn near knocked Simon across the room when he tried to stop her from bonding with Kincaid."

"Oh, please, how can Amber knock anyone—"

"With Kincaid's power. The shield he uses shot up and launched him. We were all so stunned. And Amber... her expression was so..."

"So what?"

"I don't know...fierce? Yeah... close to violent. I didn't recognize her."

Selma rubbed her eyes, trying to picture the Amber Helen was describing. "Violent?"

"Yeah..."

"How is she now?"

"It's hard to describe. Not harsh...just assertive."

"Is that bad?"

"No, just...not her."

Selma couldn't help but wonder if any of them knew who Amber really was. "She's been stuck in her own head, her own world for a long time. She's bound to have some growing pains. And didn't you say she and Kincaid were naked when you guys found Amber in the attic?"

"Yeah. Do you think that they—"

"They might have," Selma interrupted Helen. "And I don't know about you, but that's a big deal, and it's not like Amber has had an opportunity for a private conversation with another woman since Kincaid showed up. I hate to think she bonded with him because she had her first man-induced orgasm."

"You think that's why she did it?"

"Might be. The only way we will know anything is if we chat with her. Not that it matters, I guess. What's done is done. You can't undo a bonding."

"You're scaring me."

"Yeah? Well, none of us really knows Kincaid. Will he want her to go to his time? Will she want to return to hers? Who are Kincaid's parents...his gene pool?" One thing was certain. Selma had more questions than answers. "Tell you what, I have to drop something off at Jake's house, and then I'll come over. Maybe we can finally have some girl time with Amber. See where her head is."

"That would be great. I don't want to ask sex questions without some back up. And I don't think Simon wants to know, and he'd make lousy back up if he was trying to pummel Kincaid."

Selma swung her legs off the coffee table and walked into her office to gather her purse. "Not sure why he'd punch the guy. If he did take advantage of her, he married her." Selma paused. "Wow. Amber and Kincaid are married, and they hardly know each other. That has to be freaking her out."

"I'll chill some wine for you and Amber. Just get here."

Selma laughed. "You had me at wine."

Chapter Eighteen

Raine stood with her arms crossed over her chest, her dark hair pulled back in a slick rope down her back.

Mouse spread images on the digital screen, one at a time, and told her his observations.

The image of a blonde woman standing within the embrace of a man worthy of the Highlands. "Her name is Helen. From what I can tell, she and this man are married,"

"Bonded?"

"I can't say. They spoke aloud to each other without skipping sentences, so I don't think they're bonded. They're both Druid. Of that, I have no doubt."

"What's his name?"

"She didn't say it, but he did have a Scottish accent." Another picture made it on the screen, this time an old woman.

"Mrs. Dawson, I assume."

"I would have to assume that as well. She didn't leave the house."

Mouse scrolled the picture in closer until the image of another man came into view behind her. "I don't have a name for this one. I think he is someone who knew Kincaid before he arrived in this century."

Raine didn't want Mouse to think...just to relay the facts. "What did the man say to make you assume this?"

"While the others were watching Amber, he was most concerned with Kincaid."

She amassed the players in her head, attempted to place them in the manor. "Who else?"

"Only one other woman visited the house." He placed an image of a woman with unruly red curls and pale skin on the display. "Her name is Selma Mayfair."

Now *that* name Raine knew. "Of course." The descendent of Liz and Fin. "She doesn't live in the manor?"

"No."

Raine paced the room while Mouse continued. "I managed to enter the house without detection."

"How?"

"They were distracted, all of them. By the time I could hear the conversations, I learned Kincaid had bonded to Amber."

Raine turned toward Mouse. "Only him to her?"

Mouse shook his head. "I don't know the details, only that he bonded to her and they both fell into a deep sleep. Seems Kincaid was close to death when Amber woke and she bonded to him. It was in that moment I penetrated the manor. She wielded Kincaid's power as if it were her own. That's when I left to report here to you."

Laughter sat on the tip of Raine's tongue. "Kincaid bonded to Amber MacCoinnich? Oh, how unexpectedly delightful is that?"

Confusion marred Mouse's face.

"I think it's time for Amber to find out who she has bound herself to." Raine ran her hand over the screen, found the image she wanted and pulled it on screen. "This book is in Dawson's library. Probably high, unreachable. Make sure it's seen."

Mouse swallowed with a nod.

"And follow Selma. If she is out of the house, she's the link inside. I need to know her weakness...those around her. Think chaos, Mouse. When needed, we need to have mass confusion." That way no one from the future or the past would find their way to her. Not until she could fight them all. "If anyone shifts in time, return immediately so I can trace them."

When Raine turned, Mouse was still standing there. "What are you waiting for?"

"Sorry."

She blinked, and he disappeared.

"Amber MacCoinnich and Kincaid." She laughed now, deep, rich and thought of how easy it was going to be to eliminate them both.

****

Jake wasn't home so Selma let herself in, in the way only she could. She placed two small gift bags on his kitchen counter for the girls. The small card she left for the twins told them that in order for her to tell them apart, she gave them different colored necklaces. Hopefully, that would be all she needed to say to have them wear the protection crystals and keep them from harm.

She was walking out of the kitchen when she heard the front door open and one of Jake's girls call out, "Daddy?"

Kelsey, or maybe it was Sophie, ran around the corner and into the kitchen. "Oh, hi, Selma."

"Hey, sweetie. Your...a...dad's not home."

The girl threw her arms around Selma's waist in a hug, and she heard the front door shut.

"He's always late on Wednesdays."

Oh, that's right. He has the girls every Wednesday night. "I'm sure he'll be home soon."

The other twin walked into the kitchen, smiled, and hugged her as well. Selma was about to quiz them on coming alone when a tall, stunning brunette walked in behind them. *Must be Jake's ex.*

"Kelsey," the woman scolded. "Let her breathe."

"It's okay, Mom."

Kelsey peeled off Selma's side anyway.

"You must be Lindsey," Selma said as she extended her hand.

"And you must be the woman the girls have been talking about all week."

The woman? And was that a bite in Lindsey's voice? Could she be jealous? Lindsey shook Selma's hand with

169

the wimpiest shake anyone had every placed in her palm and then stepped back.

"This is Selma, Mom. Dad's new girlfriend."

Lindsey ran her eyes over Selma's frame and pressed her lips together. Her expression wasn't toxic, but it wasn't all that happy either.

"I understand congratulations are in order."

Lindsey glanced at the ring on her left hand and gave a half a smile. "Yes, ah, thanks." Lindsey set her purse on the counter next to Selma's and looked around the kitchen. "Where's Jake?"

"Running a little late," Selma told her...which obviously wasn't a lie since he wasn't there and was clearly expected to be.

Lindsey glanced at her watch with a sigh. "Figures. The man can never do anything on time."

Selma wasn't sure she liked Lindsey's tone in front of the girls. Yeah, maybe Jake couldn't punch off the clock like her paper-pushing fiancé, but that didn't make him a bad guy. "The nature of his job isn't always predictable."

Lindsey dismissed Selma's comment with a wave of her hand. "I was married to the man. You don't have to make excuses for him. He should have called me."

Ah, the you-don't-know-him-like-I-do comment from the ex. "He didn't think he needed to. I told him I'd be here in case he got hung up again."

"He expects me to just leave the girls with a stranger?" Oh, yeah...there was definitely some vinegar in her voice.

"She's not a stranger, Mom," Sophie corrected her.

"It's okay, hon. Your Mom doesn't know me. But I'm sure that will change."

Kelsey noticed the gift bags on the counter and her name attached to one. "Are these for us?"

Thankful for the distraction, Selma said, "Yeah. So I can tell the two of you apart."

Sophie pushed in and took the bag from her sister's

hand. They both removed the necklaces at the same time with tiny squeals.

"I love it," Kelsey said first as she fiddled with the clasp and placed the pendent around her neck.

Sophie put hers down to help her sister. "Did Daddy tell you our favorite colors?"

"He must have, honey." Lindsey watched her daughters and then shifted her gaze back to Selma.

"My room is green and Sophie's is purple," Kelsey told her.

"That was very nice of you," Lindsey managed.

"Completely selfish, I'm afraid. The girls look so much alike. I'm sure the better I know them, the more their personalities will shine, but until then these will help."

The sound of a car door shutting caught all their attention.

"Guess Jake's not too late after all." Selma pushed around them to head Jake off at the door.

He walked in voicing an apology before he realized she was there. "It's okay, darling, I told Lindsey you had me here in case you were late again."

Jake assessed the situation quickly as Selma walked up and slid an arm around his waist. She whispered in his ear. "Smile, buddy, I'm saving your ass… again."

His hand squeezed her close, and he flashed a smile at his ex. "I see you two have met."

"Seems we have, Jake. But you should have known I wouldn't leave the girls with a stranger."

"Of course not. Kelsey and Sophie will vouch for Selma."

Kelsey ran forward, her hand around the necklace. "We did. Mom didn't listen. Look what Selma gave us."

Sophie moved beside her sister and offered her dad the same sweet smile.

"Your favorite colors."

"So I can tell the two of them apart," Selma told him.

He narrowed his eyes, but didn't comment.

"Jake?" Lindsey caught his attention. "I'd like to talk to you about…" she paused, glanced at Selma. "something."

That's my queue to leave. "Right." Selma offered Lindsey a fake smile before turning toward Jake. "I have to go—"

"You don't have to."

I don't? Since when?

"Whatever you have to say, you can say in front of Selma."

As much as she'd like to stick around for the *ex* fight… "Remember, hon, I have a girl's night with Helen and Amber."

"Oh, ah, right. Is Amber feeling better?"

"Much. But I should go." Selma smiled at the ex. "Lindsey, a pleasure."

"Do you have to go?" Sophie asked.

"Yeah. Maybe we can hang next Wednesday?"

Selma noted Lindsey rolling her eyes as she turned away.

The girls hugged her again and Jake walked her out the front door. Once they were out of hearing range, he whispered, "Thanks. Lindsey's been crapping on me about coming late on Wednesdays."

"You could have told me. It's not a big deal for me to come by."

Jake let a rare smile through his stoic exterior. When she started to smile back at him, and her stomach did a weird-ass flip, Selma paused and took a tiny step back.

"Why are you here anyway? Not that I'm complaining."

"I was dropping off the necklaces for the girls."

"So you can tell them apart?"

She blinked. "Right."

His eyes narrowed.

She looked down, toward the inside of the house, and noticed Lindsey watching out of the corner of her eye.

"You need to work on your lying, Matilda. You suck at it."

Her eyes snapped to his. "Who's lying? Sophie loves purple. Kelsey loves green. You have cute kids, Mr. Personality, and I have a hard time remembering who is who. That happens sometimes with twins."

He was silent for a moment, and she fidgeted.

The brat saw through her.

"So you let yourself in."

She grinned. "No need for an extra set of keys for your *girlfriend.*"

"Did you know your cheeks turn pink when you're flustered?" He tapped her nose. "And the freckles on your nose stand out even more."

Her hand touched her warm cheek. "Since when do you notice my freckles?"

Jake actually laughed. "I don't know."

"Well don't. Okay? It's weird!" And her stomach was flipping around and making her uneasy. "I've got to go." She turned away and he caught her arm. "What?"

"Is that the way to say goodbye to your *boyfriend*?"

Before she could process his question, he pulled her closer and lowered his lips to hers.

Shock registered first, then the strange and completely unwelcome feeling of peace when she realized he wasn't giving her a peck of a kiss, but seemed to be moving into her so there was no doubt of whose lips were touching hers. She offered only a small protest before his hand moved to the side of her face and held her closer.

The wet quest of his tongue against her lips brought her back to earth. She ended what he began and opened her eyes to see him staring at her with the same look of awe she felt deep inside her bones.

She touched her swollen lip and sucked it between her teeth.

Jake watched the movement with a strange look of hunger.

For her?

Oh, no. Not Jake.

Water and oil had more in common.

Inside the house, she heard Lindsey clear her throat.

Funny, the noise reminded her of their ploy of boyfriend and girlfriend. Of course! Jake kissed her because Lindsey was watching.

"Very convincing, Jake. I'm sure she gets the picture now," she whispered.

His brows drew together as she pulled away and jumped in her car.

Jake stood in his driveway and watched her drive away.

Chapter Nineteen

Amber slipped into a dress after her shower, sat at the foot of the bed, and watched Gavin sleep. She felt him coming back to her...slowly.

I'm bonded. A wife.

She might not have been forced to bond, but she couldn't let him die after he'd given himself to her. In her head, Amber told herself she was raised with devotion to family, to duty and honor.

But somewhere deeper, she knew it was more than that. The vow she spoke embedded into her soul.

"You're the man my mother told me about." The words, spoken aloud, solidified them. What would her father's impression of this man be?

Fierce and protective.

"He likes those qualities in a man." She thought of Liz. "And women."

Amber?

Gavin's voice sounded in her head. She moved her gaze to his still form on the bed.

I'm here.

Alive?

She smiled. *Aye.*

And me?

Alive. Just sleep...let your body heal.

His chest rose and fell in a deep sigh. *You're safe?*

Completely.

Good. That's good.

Silence met her then, and he slept.

An hour later, a knock on the door startled her. "Amber?"

Helen's voice shocked her. When was the last time

anyone could sneak up on her? She couldn't remember. "Aye?"

The door opened slowly, Helen peeked through. "Hey?"

A strange feeling of tears welled behind her eyes. "Hey."

"Uhm, Selma's here. Is he awake?" She opened the door a little wider.

"Not yet. By morning, I think."

Helen's brows pinched. "Well, we, ah…Giles wants to sit with him for a while and give you a break."

"I'm okay."

Helen frowned. "Okay, Selma and I wanted to chat with you. Won't take long."

From the doorway, Giles poked his head in. "Hey?"

Part of her wanted to join Helen, part of her wanted to stay.

Gavin?

Go. I'll sleep. The comfort of him in her head should have felt awkward, but it didn't.

Amber followed Helen down the hall and smelled the wood in the walls, heard the squeak of a mouse far off in the distance. When was the last time that had happened? The weight of her gift simply wasn't overbearing every sense in her system and all the nuances of the home sat ready to explore.

Helen paused, placed an arm on Amber's shoulder.

She flinched and Helen pulled away. "Nay, you didn't hurt me."

"But you expected it to?"

"Aye."

Helen had tears behind her eyes. "Can I hug you?"

Amber slowly opened her arms.

The other woman's embrace brought joyful tears to her eyes. Such a simple pleasure she'd lost most of her life.

Helen's fist moved to her shoulder in a playful punch.

"Don't ever, *ever* scare us like that again."

Before Amber could respond, Selma moved into the hall. "Hey? Can I get on the hug-fest?"

By the time Selma pulled away, all three of them were holding back tears. Selma grasped Amber's hand and walked toward the library. There, she noticed a bottle of wine and two glasses already filled. "I thought you might enjoy a glass."

Once they were all comfortable, Selma started in with questions.

"I really do feel fine," Amber told them. "My head is clear, well, except for Gavin's voice."

Helen leaned forward. "You can hear him?"

Amber nodded. "It's strange. I can reach out for him with a thought, and he's simply there."

"Doesn't that freak you out?" Selma asked.

"It was worse having the thoughts and emotions of everyone else."

"That's relative, I suppose. Aren't you a little worried about being bonded to someone you hardly know?"

Amber took a moment to sip her wine and reflect on the question she'd asked herself the most since she woke. "My mother always advised me not to worry about things I cannot change."

Helen laughed. "You didn't answer the question."

"He's a good man, noble. My father would approve." Ian would approve, and he would have insisted on the marriage after their intimacies.

Selma glanced at Helen. "Still didn't answer the question."

"I've seen nothing in his character to suggest he'll be cruel to me. He's fiercely protective."

When Amber set her glass down, Selma filled it.

"Have you slept with him?" Selma asked.

"Of course. We've had to hold hands for several nights."

Both women sent Amber looks of confusion.

"What?"

"Selma's not asking if you slept beside him. She's asking if you're no longer a virgin."

Heat shot to Amber's face. "Oh, aye."

Helen's eyes grew wide. "So *yes*, you're no longer a virgin, or *yes* you are still a virgin."

Amber drew several strands of her long hair in her hands and twirled the ends. "Nay, I'm...w-we didn't. Not completely." *Oh, what am I trying to say?* From the expressions on Helen and Selma's faces, they wanted to know more. The wine was already swimming in her head.

"So you two didn't go all the way?" Selma asked.

"Just a little hanky-panky?" Helen added.

"Hanky-panky?"

Helen started to laugh. "Sorry. I forget sometimes you're not up on the slang. Let's see... you and Kincaid fooled around, kissing, touching...stuff like that?"

The fog cleared in Amber's head. "Aye. A little." The memory left a smile on her face. She reached for Gavin and felt him sleeping.

"That's a devilish smile on your face, Mrs. Kincaid." Helen handed the glass of wine back to Amber.

"Mrs. Kincaid?"

"Sure. You exchanged Druid wedding vows. That makes you Mrs. Kincaid. I guess you don't have to take his name, if you don't want to."

Amber stared into her glass, drank from it. "Of course I'll take his name. 'Tis not right if I don't." Her father wouldn't approve of her not taking Kincaid as her own.

"Don't feel you have to do anything you don't want to, Amber. I know you're married, but you hardly know the man. I don't care what you say, that has to be freaking you out. He isn't from this time, or your time. What if he wants to return to the future?"

Amber gulped more wine. "I haven't thought of that."

Helen waved Selma's question away. "They can't go forward in time."

"Why not?"

Helen blinked several times. "Because Amber belongs here, with us."

Amber realized her glass was nearly empty and set it aside. "I think food is in order if I'm to drink more wine, and I think I might like to drink more wine."

Selma pushed herself off the sofa and left the room laughing.

Helen scooted closer. "I don't want you to move away."

Amber took her friend's hand. "I don't wish to either. My mother told me my cure was in this time, but I don't know if I'm meant to stay."

"We don't know if you're supposed to leave, either."

"I think it's best to do nothing now. Gavin's not awake anyway and even then, we have many things to consider before any decisions are made."

Helen smiled. "You sound so much like your mother sometimes."

"I miss her."

Helen shrugged. "I miss them all, too. Maybe when the baby is born we can visit. It isn't like there are rules for traveling in time."

Amber grasped the pendent on her neck and thought of home. When she did, Helen slid an identical necklace from her shirt and smiled.

"Has Kincaid told you how he travels in time?"

"We've not discussed it."

Helen sighed as Selma walked back in the room with a tray of fruit and cheese. Amber's mouth watered at the sight.

A slight wave of concern struck her from Selma's direction. Amber eyed the other woman and probed. A sickening image of injured children penetrated her brain. As soon as the picture swam into her head, she pushed it away and felt Gavin's shield surround her.

"What is it?" Selma asked.

"You're worried about something."

Selma blinked, twice. "I-I thought your gift was gone."

"It is... Well, I suppose it's there, but controlled. I felt your worry and looked for more."

"I don't think that's the smartest thing to do? I mean, weren't all the emotions of others in your head been nothing but a problem for years?"

"Aye, but before Grainna I could control my gift. Use it to help others. What worries you, Selma?"

Helen swung her gaze toward the feisty redhead. "Nothing. You."

"I am not a child. You're worried about children. Whose?"

When Selma didn't deny her, she knew her gift had led her in the right direction.

"Keeping secrets is impossible in this house. You both know that, right?"

Helen shrugged.

Selma tossed a grape in her mouth. "I met Jake's daughters."

"Twins," Amber said.

"Yeah, how did you know?"

The horrifying image flashed in her head again...two identical girls lying still, unmoving. "I think Jake mentioned it," she lied.

"Well, I didn't hear it if he did. Shocked me when I saw them. Cute kids."

Helen nibbled on a slice of cheese as she moved her back to the sofa. "So what has you worried?"

"It's probably nothing."

Helen pointed her cheese at their friend. "You do know that *it's probably nothing* always turns out to be something with us."

"Don't say that," Selma scolded.

"You're worried they're in danger." Amber knew this as fact. A part of her wanted to celebrate the fact she knew this...that her gift seemed to be working the way it should. However, knowing it also meant Jake's children might be in harm's way.

"I'm just being paranoid. I had this client. He kept asking for a love potion so the woman he loved would come around. After several attempts, this guy realized that the love of his life wanted someone else. My potions only bring clarity. They don't force someone to love you when they don't."

"He knew this?" Helen asked.

"On the second shipment I always include a note highlighting what I promise. This guy didn't listen. He sent me a nasty-gram when his girl hooked up with someone else."

"It can't be the first time that's happened. You've been selling potions for several years."

Selma met Amber's gaze. "The guy lives in Arizona. I saw a report about a murder of a young engaged couple in the area that matched the description Mr. Love-Struck gave me."

Helen grew quiet.

"Why are you worried about Jake's daughters?"

It was Selma's turn to shrug. "I don't know. Just am."

"Have you told Jake?"

"Jake thinks I'm wacked. He won't believe any of my paranoia."

Amber shook her head. "Jake doesn't think you're wacked." Amber had heard Selma use the word wacked enough to understand its meaning. "He tries to keep you thinking he doesn't believe in you so you don't realize how much he does. If I had to guess, I say Jake might have feelings for you."

Selma reached for her wine while her nose turned red and the freckles on her face stood out against her pale skin.

Helen sat forward on the couch. "Oh. My. God. What happened with you and Jake?"

"Nothing!"

The denial was too quick.

The fluttering feeling Amber experienced when Gavin touched her, kissed her, warmed her skin. "He kissed you."

Now there was no denial.

Helen squealed.

"It was a ploy," Selma said. "To convince his ex that we were boyfriend and girlfriend."

Helen shook her head. "What? Why?"

Amber sat back and listened. While Selma explained the details of the pretend relationship and how Jake had kissed her, Helen filled each silence with questions. Before they drank another glass of wine, Selma was telling both of them anything romantic with Jake was a really bad idea. "I wouldn't have felt anything with his kiss if I wasn't so horny. It's been a while for me."

"Someone in the room is kidding herself. I don't buy that, do you, Amber?"

Amber shook her head with a laugh. "Nay."

Selma stood and waved them off. "You guys are crazy. Jake thinks I'm a crazy witch, nothing more."

"You're not a witch," Amber told her.

"I know that. Whatever. I'm sure he won't kiss me again. Ever."

Amber? Gavin called her name.

She stood and started for the door.

"Hey, where are you going?" Helen asked. "It was just getting good."

"Continue without me. Gavin's waking."

Amber turned to leave the room and heard Selma say, "Wow, that's some serious bond."

Amber slid into her bedroom to find Giles asleep in the chair. When the click of the door sounded in the room, his feet slid off the bed and onto the floor, waking him.

"Kincaid?"

"'Tis Amber."

Giles glanced at the bed. "He's not awake yet."

"Almost," she assured him. "Would it be too much to ask for some tea when he wakes?"

"Tea? Yeah, sure. Though I know he likes coffee."

"That may be, but tea, something weak, would be best after so many days of not eating."

Giles shook his head. "Of course. I'll make it."

He moved to the door.

"Helen and Selma are downstairs. They can help you find what you need in the kitchen."

He looked at Gavin again. "You sure he's waking up?"

Amber sat on the end of the bed, rested her hand on Gavin through the covers. "Aye, I'm certain."

Giles left the room without any more questions.

I'm here. She told Gavin through their bond.

His eyes fluttered open slowly. His gaze found hers, and his dry lips moved into a grin. "You're alive."

"I told you I was."

He moved his lips together a few times, frowned. "Water?"

Amber jumped off the bed and rounded it to help with his request.

He inched up to lay against the headboard as she brought a glass to his lips. After a few sips, she sat the glass back down. "How do you feel?"

"Like I took the wrong end of a blaster."

"That's a bad thing?"

"Yeah. How long—"

"Three days. One day longer than I."

Gavin reached out and touched her cheek. "I thought I was too late. I thought you were gone."

"You didn't have to bond with me."

"I couldn't let you die."

Aye, you're too honorable for that.

"It's more than that," he said aloud.

A knock on the door saved her from further conversation and offered a distraction. "Come in."

Giles walked in with a tray and set it on the dresser across the room. "Decided to join the living, Kincaid?"

Gavin stretched with a wince. "Not sure how alive I am."

"More than you were a few minutes ago. Gave us all a good scare."

"I hope you and Simon can hold everything down for a little longer. I think standing is going to be a challenge."

Giles lit the room with his smile. "We will. Damn good to see you awake, mate."

Amber busied herself with Gavin's tea once Giles left them alone again. "Sugar and cream will help replenish your system," she told him. When she turned she paused. His stare moved through her.

"You didn't have to bond to me," he said in a soft whisper.

"I couldn't let you die, either."

Chapter Twenty

With the excitement of Kincaid waking and making his way downstairs the next morning, Selma was able to slip out of Mrs. Dawson's home without any fuss. She knew the moment Amber and Helen remembered their conversation about her concerns about lover-boy with love potion number nine gone wrong, they'd be on her about staying at the manor.

She pulled into her parking spot, looked around the lot, didn't see anything out of place, and walked to her apartment.

Her apartment looked exactly as it did when she left the day before. The light on her answering machine told her she had a message, but instead of listening to it, she tossed her purse on the kitchen counter and worked her way to the shower.

With her favorite satellite radio station filling her room with music, Selma managed a pair of panties and a bra, and then remembered she left the hamper with her clean clothes in the living room where she'd folded them the day before. She was towel drying her hair as she walked around the corner.

The man standing in the middle of her living room brought a scream to her throat. "Son-of-a-bitch."

Jake's eyes ran down her nearly naked torso with an appreciative smile.

Selma pulled the towel to cover herself. "What the hell are you doing here?" Her heart lodged in her throat. "How did you get in here?"

"I have my ways," he told her with a grin.

"Touché."

His eyes were still taking her in. He dressed in jeans

and a tight fitting short-sleeved shirt. The stubble on his chin was shaved bare, and damn it, she could smell his clean skin from where she stood.

"W-why are you here?"

When he stepped closer and dropped his smile, she moved away. She didn't have far to go before she felt the wall at her back.

"I didn't kiss you because Lindsey watched us."

He towered over her now, his expression unreadable.

"Temporary lack of good judgment then?"

He moved within an inch of her and slid his hand into her wet hair.

Selma sucked in a sharp breath.

"Maybe."

He was going to kiss her again. She saw his dedication to the task in his eyes. Before she could remind him they didn't like each other, the towel in her hand was yanked free and his lips covered hers.

Every reason to push him away churned through her mind, but she couldn't do it. Jake had one hell of an intoxicating kiss and she forgot to breathe, forgot to think. That had never happened before.

I must be crazy horny.

From the bulge pressing into her stomach, she wasn't the only one.

She considered saying no for half a breath, and then she reached up to his shoulders and hopped into his arms, her legs circled his waist. He chuckled under his kiss and pushed against the wall. She was wet, instantly, and her mouth opened to feel the length of his tongue aside hers.

Breathless, she motioned toward her bedroom with a nod.

Without words, he carried her inside and fell onto the bed with her.

Jake's fingers made quick work of her bra, his mouth captured her breast in a near painful, but oh so enjoyable bite.

Selma rolled him over, tugged his shirt off and tossed it on the floor. He was not a doughnut-eating cop, or if he was, he worked out enough to keep himself in shape.

She found herself under him again, and her panties met his pants on the floor. With her heart racing in her chest, she couldn't think beyond how amazing Jake felt pushed against her bare skin.

They rolled on the bed so many times she wondered if they were fighting for dominance.

There was no talk, no chatter between lovers. It was raw, urgent, and when he finally pushed into her, fully naked and completely focused on bringing them both pleasure. Selma felt a little part of her hard edge toward the man soften.

She came three times before he called out her name as his release gripped him.

Too stunned to speak, she sucked in one breath after the other.

Jake collapsed on top of her, his lips pressed against her neck as he struggled to suck air in his lungs.

She lifted her chin and felt him hold her closer. Talking to Jake about her feelings, emotions she couldn't even name now, wasn't in her. So she used the only weapon she had with him. Humor.

"That's one seriously impressive concealed weapon you have there, officer."

He laughed a gut laugh that reminded her he was still buried deep inside her.

She started to pull away, but he wouldn't release her. Instead, he used his weapon on her repeatedly until she cried mercy.

When they fell in an exhausted heap, the sheets tangled, her skin raw, and her insides humming, he said. "God, I needed that."

"You and me both."

He lay sprawled in her bed and turned to look at her. He packed some serious guns under his hard-ass exterior.

187

She wanted to tell him how much she liked the view but didn't want him getting any squishy ideas about them. No, this was physical...incredible, but just a release. They hardly talked to each other, for God's sake.

His gaze softened, and she tore her eyes away. "You're not going to get over analytical about this, are you?"

"Guys don't analyze sex. That would be the girl's job."

Good! She patted his hand and shoved off the bed. "I need caffeine to analyze anything. Think you can manage a pot?"

His eyes lingered on her bare ass as she left him in her bed and made her way to the shower.

"I can make coffee."

She winked at him over her shoulder and ducked into the bathroom.

Alone, Selma looked at herself in the mirror, hardly recognizing her reflection. She lifted her chin and peered closer at her neck.

"The brat gave me a hickey." The purple love-bite would be hard to hide in summer clothing. The last time someone had placed a mark on her like that was high school and back then, it was a badge of honor, now, not so much. She was so damned relaxed after her horizontal time with Jake that she couldn't bring herself to care.

She showered quickly and slipped into a summer dress before following her nose to the kitchen.

Jake had fumbled through the cabinets and discovered the coffee cups. He'd found his pants, and left his shirt off as he padded around her space. It would be hard to look at him from across the room and not remember the expression of bliss as he moved over her.

Don't go getting squishy, she warned herself.

"Find everything?" she asked him.

He poked into the refrigerator. "You take cream, right?"

The fact that he knew, made her smile. "Yeah, top shelf behind the milk."

He pushed the milk aside, dug through some of her containers of chilled herbs, and removed the creamer. "What is all this stuff?"

"Office supplies," she told him with a straight face.

"Witch's brew?"

She laughed, not offended in the least. "You could say that."

He closed the door with his hip, and poured her a cup, mixed in the cream, and handed it to her. Selma mumbled thanks and sipped. *Not bad.*

Jake leaned against a counter. "You really believe in all that stuff?"

"What's surprising isn't that I believe in it, but that you don't. You'd think after everything we've seen, you'd be onboard by now."

"Believe none of what you hear and only half of what you see."

She'd heard him say that line before, sipped her coffee and grinned. "Fine. About the half that you've seen?"

He ran a hand through his disheveled hair, his smile fell. "It's hard to fight what you don't know. I'm used to fighting bad guys with guns and bad breath, not Druids who turn into animals or pop in from nowhere. It's damn unnerving."

"I get that. But as unnerving as it may be, it is real." To make her point she turned on the light over the sink with her mind.

He eyed it but didn't flinch. "I believe that. Crazy as it is, but potions, spells?" He shook his head.

Baby steps, she told herself.

Jake crossed the room and set his cup down, took hers from her hand and set it aside before laying one hand on the counter to box her into his personal space. He eyed her neck, and licked the sensitive spot he'd placed there

189

earlier. He reached around her, turned off the kitchen light. "I can turn things off, too."

She leaned into his lips as shivers ran down her spine. "You turn things on well, too."

He grabbed her waist, hoisted her on the counter.

Selma leaned back, catching herself, and accidentally hit the answering machine.

Her voice echoed in the room, telling the caller to leave a message while Jake traced her collarbone with his tongue.

"You're insatiable," she told him.

"I don't hear you saying no."

And he wouldn't.

The beep of her machine ended and a cold, deadpan voice froze them both.

"You think you can hide from me, bitch? Yeah, that's right…your home phone number was easy…so was your address."

Jake's grip on her tightened as they both stopped all movement.

How did he get her unlisted number? Her address?

"What the hell is that about?"

****

Everything in Kincaid's world was upside down. Amber never left his head. Her thoughts, her words, emotions. Everything was only a thought away. By morning, he was able to leave their room only to find everyone in the house staring at him, wanting to know his intentions. The fact he knew their thoughts, their needs, itched under his skin, and made his head want to explode. Was this what Amber dealt with for years, and with so many others?

To make matters worse, his body felt as if it had been pulled behind a hover-bike without a net for a hundred miles. He hoped to hell the relative peace he'd managed for the better part of a week would continue. He didn't need any unexpected battles, or he'd have to shelter

Amber and himself until he was strong enough to fight.

Instead of inviting chaos, he holed up in the library with Giles and suffered his friend's concerned state.

"Stop staring at me," he finally told the man.

Giles shook his head with a laugh. "Can't help it. We thought you were going to die. Then when you didn't, I realized how dramatically your life has changed. Makes a man think."

"My life isn't so different."

"You're married to a MacCoinnich, Kincaid...an original. Not some descendent passed down through bloodlines over hundreds of years. But the daughter of Ian and Lora. Good God man, do you have any idea what that means?"

Kincaid crossed his arms over his chest. "It means I'm sworn to protect her."

"It means we're all sworn to protect her and your children for generations to come. Your own power will grow with your bond, and you were damn near untouchable before your vows."

That he knew. Perhaps that was why it was taking him so bloody long to recover from his brief illness. He'd not experienced anything close to near-death in all his years of battle, in all the lives he'd taken.

He didn't want to think of the boost to his gift or the weight of hers that had been with him since he first grasped her hand. Instead of addressing his abilities, he spoke of what didn't have to be. "There are no guarantees we'll ever have children."

Giles laughed outright. "You're bonded. It's only a matter of time."

"We hardly know each other."

"Yet you're married."

Kincaid couldn't argue that. "Still."

"You were attracted to her before we found her."

Kincaid stood, ignored the slight spin of the room, and walked along the wall of old books. "If bonding has

191

sealed our fate of many years and children, why don't your books talk of us? Why didn't you find any word of us in the future?"

"I haven't found a word about Simon and Helen, either."

"Who would know of them other than us?"

"Good point. Maybe I'm the one who needs to write their story...and yours," Giles suggested.

"Maybe." Yet if he did, there would still be a story told somewhere.

"If your story takes place from this time forward, there wouldn't be any evidence in this library today."

"And if we all return to our time, the story hasn't been told yet."

Giles stood and rolled the ladder along the wall of books. "Would you want to read your story? Know your future? If you knew what would happen between you and Amber, would you have come to this time?"

Kincaid felt his arms grow cold. If he hadn't come, she would be gone by now. Of that, he had no doubt. "I'm sworn to protect her."

"You didn't answer my question."

Kincaid felt the headache he'd finally managed to shed returning.

"Maybe instead of asking about the future, we need to look in the past. Who knows, maybe you both return to her time and you manage to wear that kilt you love so much."

He ignored his friend's sarcasm, knowing damn well Giles understood his discomfort in a skirt.

Before Kincaid could comment on living in the past, he felt the presence of others and turned toward the door of the library. The sound of the front door slammed at the same time a book fell from one of the top shelves.

A rough voice of a man shouted Simon's name in the hall.

Jake stood grasping Selma's arm in the hall while the members in the house took little time to meet them.

Jake held a suitcase, which he promptly tossed at Simon's feet, and said. "Selma's staying here."

"Not necessary, Jake!" Selma pulled out of his grasp.

"The hell! You have some nutcase stalking you. You're staying here!"

"Nutcase?" Simon asked.

"Yeah, some freak threatening her life." Jake turned his back to Simon to glare at Selma.

Helen moved to Selma's side. "I told you Jake would believe you."

"Wait? You knew about this?" Jake asked.

Selma pushed between Jake and Helen. "I told Helen and Amber about the email last night."

"That was before the personal phone call," Jake said.

"A phone call?" Helen asked.

Simon shoved in. "Wait, what are you talking about? Some of us in the room have no idea what's going on."

Kincaid was glad the other man asked. He for one was clueless. He did know, however, Jake was acting out of fear, and even though Selma was defensive and combative, she too was scared. Their emotions were as real as his own.

He met Amber's gaze and silently said, *He believes she's in real danger.*

Agreed. Do you feel this or are you assuming?

Just a knowing. Your gift?

Aye.

"I sent a love potion to a guy in Arizona," Selma started to explain.

"Several potions." Jake rolled his eyes.

"Several. And they worked! Just not for him. The girl he wanted ended up realizing her love for someone else."

Kincaid glanced at Giles and laughed. "Love potions? Seriously?"

"Hey! Don't judge. A girl has to make a living. Anyway," Selma tossed her hair over her shoulder as she explained. "The guy was pissed and sent a nasty email—"

"*Threatening* email," Jake corrected.

"Then he left a message on my home phone," Selma told them.

Now that wasn't a laughing matter, Kincaid thought. The nutcase was probably only that, but that didn't make him any less of a threat.

"This is the man you think murdered the couple in Arizona?" Helen asked.

Jake swung his gaze from Helen to Selma. "Murdered? What are you not telling me, Matilda?"

"I don't know if he was *that* nutcase or not. I got spooked after I saw a newscast. I'm probably paranoid," Selma told Jake.

Jake rested his hands on his hips and stared at her. "And when did this newscast air?"

Selma shrugged, glanced at her feet. "I don't know...last weekend."

"When you came over to my house?"

"I don't know. Maybe."

She's lying.

"I knew there was something bothering you!" Jake yelled. "Why didn't you say something then?"

The two of them had their fight while everyone else watched. Seemed Jake was handling everything perfectly. If Selma had been threatened, she needed to be with others. Why she lived outside of the manor was a puzzle to Kincaid anyway. They were stronger together. Always had been.

"Oh, c'mon, Jake. Like you'd believe me. Besides, I didn't want to bring it up with your girls around. You have enough to worry about."

"You don't get to tell me when I can and can't worry." Jake moved within three inches of her body.

She glared at him. "And you don't get to tell me what to do just because we slept together!"

Helen gasped.

Oh, my. Amber's words shot into Kincaid's head.

I take it, that's a new thing? He asked her.

Aye.

Kincaid smiled. He liked this new gift, he decided. The ability to talk to Amber without anyone else hearing them was already turning out to be beneficial.

"You're right," Jake told Selma. "It doesn't. I'll let everyone here tell you how stupid it is to try and fight an unknown enemy by yourself. My guess is they've all done it more than once." He poked a finger in her chest. "You, on the other hand, haven't."

"Jake—"

He placed a finger over her lips. "I'll find the bad guy. You keep your skinny ass here and stay out of my way."

"But—"

Kincaid spoke at the same time as Simon. "He's right."

"Selma?"

Kincaid nodded for Simon to continue.

"Jake is right. You know he is. You're safe here."

The tension in the room slowly drifted to a low purr. From down the hall, Mrs. Dawson issued a request.

"Amber, Helen? Why don't you prepare one of the rooms for our guest? Selma, dear, can you please help me in the kitchen. You do seem to have a way with herbs."

Selma growled at Jake as she walked past him, and Helen and Amber moved in the opposite direction.

"Stubborn woman," Jake whispered under his breath.

Chapter Twenty-One

After two painfully quiet days and nights, Kincaid wanted, no needed, to break free.

He purposefully let Amber have the room and slept anywhere but at her side. He didn't want her feeling pressured, didn't want her questioning his intentions. Not that he knew his intentions. He was a married man in the blink of an eye, and he had no way of knowing how to handle the new status in life.

He'd watched his wife slowly come out of the shell he'd seen her in since they met. Her smile was brighter, her personality bigger. She wore pants with the encouragement of Selma and Helen, and managed to keep herself out of his head whenever she wanted. Something he had yet to master.

Still, when he cornered her in the yard, she appeared shocked. "You and I are leaving here in one hour," he told her.

She blinked. The smile on her face didn't fall as she turned away from her friends to speak to him. "Leave?"

"A date. You and I. One hour." He turned then and left the other women to explain the word that circled in her head like a cloud.

A date?

Ask Helen and Selma. They'll explain.

She was quiet then, until a half hour later when the inevitable question was asked.

What shall I wear?

Kincaid stood before the bathroom mirror and smiled as her question popped in his head.

Women were predictable about that same question throughout all times. *What you have on is fine.*

He found Simon in the library with Giles. The two of them had been bent over the books for some time, neither of them taking notice of him. "Amber and I are leaving for a few hours."

Simon and Giles sat motionless as they took in his words.

"Leaving?" Simon asked.

"A date. We won't be gone long."

"A date?"

Kincaid held his ground through Simon's stare.

"Yes." He lifted his hand. "I need the keys to the R8."

"My car?"

"I'd take Mrs. Dawson's Lincoln, but I'm more familiar with the power of yours."

Giles sat forward. "You have an R8...as in a combustible engine Audi? Really?"

Simon gave a curt nod, his eyes never leaving Kincaid's. "Where are you going?"

"Dinner. Alone. We're bonded, Simon. She's safe with me." The man took his role as protector seriously, but Simon had no idea how seriously Kincaid took the role.

"The key is on the hook in the kitchen. There's a cell phone in the car."

Kincaid offered thanks and moved through the library with purpose. The western wall, three shelves up, he found the book titled *Contingency*. The same book was situated in the exact space in his time. There, he removed the book, opened it, and found several bills of the currency of the time.

"What the—?"

"Mr. Dawson's legacy is embedded in this library. The man knew more than he let his wife know."

Simon stood, crossed the room, and looked at the hollowed out book filled with hundred dollar bills.

"Emergency money is always here, no matter the time or the currency used."

Simon frowned. "What do you need all that for?"

197

Kincaid sucked in a breath. "My wife."

Showered, clean, and ready to take his wife on their first date, Kincaid met Amber at the foot of the stairs as she walked toward him. She wore black slacks with a tiny black halter shirt and sheer black cover up. She was dressed like him, and it didn't go unnoticed. It was impossible to notice the little things that hadn't been there before. The small amount of makeup, the way her hair was slicked back. Put her in tight leather, and she would resemble the exact image of a female warrior of his time.

Damn she was beautiful. The large dark gaze, the full sensual lips…the smile.

He envisioned the stream he'd seen in her head for days to keep her from seeing every thought inside his mind.

He offered his arm, which she took with a coy smile.

"You're beautiful," he told her.

A rose blush filled her cheeks.

What are you up to?

Her voice pushed through his head.

"Let's try and speak out loud," he suggested.

"All right." She stood back, only her fingertips touched his arm. "Where are we going, Mr. Kincaid?"

The stream ran in his head, he hoped his thoughts were hidden. "You don't know?"

"Nay," she told him. "I do not."

"Good." He winked and pulled her out the door. "My guess is you haven't been outside of this house much since you've been here."

They walked down the steps of the manor to the waiting car.

Amber hesitated at the door of the car, and her anxiety wavered over him.

"Twice. I've left this home two times since my parents left me here."

Kincaid paused and opened his mind. *You're safe with me, Amber. Always.*

She offered a nod, but her anxiety was palpable.

He tucked her in the car and moved to the driver's seat. He hadn't driven a gas-powered vehicle in years, but much like anything learned as a child, he knew enough to make the car work.

As they left the sanctuary of the manor, Amber's anxiety increased.

With purpose, Kincaid reinforced the barrier between the two of them and the world. "I won't let any other emotions hit you," he promised her.

"I keep waiting for their return," she told him. "The voices."

"You've managed to wield my power since our bond. Have the emotions of others returned?"

She watched the world pass by. Her hand gripped the handle on the door. "Nay...well, only when I searched for them."

"What about my gift? Do you have to concentrate on it for it to be there?"

"Aye...nay."

"Which is it?"

"I need to think on it now, out here. At the manor, I don't think about it. It's just there. When I feel burdened by the thoughts of others, I bring up your shield."

"Our shield."

"I suppose you're right."

He wove through traffic; his destination embedded in his mind.

"I don't have to think about your gift. I sense others, their feelings. I thought it might be important for both of us to experience life outside the manor for a couple of hours. It's hard to judge other's true feelings when you trust those around you the way we do."

"I trust my family," she told him.

"Trust is important in the manor. Always."

"Throughout time?"

He moved off the highway and toward his

destination. "If someone isn't trustworthy, they're banished. There are few exceptions."

"With the gifts of perceptions and premonitions, it would be very difficult to deceive the occupants."

He nodded. "In my time? Yeah, that's true. Not in this time. It's something Simon and Helen need to fortify."

"Why Simon and Helen? Why not us?"

He glanced at her. "I'm not sure we're meant to fortify the future of the manor, are you?"

"I'd ask my mother if she were here. But nay, I don't know if we're meant to stay in this time."

He wanted to ask if her desire was to stay here now, but he wasn't sure he'd like the answer.

Kincaid pulled into the parking lot and ignored the stares of those as they exited the sporty car.

Amber moved close to his side and watched the mass of people as they walked by them.

"I have you," he whispered in her ear.

The tight smile on her face had him squeezing her hand. He ushered Amber inside the high-end mall and guided her into a jewelry store.

"What are we doing here?" she asked.

He pulled her closer. "We're married, Amber. I don't want anyone thinking you're not taken."

She turned toward him. "I'm not around anyone who doesn't know of our status."

Kincaid shrugged. "Humor me."

She did.

They picked out a diamond-studded band that Amber insisted reminded her of her mother's. He in turn, placed a titanium band on his finger before they left the store.

Amber's anxiety hovered like a mist. Unlike any other woman who might enjoy a shopping trip, she kept pace with him for a speedy exit. The threat of so many people around her sent a cold sweat over him.

"Should we find a quiet place to eat?" he asked.

"The manor?"

He shook his head. "I was thinking a restaurant."

She glanced at those coming and going from the mall. *Is it safe?*

I wouldn't take you if it wasn't.

Inside the car, Amber followed his lead, buckled her belt, and sat back with a heavy sigh. "I keep waiting for everyone to crush in."

He covered her hand with his. "I know you do. Just think of my shield, see the blue color grow solid, and know it will hold. It's never failed me."

The car started to shudder as if it were in quicksand. "Okay, perhaps a little less would help us actually move," he told her.

Amber's brow pitched together. "Is that me?"

"Just pull it back to reach only inside the car."

The thick band around the car eased in slow degrees. *Distraction. She needs a distraction.*

"So..." he began, "Jake and Selma?" He could care less about the gossip of the two in question, but the car instantly surged forward when Amber thought of the couple and released his shield from around the car.

"I should have seen that coming," she told him as he pulled the car into traffic en route to the restaurant.

"You didn't?"

Amber shook her head. "When I met Selma and Jake, everyone's emotions were rampant in my head. Concentrating on any one person was difficult."

"He cares for her."

"Agreed. She has no idea how much," she told him.

"Agreed."

They sat in silence for a moment. "It's not easy for the others," he said. "The ones who join us and aren't Druid."

She stared at the passing traffic and a sense of peace washed over him.

"I was a child when Todd joined us. Myra's husband is from this time—Jake's brother in arms. He adjusted eventually."

"There are plenty of Todd's out there. Men and women who join the manor and keep order. Not everyone picks a spouse who shares his or her Druid heritage. Those of us who do understand the risk or the gain."

"You make it sound as if the manor is filled with people from all walks of life in your future."

"It is. Though the manor is larger than it is now. The houses surrounding Mrs. Dawson's home become sanctuaries for families who attempt to raise their children in relative normalcy."

"Not unlike my parent's home."

He laughed. It was hard not to. "MacCoinnich Keep is much more than a home."

Amber shrugged, looked out the window. "For me it was home. Nothing more or less than Dawson Manor. I kept up with the cats in the barn, knew when they were giving birth. Those who roamed the halls—the maids, the cooks, the knights—all were essential in the movement and protection of my childhood home. But it was still my home."

The thought sobered Kincaid as he parked in the lot and jumped out to help Amber.

His wife had grown up the youngest child in a medieval Keep…during medieval times. She had family members who had crossed centuries and would again to keep her from harm. He however, grew up with menial financial means in a single room apartment with strangers. Growing up, even his own father was nothing more than an unapproachable enigma. Kincaid had leapt at the opportunity to belong to something, anything.

The host sat them at a table in the back of the restaurant where Amber picked up the conversation from the car.

"Where is it you grew up?" she asked.

"Outside the manor," he told her. "My mother disappeared early on and my father was stuck with the burden of raising me."

"She left you?" *How can a mother leave her child?*

"Not all mothers are the same. Mine spawned and left."

"How very cold." She looked away.

"It's hard to feel anything for someone I don't know." Anything other than hatred and disappointment, that was.

Amber sat rod-straight, her eyes never left his. "I'm sorry," she told him.

He was about to ask about what, when he heard her.

For the loss of a childhood.

He shook his head. "My father knew I was a powerful Druid early on."

"How? You were a child, how did he know?"

The memory of his father out of control swam in his head. Kincaid wasn't sure what his father's drug of choice was... he just knew good ole' dad wasn't often lucid and logic and loyalty to his family wasn't there. "I got into a fight at school. The other kid tossed his fists, but they never landed where he intended them. My dad...he knew, said something about my mom being un-human. He mentioned the word Druid...I thought it was a joke."

"Druids are human."

"Not to my dad."

Amber's eyes turned cold. "He treated you differently."

"He treated me indifferently. Like a dog that needed to be fed and housed."

Amber reached across the table, took his hand in hers. Warmth and the feeling of home settled over him. He'd never, ever, said any of this to anyone in his life. Hell, he hadn't thought of the man who fathered him in years. "I'm sorry," his wife said in a soft whisper.

Kincaid offered her a smile. "He had a hard time keeping a job, and when he had a chance, he pushed me off his to do list. I found the manor and those like me, and I made myself useful. It wasn't long before my new family understood my worth." He shielded her from his thoughts, the memories of those early years and how painful they were.

"Your ability to shield others?"

"Yeah." He removed his hand from hers, patted his leg where one of his weapons was concealed. "I'm not a bad shot, either."

"I'm sure you're a valiant warrior," she told him.

"Even in a kilt."

She laughed then, and he felt the need to make her do that again. He liked her innocent laugh, and she didn't let it out often enough.

"I have a hard time picturing you in a kilt."

The waiter arrived with their wine and left a helping of bread. Remembering the time she was from, he removed a chunk of bread and placed it on her plate.

"My kilt is modified, but I do own one, or two, actually."

"The plaid of my family?" she asked.

"Is there another?"

His question pleased her and brought the smile he loved to her lips.

He told her about his travels in time—how he'd always battled alongside her ancestors and probably even some of his own at some point.

Their dinner arrived and for the first time since Kincaid had landed in this century he felt like himself again. When the emotions of those around them started to leak in, he'd bring up his shield stronger and force them out.

It was just him and Amber.

"My father would like you," she said between dinner and dessert.

He sat back, drank his coffee. "Your father would question every move I made."

"Aye, he would. But in time, he would approve."

Kincaid leaned forward and laid his hand across the

table. She hesitated for a moment before laying her hand in his. Their connection sparked and a sense of peace filled his blood. "Your father's approval is important to you?"

"Aye."

"Then we should return to your time. Inform your family what has happened." If he ever had a daughter, he'd want to know if she was safe. Ian MacCoinnich might be the patriarch of damn near his entire race, but he was still a *man*…a father.

"You'd do that for me?"

"Amber," he uttered her name in a whisper. "My life is in as much turmoil as yours. We have both leapt into this bond, but I'd like to think there was something there before the leap. Your portrait on the wall drew my attention, and you've captured something deeper than just an attraction."

The edges of her embarrassment developed in her blushing cheeks.

"I find you attractive, too," she said in a whisper.

He wanted to laugh, but held it in. "That's a start."

"Is it enough? We're bonded…married."

The thought chilled him. Her worry? Or maybe it was his. "We'll figure it out. Families arranged marriages for years, especially in your time."

"That was never a concern of mine. My father didn't follow that tradition."

Her father was obviously the obstacle to help her past her fears. The thought of meeting Ian face to face didn't sit well in his gut. Once again, Kincaid shielded his thoughts as best he could from his wife. They would need to visit her family as soon as time permitted. She needed their strength and their approval to move forward.

And moving forward, in order to find their place in life, was essential for him to return to his world.

He paused and realized he wasn't sure where that was anymore.

Past, present or future? He didn't know.

****

Giles huddled over the book that had fallen off the shelf and ran a frustrated hand through his hair.

Why was this information coming to him now? To confuse him or to make him question all he knew? Did he dare look for answers?

Grainna, the evil one the MacCoinnich's removed from all time, had bore one child. A product of a union, a ritual that gave her immortality that only the MacCoinnich's could remove. She discarded her child as if it were garbage.

Giles cross-referenced his books—found other information on the lineage of that child, of their children. The story was always the same…a child was born and discarded. In early times, the legends said the adult child understood the power they held, and attempted to exploit it and others. In some generation's accounts, the child did not know of their bloodline.

Then, in the last pages of the book Giles held, he read the most cryptic and disturbing prophecy of them all.

Only when the powerful one bonds and complete their union with one of equal gift, will the cycle be broken…and then the gifts of the forefathers and mothers will come together. This bond will come from two opposing families…enemies.

A crossroad will follow where the path of good or evil will be chosen. Power, in this time, will mean everything, and the path of right will have been nearly forgotten.

From this day forward, the path will not be recorded to protect and preserve the future.

May God be with us all.

Giles slammed the book closed, crossed his arms on the desk, and laid his head down.

Chapter Twenty-Two

Raine knew the moment Mouse returned to their time. The shiver up her spine was a physical sign of pleasure, much like a cat purring or a dog rolling on his back for a rub to its stomach.

Mouse arrived with enough information to dent the armor of the MacCoinnich lineage—possibly even change history. What good was time travel if one could not alter the outcome in favor of oneself, anyway?

She sensed him at the door of her chamber and bid him enter.

The man had circles under his eyes, the effect of lack of sleep and too many trips through time without rest.

"Well?" she asked, skipping all pleasantries.

He held onto the back of a chair as he spoke. "The librarian has the book."

"And?"

Mouse shook his head and closed his eyes. "Is Kincaid really a descendent of Grainna herself?"

"You're not here to ask questions, Mouse. Just tell me what you know."

"There isn't much to tell. Selma Mayfair moved into the manor." Mouse pressed a button on the timepiece on his wrist and accessed the holo projection in Raine's room. A picture of a law enforcement officer of the twenty first century played on screen. "This man is not Druid." The images shifted and two identical children appeared next to a woman. "These are his children and his former wife."

Raine smirked. "So many broken marriages in this time. Who are they to Amber and Kincaid?"

"No one directly. However this man," the image flipped back to the officer. "He was a close colleague to the second sister's husband."

"The second sister?"

"Amber's sister."

Raine pushed from where she was perched and started to pace. *Now the pieces fall into place.*

The pieces and the path.

"Tell me of the manor. And then tell me the routine of these children."

Because nothing created chaos quite like a child in need.

****

Amber exited the car with Gavin's hand in hers. He paused under the moon and stroked a stand of hair that had fallen in her face. "We're going to be okay, Mrs. Kincaid."

"I want to think so." They'd talked all night of their lives before he entered hers. Just under the surface lay worry. The fact she had trouble hearing all his thoughts and that he had managed to keep her out of his head as much as she had kept him out of hers, troubled her. She wanted to mask her insecurities, her worry of being inadequate as a wife and companion. What did she know of anything other than being a child? The opportunity of living her life hadn't presented itself until Gavin entered her world.

Adding to her unease was the strong desire to see her family, to speak with her mother, and seek her father's approval. They would want to see her well and alive, but would they approve of her rash decision to bond with a stranger? And why did it matter so very much?

She knew the answer to that.

She'd lived under the protection of her family her entire life. Never once had she been in a position to make a decision for herself.

When she had made a decision, it was the ultimate one.

"Hey?" Gavin ran a finger along her face. "What's going on inside this beautiful head?"

Instead of answering him, she opened her mind to him and let everything flow between their link. His palm paused alongside her face as a play of emotions...hers, passed over him.

"Wow."

"I feel more like a child than a woman sometimes. I know I have the body and the age of a woman older, but inside..."

Gavin stepped closer and folded her in his arms. "Shh. You're not a child, Amber. Quite the opposite. Seems you've had to take on the persona of someone much older at a very young age. Somewhere you were lost in all of that."

She buried her head in his shoulder and sucked in the masculine scent of his skin. "Is it wrong to want the council of my parents...my sister?"

Before Gavin could shield his thoughts, she heard him admit he had no desire for that in his life. Yet his words encouraged her. "Women have always asked their mother's and sister's advice. You're not unique there."

"Mine are harder to reach."

He pulled back and sought her eyes. "They are a thought and a chant away, Amber. Closer than most people need to reach across town."

"I suppose you're right."

Of course, I'm right.

His thought made her smile.

Humble, too? she asked in her head.

He looked away and she couldn't read him. "Your life...your family...the entirety of them is something we both need to be prepared for. Before we visit them."

Maybe she wasn't the only one feeling a wee bit insecure in their union.

"Should we go inside?" he asked as he stepped away and held her hand.

She nodded, but didn't move.

"What is it?"

209

"Why are you sleeping away from me?"

He shook his head and laughed. "It's not easy."

"Then why? Before our bond, we shared everything. Now it seems as if we are strangers in the same mind."

Gavin moved into her personal space again. "Believe me. I want nothing more than to return to your bed. But the pull to be with you, in every way, is stronger than I've ever felt."

"Then why stay away?"

He ran a thumb along her lower lip, licked his own. "Are you inviting me into your bed, Amber?" She pictured the two of them in an intimate embrace and realized the thought came from him.

Oh! How naive of her. Where she was looking for acceptance and security, he was looking for complete intimacy.

Gavin laid his lips to hers for a brief kiss and pulled away. "I'll come to your bed when you don't flinch at my thoughts."

"I'm sorry."

"Don't. Don't be sorry for what you don't know. When you're ready, we'll both know and neither of us will flinch or question."

She tilted her head. "You're a patient man, Gavin Kincaid."

He draped his arm around her shoulders and walked her toward the manor. "Do you see that stream in my head?" he asked.

"Aye."

"It's there so you don't realize just how impatient I am to have you."

She stumbled, but he kept her upright. "Why tell me that?"

"So you never doubt how much I desire you."

Oh!

For such a cool night, she certainly felt as if she had a fever.

****

"Kincaid, can I have a word with you?" Giles asked the question from the Library door the next morning.

The previous night with Amber had left him strangely comfortable and confident in his decision to bond with her. It might take some time to get used to the fact he had a life mate, but for the first time since he woke from their bonding, he was ready for the next step.

The dark circles under his friend's eyes shadowed Kincaid's good mood. "You really should try and sleep, Giles."

He hid a yawn behind the book in his hand and nodded toward the empty room. "I can sleep later."

"I'm not sure why you're avoiding sleep now. Amber and I are bonded, and she's out of danger."

Giles closed the door behind them, something he seldom did, and didn't make eye contact as he strode in front of Kincaid.

"She *is* out of danger, right?"

"What? Yes. I mean, I think so." Giles rubbed his eyes under his glasses. "I think so."

Not the answer Kincaid was looking for. He crossed his arms over his chest. "Explain."

"I'm not sure I can."

"Try."

Giles lifted his arms to the walls of books surrounding them. "In all these books, the ones handwritten or those that have writing added to them, is the most significant source of knowledge of our past. In the past few days, I felt it was my duty to record what has occurred between you and Amber."

So far, Kincaid wasn't alarmed by his friend's actions. "Librarians have always added their input to these tomes."

As if to emphasize his point, Giles moved to the ladder, pushed it along the wall, and stepped to a higher shelf. He removed a dusty book, stepped down, and laid it on the table in the center of the room. He opened up to a spot that must have been familiar to him and noted writing in the margins. "Some notes are connected to occurrences of the day. Others are there to help future keepers of the books cross reference the information to provide clarity."

"You're not telling me anything new."

Giles nodded repeatedly. "I know. Bear with me."

Kincaid leaned against a shelf and watched Giles pace.

"I considered writing in a book I've seen many times in our future so we would know what you were sent here to accomplish. Then thought better of it. Although it might have been a painful bonding for the both of you, you both did so of your own free will. Better to not alter what has happened thus far."

Kincaid nodded in agreement. Time travel and the affect it has on one's future suggested they tread carefully always.

"I removed this book," Giles waved the book in the air when he called Kincaid in the room. "I've never opened it, but I know it sits on these shelves in our time. I wrote your and Amber's names in the back of the book, with the date and time of your bonding."

"Seems reasonable." Those things were written in many books. "You chose this book because you know you've never opened it."

"Yes. Imagine if I'd told you I had once read you moved forward in time and bonded with Amber MacCoinnich."

Kincaid couldn't imagine taking each journey in time wondering if that was the one where he'd meet his bonded mate. Distraction might have killed him.

Giles thrust the book into Kincaid's chest. He uncrossed his hands and took it.

"The last page is where I placed the note."

"Okay."

"Open it," Giles told him.

212

Kincaid flipped to the last page and found it blank. He flipped a few pages more, found nothing written in Giles's hand.

"Are you sure this is the book you used?"

"Positive."

The room grew cooler. "What does this mean?" Kincaid tossed the book on the table and looked at the others gathered.

"Don't you find it strange there is no mention of Amber coming to this time? Of her surviving?"

"There are hundreds of books here. I'm sure the information is somewhere."

"Perhaps. Or there is some reason why her history...or future as it is, isn't recorded for a purpose. Like my writing your bonding date on the page of that book, it is not meant to be recorded."

"Why? Why keep that information only to us?"

"With that question in mind I found this book. There's a passage in here I've never heard of. In fact, I don't think any of us have heard of it."

"Which is?"

Giles hesitated, and then said, "Grainna had a child."

Kincaid blinked once. "Go on."

"She bore one child, a product of a ritual that gave her the immortality that kept her alive for centuries. She discarded the child shortly after birth."

Kincaid understood that all too well. "I don't think she was a maternal woman."

Giles offered a half smile. "This book tells of that child and the others that followed. They all bore one child. Man or woman, they abandoned the infant to others to raise. Some of these decedents knew of their power, but none knew where it originated. Their family tree had missing limbs and no clear path back to identify who their family was."

Kincaid huffed out a laugh. "There are many of us who share similar stories."

213

Giles caught Kincaid's eyes and stared. "Yes. But those who are most powerful know their kin."

"I'm powerful and have no knowledge of the mother who gave it to me. Or any of her family."

"I know." Giles stared directly at him and didn't let his gaze stray.

A chill, so powerful it shook Kincaid's entire body, rolled over him. "You don't think... No! I'm not."

Giles pushed another book across the table. "Read this."

Kincaid clenched his fist to keep it from shaking. With his back rod-straight, he pulled to look closer and read the passage.

Only when the powerful one bonds and complete their union with one of equal gift, will the cycle be broken...and then the gifts of the forefathers and mothers will come together. This bond will come from two opposing families...enemies.

A crossroad will follow where the path of good or evil will be chosen. Power, in this time, will mean everything, and the path of right will have been nearly forgotten.

From this day forward, the path will not be recorded to protect and preserve the future.

The passage was an omen. That was obvious.

"This could be anyone."

"It could be the two of you."

"I'm not a descendent of Grainna."

"Are you sure?"

No. "Of course."

"Your shield makes you nearly immortal."

"I assure you, I can bleed." Yet when was the last time he had?

"Explain why when I do this..." Giles placed his pen to the book and wrote Amber's name in the margin. As he wrote, the words swiftly disappeared before their eyes. "It won't keep."

"I don't know."

"*From this day forward, the path will not be recorded to protect and preserve the future.* I have written other passages, that of Helen and Simon, those have all preserved. But not one word of you and Amber. Not one, Kincaid."

"There must be some protection her family put upon her."

Giles shook his head. "Or this passage is speaking of the two of you."

Kincaid slammed the book closed and the fireplace behind him sprang to life. "It isn't me. I am not the son of Grainna!"

Behind him, he heard a gasp and felt the presence of his wife before he turned around.

She'd gone sheet-white as she stumbled backward toward the door. "God's teeth."

"Amber?" He moved toward her and she flinched and backed farther away.

You're her family?

"No."

The words in his head dried up as she successfully shut him out.

He took another step in her direction, and she pushed the shield up between them. "Don't."

Before he could say one word, she fled the room.

"Wait," Giles called him.

Kincaid twisted toward his friend. "Quickly, Giles."

"I-if you're her descendent—"

The sound of Amber fleeing couldn't be ignored.

Giles backed away, clearly uncomfortable. "Never mind."

"I'm *not* a son of Grainna!"

"I hope you're right."

He pursued his wife up the stairs and found her door closed and locked. "Amber?" How had she shut him out so completely? He barely felt her. He lowered his voice in an attempt to coax her out. "Giles doesn't know anything for certain. We can figure this out."

He waited.

Nothing.

"Amber?"

Amber?

He swallowed a wave of nausea and pushed his shoulder into the door, forcing it open. The room was empty. In the middle of the room stood a circle of candles still flickering.

Amber was gone.

Chapter Twenty-Three

One moment Selma was drinking coffee on the back porch of her temporary home and the next the cup fell from her hand, hitting the wood and spilling the dark brew everywhere. The charm around her neck grew cold and spread over her body. The image of the twins swam in her head, their tiny voices screamed with fright. "Kelsey, Sophie," she murmured. "Oh, God."

She jumped from her chair and ran in the back door. "Simon? Helen?" *Where are my keys? My purse?* Something was wrong. She tore up the stairs, colliding with Kincaid as he moved franticly in the opposite direction.

"Where's Amber?"

The question got stuck in a loop in Selma's brain. "What? I don't... something's wrong with the girls. We have to get to them."

Kincaid offered the same confused looks she most likely gave him.

From opposite directions Helen and Simon appeared both above and below them in the stairwell.

"Amber's gone!" Kincaid told them.

"Gone?" Selma froze.

"Gone. Moved in time, I think."

"She wouldn't. Not without you...without one of us," Simon told them.

"Go look for yourself."

Simon passed Selma on the stairs while the charm on her neck felt as if a brick of ice surrounded it and burned her skin. "I've got to check on the girls. Something awful is happening."

Helen swung in Selma's direction. "What are you

talking about?"

"I gave the girls charms. I linked them to this." She moved up a few steps and extended the necklace to Helen's hands. As soon as Helen touched it, her face grew white and her eyes closed. "Oh, no."

"You see something?"

Helen nodded, her eyes pinched together. "They're scared...in a closet. There's blood."

"Where? Where are they?"

"The closet is painted green... lots of toys and clothes."

"Their mom's house."

Helen dropped the necklace. "You need to call Jake."

"Helen?" Simon called from above.

Both of them ran toward his voice.

The room was empty.

Candles that sat in a circle flickered.

Giles ran in behind them and stopped short at the door. "Damn."

Kincaid glared at his friend, pointed a finger in his direction. "Keep searching for other answers, Giles. I need to find my wife."

"What happened to make her run?" Simon asked.

For an uncomfortable moment, Kincaid stared at the floor. He then stared at Giles. "I'll let him explain." Kincaid swiveled his head toward Simon. "Trust what you've seen and not what you hear."

He took a giant step back and the blue aura of his shield swam around him. Though he mumbled under his breath, Selma knew he was about to move time. Unwilling to get caught up in the vortex, she moved away and watched as Amber's husband disappeared into thin air.

They stood there, stunned, and all eyes turned to Giles.

Before anyone could question the man, Selma felt her stomach cramp, and she doubled over with a pain so intense she felt her coffee erupt.

"Selma?" Helen knelt beside her. "You're cold."

All she could see were the twins. Their anguish and pain. "I have to get to them."

"What is it, lass?" Simon asked.

"The twins...they're in trouble. I have to go."

Helen helped her upright. "Should we follow Amber?"

Simon frowned. "Amber will go home. She has protection there."

"The twins are children," Selma reminded them all. "Innocent."

"Then we go there first."

Selma turned from the room and darted around Giles.

"Stay here with Mrs. Dawson," she heard Simon order Giles "We'll discuss Amber and Kincaid when we return. Call Jake. Tell him we're en route."

****

A vortex of color surrounded Kincaid as his mind reached for the energy of his other half. Find her, he chanted. *Amber. Find my Amber.*

His stomach pitched, his head felt heavy enough to explode. All the while he grew closer, knew she was near. His hands stood at his side, his weapons at the ready. When the world shuddered to a grinding halt the gasps of women drew his attention first.

Stone walls. Large hearth with a fire blazing. MacCoinnich Keep.

Farther in the past than he'd ever seen.

Four witnesses. Two men, formidable foes...allies? Two women, one younger than the other, dressed as mistresses, not common servants. His assessment clicked off in rapid fire.

The older man tensed first as he dropped the object in his hand and unsheathed his sword.

Amber was there...somewhere. He felt her.

Kincaid removed his weapon by instinct, pointed at the man with the weapon.

From the other younger warrior, a knife flew. With a flick of his hand, his shield stopped the weapon a foot away and it fell to the floor.

"Where is she?" he yelled.

"Who?" the older man questioned, his eyes never wavering. The dim light in the room left the man in shadow.

Kincaid met the other man's stare. "Where is Amber? Where is my wife?"

The only emotion on the older man's face was the flare of his nostrils. Inside the man steamed.

The women were harder at guarding their reaction to his words.

The younger man shielded the women as he came to rest in front of them, shoulder to shoulder with the older man.

Before Kincaid could ask who these men were, he felt her.

Who they were could wait. He needed to find Amber before she ran again.

Kincaid bolted from the room, the beat of his own heart moving faster as he rounded the halls and ran up the familiar steps of the Scottish fortress. The room was cooler, the tapestries different, but it was the same space. He knew the others followed, but he had one goal. Find her. Keep her in one place long enough to talk to her. Explain.

He twisted a corridor, rounded another, found stairs, and moved up and up. Away from the warmth of the main floors. Away from the nagging emotions of everyone in the Keep.

The door he sensed her presence behind was massive, its hinges made of thick iron and not easily breached.

Inside Kincaid's head, he felt Amber's confusion, her worry. But he didn't sense she knew he was near. Instead of giving her warning, he aimed his weapon at the door and quickly dissolved the iron with two blasts before kicking her door in.

She stood in the center of the room with a gown in her arms.

He drew in a relieved breath and lowered his weapon. "You found me."

He heard the others behind him, ignored their presence.

"We're bonded, Amber. You can't escape me."

"God's Blood," someone said behind him.

Amber looked past him and the harsh expression on her face softened. She opened her arms. "Mother."

Kincaid grew cold.

The older woman moved past him and into his wife's arms.

Of course.

Where else would a scared newly married woman flee but home?

Which meant he, Gavin Kincaid, had actually drawn his weapon on his father-in-law. More than that, he drew his weapon on the man he'd sworn to protect through time.

Could it get any worse?

Then Kincaid remembered the information Giles delivered before he'd left the twenty-first century.

Yes. It can get worse.

****

They piled into two cars. Helen and Simon followed in the R8 while Selma sped through traffic in her beater en route to the address on the portable navigation. "I'm coming, girls. Hang tight."

The phone on the seat beside her rang. Unlike any other time, she didn't think twice about answering it. "Hello?"

"This had better be good, Matilda."

"Jake?" God it was good to hear his voice. "The girls. God…get there."

He was silent for a moment. "What's going on?"

"I feel them Jake. Something's wrong. Really

221

wrong."

"This witchy shit doesn't—"

She slammed on the brakes to avoid oncoming traffic. Horns around her blared.

"Dammit, Jake. Your daughters need you. Put the fucking phone down." With that, she tossed the phone to the floor and blew through a stop sign, swerved around a pedestrian in a crosswalk, and gunned her gutless engine down the street within a block of the girls' home.

She saw a wave of blue over the house and pulled her car to the curb. Behind her, the sports car pulled in and from it, Helen jumped out, a wolf at her side.

Simon.

"Wait here," Selma told her friend. Helen didn't need to get any closer until they knew it was safe.

Simon shook his head and bolted toward the house. The fact he didn't need to be told which one it was bothered Selma on so many levels.

Simon ran in front of her, cutting her off with a growl.

Selma hesitated outside the splintered and cracked front door.

Simon pushed through and Selma waited for several seconds before she heard his bark.

Without hesitation, she shoved her way inside and nearly stumbled over the sight.

Blood splattered a path through the house, throughout the living room, the kitchen. Her head spun and she swallowed back nausea. *Not the girls. Please, not the girls.*

At the end of the blood bath lay two adults.

The man Selma didn't recognize, but the woman was Lindsey. The wide deathly stare of their eyes and the carnage of their bodies were evidence of the vicious, lethal attack. Animal, if she had to guess.

From the stairs, she heard Simon bark.

She ran up and found Simon at the top. Seeing him naked wasn't something she wanted to get used to but by now, she didn't even flinch.

He stopped her from running into a closed door.

"They're in there."

For one awful moment, she thought he was shielding her from the unthinkable.

"Alive."

Her body collapsed against him. From the distance, she heard sirens.

"An animal killed them. I need to leave here in a different form."

Selma nodded.

"I'll scout, but I think whatever did this is gone."

"Whatever?"

"It wasn't human."

The charm on her neck started to thaw, as the noise of sirens grew closer.

"Go," Simon told her. "They need you."

Selma nodded and Simon shifted form and spread his wings. Without a thought, she opened a window and watched briefly as Simon flew away.

She opened the door to what had to be Kelsey's room.

The color green penetrated every surface. "Girls?" she said once, then again a little louder. She headed toward the closet and felt the charm warm. "It's Selma. You're okay... I'm here."

Without waiting for them to open the closet door, she inched it open to see the two of them huddled together, shaking. They rushed her, their large eyes opened wide as tears ran down their cheeks.

"I'm here, baby." She kissed the top of each of their heads. "I'm here."

Chapter Twenty-Four

From the corner of her eye, Amber saw Gavin take several steps back as her family moved in to surround her. Her father positioned his back to her to face her husband while Lizzy pushed forward.

"My God, we just left you," Lizzy said.

"Only minutes ago," her mother, Lora, said.

"'Tis been a few months in my time."

From the hallway, footsteps announced new arrivals.

Duncan and Tara arrived first followed by Todd and Myra whose chambers were farther down a distant hall. Her family was a welcome sight, a relief beyond any she could imagine. So many questions swam in her head. So much doubt. Finally, Cian filled the doorway.

She'd missed them. All of them.

Lizzy turned her gaze toward Gavin. "Who is he?"

Amber met Gavin's stare, said nothing.

"I'm her husband."

Her father tensed.

"And you're standing on opposite sides of the room... why?" Lizzy asked.

Amber lifted her chin, recalled Giles's words. "I've learned he is a descendant of Grainna." Every eye in the room shot to Gavin.

He looked at her, only her. His thoughts were a jumbled mess inside her head.

"We don't know if that's true," he told her.

"We don't know if it isn't."

He advanced on her and the men in the room moved to stand before her.

"I heard Giles. He spoke of a passage—of proof."

"He recited from a book, Amber. That's all."

Gavin kept moving forward. Her father attempted to move in his path only to jump back from the shield.

Duncan drew a dirk and rushed. He too was pushed to the floor.

It took every ounce of willpower to stand still as Gavin used his shield to clear a path to her side.

Everyone in the room grew uneasy as they found themselves held back.

"Have I given you any reason to question me? My trust?"

"Grainna was a master manipulator."

Is that what you think I am? His question sounded angry in her head.

He reached her and lifted his hand slowly to her face as if she were a frightened animal. Which she had to admit, if only to herself, she was.

"Don't hurt her!" she heard her father growl under his breath.

"If I wanted to hurt her, Laird Ian, I wouldn't have saved her." Gavin's gaze never left hers. His deep abiding stare soaked into her skull, leaving her head with pain. His long fingers skimmed around her neck in a near intimate caress. The heavy chain holding the sacred stone that afforded her the luxury of traveling in time fell into his palm.

His hand fell away with it.

He twisted and tossed the necklace at her father. "I'm sure you'll want to hold onto this," Gavin told Ian. "Amber, running off scared to times unknown can get her killed."

She opened the link in her head to his. *You think I'm a child.*

No, Amber. I think you're scared.

"God's teeth, Amber...you're not cloaked," Myra said as she pushed in only to hold back outside Gavin's shield.

Gavin's eyes traveled to Myra's heavily pregnant

225

belly and he stood back, sucking in his shield so it only layered his skin. Amber did the same and opened her arms to her sister.

While the women moved to gather around her, the men regarded her husband with thinly veiled anger.

"You're cured," Tara said.

"It seems I am."

"But how?" Tara asked.

Amber glanced at Kincaid and lifted her chin. "The same shield that protects my husband protects me."

"They're bonded," Lizzy told those who hadn't heard the earlier exchange.

"Really?" Myra asked.

While the other women asked questions, Amber stared directly into his eyes. "Aye," she said softly. "We are."

Bonded and wed, Amber. Running from me won't change that. He opened his mind to her...every thought, every emotion. *I have nothing to hide.*

She blinked several times. *I am frightened.*

Kincaid faced her father. "Laird Ian," he said with a slight bow of his head. "Gavin Kincaid, m'lord, at your service." He extended his hand and waited to see if he was to be accepted or denied.

Ian swept his eyes up and down Gavin's frame, his eyes landing on his extended hand. "Are you kin to Grainna?"

Gavin sucked in a deep breath. "I want to tell you I'm not. But the truth is I have no knowledge of my extended lineage."

For one awful moment, Amber noticed her father's shoulders tense and felt the static in the air charge.

"He speaks the truth, Father."

Several seconds passed before Ian nodded and slowly extended his hand.

The men regarded each other in silence, and Gavin then turned to Duncan. "Duncan MacCoinnich, I

226

presume?"

"Aye." They shook hands.

"And Finlay?"

When he turned to Cian, her brother stared at his extended hand but didn't offer his own.

"I won't shake the hand of evil incarnate."

"Cian!" Ian scolded.

"Nay, Father. If this man has an ounce of *her* blood in his veins, then he is our enemy."

"We *will* withhold judgment."

Cian offered a cold stare in Amber's direction. "How clever to penetrate our family through the bed of the most innocent one among us."

His disgust shot like a dagger into Amber's core.

Gavin dropped his hand, his jaw clenched. "Apologize to my wife."

Amber's gut twisted. To see her beloved brother denying her husband left her ill. This wasn't what she wanted when she'd run home. What had she expected? Watching her brother's stone-cold stare directed at Gavin made her realize how thoughtless she'd been in running away.

The air cracked with the force of her father's gift. "You're out of line, Cian."

"Better to die a noble death than to spawn with the devil."

Gavin pulled his arm back and swung. His fist connected to her brother's face with a loud clash.

Fin grabbed a hold of Cian and Duncan and Todd pushed Gavin away.

Instead of backing away from the violence, Amber pushed in, placing herself between her brother and her husband. "Stop!"

Get out of the way, Amber! Gavin pushed around Duncan only to have him keep hold of his arm. The fact that Gavin didn't use his gift to push off Duncan proved her husband was distracted by the chaos in the room.

Chaos that left him vulnerable. She left him vulnerable.

Instead of addressing Gavin's words, she leveled her eyes to her brother. "Gavin has not been in my bed. Not in the way you mean. I was close to death and he bonded to me, extending his gift. He did so without any assurance he would survive. We only just learned of his possible lineage."

"Yet you ran," Cian told her.

"Aye. I wanted the council of my family. I too fear what I don't know. But do not lay blame on an affair that hasn't occurred."

Cian pulled out of Finlay's grasp and squared his shoulders. "You call him your husband."

"And he is. I spoke the vows. We *are* bonded."

There were voices in the hall that told her they were about to be discovered by either servants or knights. None of which would understand the presence of Gavin and herself.

"Mother?"

"Ian," Lora said with the calm voice Amber wished she had. "Shall we find something for our son-in-law to wear while we," she indicated the women in the room, "assist Amber with an appropriate dress?"

With the distraction, Cian slid from the room without a backward glance.

Ian watched his youngest son leave and said nothing. "Finlay, Todd, see to Gavin's needs. Duncan, we will speak downstairs. Myra, tell the others we expect Amber and her intended to arrive before dawn. Tara, take your son from his bed and lead a horse to the south wall." Ian paused, glanced at Gavin. "Do you ride?"

"Of course."

"Elizabeth, prepare the children."

The room started to buzz with activity.

"Father?" Amber stopped him from leaving the room.

"Aye, lass?"

She opened her arms and embraced her sire. "He's a

good man," she whispered into his ear.

He kissed her forehead and gave her a slight smile. "We'll speak later."

****

The drizzling rain of Scotland wasn't something he'd ever get used to. God help him if his wife wanted to stay.

He stood under a tree with a horse at his side while he waited for the women…or maybe it would be one of the men, to bring his wife to his side.

It was surreal, really, to have Ian MacCoinnich orchestrate his entry into the family, into the fortress with little more than a few barked orders.

Dressed in a kilt, and not one that had enough pockets to house his weapons, Kincaid stood by the dark horse and waited.

How had his life been reduced to this? He was a warrior, for God's sake. He'd battled men throughout time, saved lives…taken others. And here he stood in the damn rain waiting.

Waiting.

When he started to contemplate what was happening in Simon's time, his head felt as if it was going to explode. *Too damn much turmoil.* Once Kincaid was brought into the Keep with enough pomp and circumstance to secure his welcome, he would be able to take all the men aside and discuss life in the twenty-first century.

Well, all the men save one. Cian's reaction needed to be analyzed.

The muddy sound of a horse approaching brought his attention to the misty darkness in front of him.

Amber?

Aye.

Listening to her in his head held a strange comfort. Even though she didn't offer anything other than confirmation, it was her approaching.

She sat on the back of a horse; her brother Fin sat in front.

Fin swung from the horse and captured Amber's hand to help her dismount. The hood of her cloak covered her face, masking any emotions he might see.

Long layers of dark fabric covered her lithe frame. She moved in the gown with the ease of a woman born in them, ever so much a lady.

Fin handed her over to Kincaid, who happily took her hand.

"Give me time to make it back and circle in from the North."

"I'm familiar with the land, Fin."

"As am I," Amber said.

Fin returned to his horse and kicked it into a run.

Alone, Kincaid watched his wife.

"You missed your family."

"Desperately. But I shouldn't have come here the way I did."

"I won't argue that."

"I'm sorry, Gavin. I was scared."

He pulled her farther under the tree to add some protection from the drizzle. "You have to learn to trust me, Amber. Maybe that would be easier for you to do if you didn't work so hard to keep me out of your head."

"But I'm not."

"You are. Even now. I see the stress in your eyes, the tension in the way you stand, but your emotions are highly detached from inside my head. Emotions I felt before we bonded."

"I haven't learned to separate your shield from my gift. Not completely."

Then simply open your mind to hear my voice. Can you do that?

I'll try.

He lifted her hand to his lips and kissed the back of it.

For the first time since they arrived in this time, she offered him a smile.

You're so very beautiful.

Her cheeks started to resemble the pink rays of sun starting to lift over the horizon.

Thank you. She lowered her eyes.

"I'm embarrassing you."

"I'm not used to the compliments."

"Well prepare yourself, Amber Kincaid. I plan on complimenting you often."

She giggled and he felt a smile on his lips.

"C'mon, m'lady. Your family awaits. I really don't want them to worry more than they already are."

He helped her onto the back of the horse and pulled himself up behind her. He held her slim waist with one hand and the reins with the other.

He led the horse to the north in a wide berth before heading toward the Keep.

"Should I worry about Cian?"

"I want to say no. He lost the most when we battled Grainna. The girl he loved fell victim and died before we could destroy the witch. I suppose if any of us knew of a child of Grainna's we might have searched them out."

"Guilty by association?"

"I don't know. Men in these times battle families based on the past deeds of their ancestors. My father has never ruled that way, but 'tis hard to say if he would have, had he known of a child."

The fog pulled in around them, and he slowed the horse down to see the silhouette of the Keep.

"And if I carry her blood...will your father damn me?"

He felt her answer before she said a word. "Nay. My father will judge you on your merits. He will worry and question. Grainna held so many powers, dark menacing power. Yet she was beautiful on the outside. Only her dark eyes gave away her evil. The contradiction is what will keep my family on alert."

"Hmm. What about you, Amber? Will you damn me?"

231

She twisted and looked up at him.

Kincaid pulled the horse to a stop and opened his mind for her to search for answers.

"You're worried Giles is right."

"I am." Because the evidence Giles found in the past seldom led them down the wrong path.

"Then we'll battle whatever internal conflict might occur together."

His chest warmed with the conviction of her words. He leaned down and briefly touched his lips to hers.

She didn't flinch.

"Let's get you home," he told her.

Without effort, the horse started to move again, carefully picking his way through the fog.

Chapter Twenty-Five

"I did what I could, but the children were charmed...protected."

"I wanted you to bring them to me."

Mouse barely held himself up. "I couldn't touch them. The power surrounding them was too great. You wanted to create panic, which was achieved with the death of the parents."

Raine seethed, gripped the back of the chair.

"Did you at least penetrate the manor?"

"Yes. Briefly."

Mouse wasn't meeting her eyes.

"Well?"

"Kincaid and Amber were both gone. Slid in time."

"Forward or back?"

"Back. Far back."

Raine hid a smile. At least that part worked.

The manor would fill quickly now. Because Mouse had been inside and laid his own blood, he would be able to penetrate the wards that would undoubtedly be placed. Only Mouse wasn't cunning enough or strong enough to finish the job Raine was preparing for.

No...she needed eyes back in time and the blood of another.

Mouse barely kept his eyes open.

She still needed him, but needed him more alert than he currently was. "Seek your bed, Mouse."

He nearly collapsed with pleasure.

"Before you do, send Clarisse to me."

Raine waited for the woman and smiled when she entered the room. "Just the talent I need."

****

It was impossible not to smile.

She was home. Alive and home.

The laughter of the children was more welcome than it had ever been before. With Gavin's shield, she didn't feel their worry or their overriding emotions that once caused her pain. No, she only heard their excitement, constant chatter, and questions. All of them asked about the manor in the future. The manor had briefly been a sanctuary for them. A wonderful escape into a future they will hear a lot about but would probably never live in.

Aislin, Myra and Todd's youngest daughter, sat curled in Amber's lap and listened to all the chatter.

"You look so different," Fiona told her. Tara and Duncan's only daughter sat beside Selma, her cousin while all the boys grouped together and kept a watchful eye on Gavin. Her poor husband had no less than six sets of eyes on him at all times. If not the children's, then the adults in the room. Except for Cian. He decided to ride to the village and avoid any more words on the touchy subject of Grainna's blood.

Amber hated the divide from her brother, but there wasn't anything she could do now that she and Gavin were bonded.

Family filled every corner of the massive room.

"You look like yourself again." Lora smiled when she spoke.

"I feel like myself again," Amber told her.

"Amber tells me you're the one who knew I'd come," Gavin said.

"I didn't know who would come, only that someone would."

"Are you truly married?" Briac asked.

"Aye, son, they are," Duncan spoke for them.

"But doesn't grandpa need to approve? I mean, you are his daughter."

Most of those in the room turned their gaze to Ian.

"'Tis a little late for that now, lad. Though I would

have preferred some knowledge before any vows were exchanged…"

"There was no time, Father," Amber told him.

I don't think your dad likes me. Gavin's words spoke inside her head.

Give him time.

"Simon stood as witness. He understood the urgency," Amber said.

"Why didn't he return with you?" Lizzy asked.

"He didn't know I was coming home."

"How could he not know, lass?"

Guilt about the way she left swelled in her chest.

"He couldn't have come even if he knew," Gavin said. "There were important matters to attend to when we left."

"What matters?" Fin asked.

How much should I say in front of the kids? Gavin asked her.

How much is there to say? Did I miss something?

Things were erupting after you disappeared.

Are they in danger?

Someone in the room cleared their throat.

"Selma, can you take the children outside so we might speak?" Amber asked Liz and Fin's oldest daughter.

A collective sigh of disappointment rose from all eight kids. But not one of them argued as they stood and left the room.

Gavin sat on the arm of the chair beside Amber while the rest of the family waited for some explanation.

Amber rested her hand on Gavin's leg. "What happened?"

"I felt you running, knew when I went to our room that you wouldn't be there. When I didn't find you, panic filled the house. Selma's panic."

"Selma?" Lizzy asked. "Do you mean Selma Mayfair?"

"Yes. She's been staying with us for a few days.

235

Someone threatened her, and Jake insisted she be around others."

Todd sat up. "Jake? My partner Jake?"

"Aye, Todd. It seems the two of them are attracted to one another. He seemed quite worried when she was threatened."

"Was the threat magical?" Duncan asked.

"It didn't seem that way at first," Gavin told them. "But when I was leaving I knew Selma's panic matched my own. She was terrified for Jake's daughters. She believed something awful was happening to them."

"Jesus," Todd jumped to his feet. "We need to help him. Jake's girls are all he has."

Ian lifted his hands in the air. "Calm yourself. We will not rush into anything."

Gavin nodded. "And traveling in time to alter a single event for one's own personal gain is forbidden. Besides, the Ancients only allow us to travel where they want us to go."

"But Jake—"

"He has Simon, Helen, and Selma with him."

"And Giles," Amber added.

"Who is Giles?" Tara asked.

"He's from my time," Gavin said.

"Your time?" someone in the room asked.

"When were you born?" This question came from Tara.

"Twenty-one ninety-nine."

"Really?"

"Wow! What's it like in your time?" Tara asked.

It seemed as if everyone in the room focused on Gavin.

"Harder...some things are easier. The political world is volatile and on the brink of civil war in nearly every 'free country'. Our natural resources are waning, as would be expected with the population growth and the advancement of medicine. Many of us live as far off the grid as we can to go unnoticed."

"Off the grid? What is the meaning of that?" Ian asked.

Gavin grinned. "Much like how you live here. Your resources for living…food, shelter, and power…manpower are all provided within the walls of the Manor. I live in Dawson Manor, which is much different from the Manor you know. The home is the same, but larger. The grounds extend for acres. The homes there now are occupied by those in our brotherhood."

"Brotherhood?"

"Or sisterhood. Many of us are Druid. Some are family or sworn friends to our cause. Not unlike what you have here. Laird Ian has his family and those watching the walls of this fortress. his men, and his servants making sure everyone is fed, clothed."

"And who manages this fortress?" Ian asked.

"It's more of a collective of Druids that manage and protect those who are not. We follow the leadership of a brother and sister whose powers help guide our path."

Duncan pushed away from Tara's side as if he couldn't stand still. "You said something about a cause? What cause do you speak of?"

Gavin narrowed his eyes and paused. "Yours. All of yours. We serve you."

"How is that possible?" Lizzy asked. "You don't know us."

"But I do. I know all of you. More than you will ever know me, I'm afraid."

"Do you meet us in the future? I don't get it." Tara exchanged confused looks with her sister.

"No. Nothing like that. You set into motion many things. The recovery of the trunk that Selma Mayfair retrieves with a stone in the twenty-first century?" Gavin paused. "That trunk needs to travel in time undisturbed for hundreds of years before it reaches its destination. We, those of us who are branded warriors, make tasks like that happen."

"Wait." Todd tossed his hands in the air. "How?"

Gavin smiled and Amber felt the entire room riveted to his words. A level of honor washed over her as she watched him speak.

He slowly lifted the sleeve of his shirt and exposed the embedded ink circling his upper right arm. "The ink used in this mark is derived from one of the original stones. Those stones are spread throughout the globe in my time. I believe at least two reside in this home throughout time. Only warriors, strong Druid warriors, are given the ability to shift time. We have learned, from the librarians, of your trials and the risk that Grainna posed to all. Imagine if the one stone had not made it to Selma when it was needed most? How would that one task have changed all of our lives?"

Amber remembered the final battle with Grainna, how each of them was needed to fight against her in order to win.

"There are other times, when the knights of this Keep are outnumbered and would have been overthrown if not for our intervention."

"Wait! Are you saying you've fought in this very hall to protect the stones?"

Gavin nodded. "Yes. Many times." As if to make his point, he stood and walked to the hearth and ran a hand over its massive stone mantel. When he reached the third stone on the end, he placed his palm over it and watched it turn. Inside, a sacred stone lay alone.

"One of the original stones?" Gavin directed his question to Ian.

Her father said nothing, but she noted the flare of his nostrils and the rigid set of his shoulders.

"'Tis but a rock."

Gavin lifted the sacred stone she knew was anything but a rock and grinned. He moved the stone closer to his arm and the Celtic marking on his arm appeared to glow.

"More than a rock. But I understand your need to protect it." Gavin returned the stone and closed the strange door.

"I have served this family, our cause, since I knew of your existence. I am but one of your knights, Laird Ian, sworn to protect this family and all the secrets you hold."

Amber's gaze shifted from her father to her husband and she held her breath.

"How is it you came to know my daughter? Did someone in your future tell you to find her?"

Gavin settled his eyes on her. A soft smile met his lips. "I noticed her portrait hanging in the stairway of this hall. It captured my attention because I'd never seen it before." *And because of your beauty.*

Amber smiled.

"I asked Giles to search for the name behind the picture. After that a series of events brought me to your daughter's side."

"If your one purpose is to protect this family then how is it you didn't know Amber on sight?"

Gavin turned to her family. "I have seen every one of your pictures. Portraits that even in my time are preserved in this Keep. But not Amber's. The books say very little of her. Giles and I thought perhaps she'd passed away as a child. Obviously that isn't the case."

"You should tell them what Giles learned right before we came here," Amber said.

The prophesy?

Aye.

Kincaid shook his head but launched into the driving force behind Amber's speedy retreat home. "Giles found out that Grainna had a child. And that the powerful child was thrown away by her at birth. Throughout time, each offspring has only one child, only to give the baby up. A mother giving away a son, a father giving away a daughter. It's repeated, making it difficult to follow the child's ancestry." The mention of Grainna's name brought every eye in the room on him.

"Go on." Ian's strong voice ordered him to continue.

"The passage Giles believes pertained to Amber and myself said this: Only when the powerful one bonds and completes their union with one of equal gift, will the cycle be broken...and then the gifts of the forefathers and mothers will come together. This bond will come from two opposing families...enemies. A crossroad will follow where the path of good or evil will be chosen. Power, in this time, will mean everything, and the path of right will have been nearly forgotten. From this day forward, the path will not be recorded to protect and preserve the future."

Amber noticed the sobering expressions of her parents.

"I have no proof I am or am not, a descendent of Grainna. However, I do know when attempting to record our marriage and our bond in the books we leave for the future, those recordings do not keep."

"You mean the writing disappears?" Lizzy asked.

"Nearly as fast as it's written. Which then leaves only word of mouth, but it seems even that doesn't stand in time."

"What of this crossroads?"

Gavin shrugged. "I have no idea. Amber and I bonded less than a week ago. I know she worried about not seeing any of you again, and I have concerns about where and, more importantly, when we are meant to live our lives. Those are the only crossroads I can see." He turned to Amber. "Do you feel anything looming?"

"Only the approval of my father and my mother. I too wonder where it is we will live. It seems a fortress needs to be made of Mrs. Dawson's home and with only Simon and Helen there to do the task—"

"Oh, Amber, this is not a crossroads." Lora, who had remained silent, spoke now commanding the attention of everyone in the room. "You are not meant to live in this time. That I know. Your time will be in the future, that I felt when I saw your knight saving you. When in the future I cannot say, but I do know your time here with us is limited."

Amber's heart sank in her chest.

You didn't want to hear that.

Amber looked at her husband. *They are my family.*

"I'm sorry, m'dear. I too wish it were different. Perhaps I will have another premonition giving me more details of our future."

"Maybe the passage has nothing to do with you. You're obviously bonded, the union complete. Do either of you feel the weight of new gifts inside of you?" Myra asked.

"I feel Gavin's shield. The strength of it increases every day. My gift is difficult to reach."

"Or you fear its return," Gavin said.

"Aye. I do fear the pain."

"Amber's gift hovers over me. I felt your fear when I arrived, sensed your distress about our union, and experienced your joy that Amber will survive what once was killing her. As for multiple gifts? There's nothing I didn't have before."

"Perhaps the passage isn't about us after all," Amber whispered.

"Or your union isn't complete," Tara's small voice said from the back of the room.

Gavin reached for Amber's hand and weaved her fingers together with his. "I assure you, we are bonded. Before we spoke the vows I couldn't let Amber go without her gift crippling her."

Amber nodded her agreement. Tara was mistaken, which must mean the passage didn't apply to them.

Chapter Twenty-Six

Selma and Jake held the girls long after their tears had dried up, and their swollen eyes finally closed in sleep.

Jake was reluctant at first, but he decided Mrs. Dawson's was the best place for all of them while the police feverishly attempted to find his ex-wife's killer.

He eased off one side of the bed while Selma did the same on the other. The girls snuggled closely together in their sleep.

After propping the door open, she and Jake made their way down the stairs in silence. They hadn't had time to really talk once the police arrived and the investigation began. She'd kept it together during the entire ordeal—a show of strength for the girls in an effort to alleviate their pain. The adrenaline that fueled her hours before now short-circuited in her veins and made her dizzy enough to sway on her feet.

"Hey?" Jake caught her elbow and steadied her.

She started to shake. First the tremor in her hand moved up her arm and then waved over her body and down her legs. "I thought I was too late."

"Shh! You weren't." He pulled her into the safe warmth of his arms. "They're upstairs, alive."

Selma buried her face in his shoulder and released the sob that had been lodged in her throat for hours.

Jake held her, just held her as she cried on his shoulder. The man could have lost his kids and yet he was comforting her. It was her fault. Whoever was after her managed to touch the girls. "You should take the girls. Go far away from me."

"Shh!"

She pushed away and met Jake's eyes. "I-I mean it.

The crazy after me is probably behind this."

"We don't know that."

"But it could be."

Jake's jaw bulged. "I've been a cop for a long time. It could be anyone from my past too. Where would you suggest I go to escape it?"

She hadn't thought of that. "But if it's because of me—"

"Then we deal with it."

She couldn't look at him. His trusting eyes, his calm voice. How could he be so calm?

Jake lifted her chin with one finger. "You protected them, Selma. You and your cauldron crap."

The snark in his voice made her hiccup and smile. "You don't believe in my cauldron crap."

"I don't want to believe in it. Doesn't mean I don't. I'm all about facts, and I sure as hell can't ignore any of you. Especially you."

God, when had Jake become so human? He'd always been such an ass with everything Druid.

"We almost lost them," she whispered.

"But we didn't. And we won't. Now…" He slid a thumb over her cheek to dry her tears. "Let's find the others and figure out how to protect my girls in this house."

"O-okay."

****

Amber didn't see a lot of Gavin over the next couple of days. On the day of the gathering meant to welcome Gavin into their family, she retreated with the women while her father took Gavin and her brothers outside the Keep for a more private talk.

The sun sank low on the horizon, and she smelled the cooking fires and the rich aroma of roasted meats and fresh bread coming from the kitchens below. They would have a feast in honor of her and Gavin's joining.

"The longer you stay the harder it will be for you to

leave," Tara said from where she sat next to her sister. Myra and Lora were perched in chairs across from each other, and Amber stood by a window staring at the land surrounding her childhood home.

"I know. Gavin reminds me we can visit, but I can't help but wonder if doing so would alter the future."

"Your father worried of that when we first sent Duncan and Finlay to the future. The responsibility of traveling in time isn't something we can ignore. It seems Gavin understands that better than even we do."

Myra stood and started to pace. Her overburdened belly filled with a new life led the way. "I wonder how Gavin and those in his clan police others. Certainly, tragedy must occur in the lives of those who time travel. The desire to alter the outcome would be difficult to overcome."

"I've thought about that," Lizzy said. "What would any of us do if something awful happened? Would we be tempted to go back and change the results?"

"We have to believe there are reasons for our journeys in life. To alter them, no matter how painful, could prove more tragic."

"Isn't that what Gavin does all the time. Changes the course of time?" Myra asked.

"Not entirely," Amber said. "There are gifted Druids who guide the travelers to where their premonitions tell them to go."

"The Ancients must be guiding them." Myra rubbed her back as she talked.

"As they did us," Lora said.

"Still, there have to be rogue warriors. Those who desire personal gain, love and power."

"There are, Lizzy. According to Gavin, men and women throughout time have simply disappeared. Some band together, others stay apart from their own. Many want to be the next Grainna. They collect power, as she did, and fight against Gavin and his men."

"For not knowing Gavin for very long, you certainly understand his cause."

Amber smiled. "Before we bonded the only thoughts in my head were his and mine. The peace of only him being in here," she tapped her head, "was a blessing. Escaping the pain wasn't something I ever imagined happening in my life."

"Is that why you bonded with him?"

"Nay, Myra. I bonded with him because he saved my life... twice. I couldn't let him die." Just the thought of him laying there lifeless, or nearly so, chilled her core.

"How did he save your life twice?"

She wasn't proud of her weak moments, but talking about her fears with the women in the room wasn't something she would have the luxury of repeating often in her life. "I was dying. I felt my body weakening, my will to live with the world crushing in was simply too much to bear." She turned away from her mother's watering eyes and stared out the window. "In a moment of weakness I prepared myself to return here. I didn't want to die without seeing all of you again." She paused.

"What happened?"

"I collapsed before I could shift time. When I woke, Gavin was beside me holding my hand, and the world had gone silent. His gift surrounded us both and pushed everyone else out."

"That's one hell of a gift," Lizzy said with a weak laugh.

"What happened when he let go?"

Amber's eyes drifted to her mother briefly, then back to the green landscape. "He couldn't, not without everything rushing back in. We learned that quite by accident. Giles searched feverishly for a cure, a way to use Gavin's gift to seal everything out, or at least control it, but all we found was talk of bonding and marrying our gifts."

"So you had to bond. That or die," Tara said.

245

Amber pushed away from the window and moved to her sister's side.

"I chose to die. I couldn't ask Gavin to bond to me. His loyalty to us, his honor would have forced him to bond. I couldn't let him."

"But you didn't die."

"No. I left his side one night but only made it as far as the attic. I'm told when they found me I was on my last breath. Gavin took hold and spoke the vows."

Lora sucked in a breath. "To a dying woman?"

"Aye, mother. My gift crippled him while I slowly began to heal. So you see, when I woke I had to save him. I couldn't let him die—not after all he sacrificed for me."

Lora stood and walked to her side. She lifted a hand to her cheek and pulled her into her arms with a sob. "I'm so sorry for your pain."

Her mother's sorrow struck her gut as the emotion leaked through Gavin's shield. Instead of fighting it, Amber let the feeling in. "I'm well now. We simply need to determine how we will live our life together."

"At least he's cute," Lizzy said evoking a laugh from all of them. Lora and Amber pulled away from their hug and the grief in her mother's heart started to mend.

"He is handsome, isn't he?" Amber asked with heat filling her cheeks.

"I'm happily married," Tara said. "But I'm not blind. He's hot."

Myra started laughing while holding her belly. "You're going to make me wet myself."

Lizzy curled her legs under her skirt and leaned her elbows on her knees. "So if he couldn't let you go until after you bonded...that means you guys slept together...bathed together?"

Tara's eyes widened. "Oh, yeah, how did that go?"

Amber gauged her mother's reaction to the question before answering. "We didn't have a choice."

"I'll bet *that* was scary."

"At first."

"Didn't you say the two of you haven't been intimate?" Myra asked.

"We haven't." If she didn't take into account the moments in the bathtub, they had very little knowledge of each other.

"Do you want to?" Lizzy asked.

Amber blinked several times, not sure how to answer the question. She moved her gaze to her mother and chewed on her bottom lip.

"Don't hold back for me. Intimacy is part of a marriage."

"I never thought I could stand the touch of anyone, let alone—"

"I'll take that as a yes," Lizzy said with a laugh.

Tara stood and arranged her skirts. "Well if Gavin is as considerate with your body as he was with your life, I don't think you have anything to worry about."

"She has a point," Lora said. "But if you have any questions—"

"Nay, Mother. I've heard all of you speaking of intimacy, and dare I admit when I couldn't control everyone's emotions from taking root in my brain, I have more knowledge than I probably should."

Lizzy giggled. "Our own little voyeur. Who knew?"

"The men are back," Tara said. "Duncan is suggesting we make ready for dinner." Tara and Duncan's bond was as seamless as walking. She was obviously speaking to him in her head where Amber felt the need to pause her thoughts before connecting to Gavin.

"I think we should dress you as a bride." Lora played with a strand of Amber's hair as she spoke.

"What a grand idea. I know just the gown." Myra waddled toward the door, and Amber trailed behind with Lizzy at her side.

"Uhm, Lizzy?"

"Yeah?"

"What does the word voyeur mean?"

****

Please tell me you're on your way down. Kincaid pushed the words into Amber's head long after he had returned to the Keep with all the MacCoinnich men. Well, again, Cian wouldn't join them, but Duncan, Finlay, Todd, and Ian had insisted on spending time with him away from the Keep and away from the women.

Kincaid wasn't a father, and could only imagine how difficult it was for a medieval man to meet his daughter's husband after they'd already wed. If not for the fact that Kincaid's gift saved Amber's life, he thought Ian would have forced an annulment and banished him from his home.

Their ride in the Highlands had been a testing ground. Apparently, Kincaid passed the riding test, and the sparring, because at one point Duncan suggested a friendly fight. There was not one word of praise or acceptance, just a nod before they returned to the Keep.

Todd seemed the most accepting and offered words of encouragement.

"At least you married his daughter before sleeping with her."

"You didn't?"

"I'm sure Amber will tell you the story. But no. And without any powers, I was completely out armed when I ended up here."

The hall was filled with family, servants, and knights. Many an eye followed Gavin as he and Todd spoke.

Kincaid drank ale from the goblet one of the servants gave him.

"If Ian didn't approve, you'd already know it. It killed him to leave her with Simon and Helen."

"Seems he's testing me to see if I can keep her safe."

Todd nodded. "Wouldn't you? If you had a daughter?"

"I guess I would."

Todd nudged his arm and said something, but he didn't catch it because Amber's words filled his head.

Is my father being difficult?

Kincaid caught Ian's eyes on him before looking away.

I believe I've passed all his tests. Are you on your way?

We're nearly done.

"You'd think I'd be used to this thing by now," Todd said as he scratched his knee under his kilt.

Kincaid wore one identical to Todd's and since there wasn't a threat looming, no sword accompanied the costume. Not that Kincaid didn't have one of his modern weapons hidden in the layers of the plaid. He was a warrior, and being unarmed was against his nature. "I'll be sure and tell Jake about your distaste for a kilt."

The grin on Todd's face fell. "Do you think he's okay? His kids?"

"When we go back, I'll try and return close to the time we left," he said under his breath to avoid anyone overhearing him. "If there's something I can do, I will."

Todd patted him on the shoulder. "I appreciate it."

A hush went over the room, and Kincaid followed the collective gazes to the stairway.

From the first moment he set eyes on the portrait in that very hall, he always knew Amber was lovely. But the woman standing at the top of the stairs staring down meeting his gaze was stunning. Dressed in layers of white and gold fabric, she stood in contrast to nearly everything in the room. Her dark hair was partially piled on her head with much of it draping down her back and over her shoulder.

Without realizing he moved, Kincaid found himself at the base of the stairs, while someone took the goblet from his hand.

Everyone is staring at me.

You're amazing. Your beauty makes everyone else

pale.

Her smile grew wider as his words sunk in.

When Amber reached the bottom step, she extended her hand and placed it in his and he kissed her fingertips. "I'm a lucky man," he told her. Her dark eyes stared into his.

I'm the one who is lucky you found me.

He kissed the back of her hand again and rested it on his cheek. He knew the gesture was one that laid claim to her. But more than that, he felt the need to be close—to keep her at his side. There were too many warriors in the room watching her who weren't her kin.

Her gaze moved to the floor and her color rose. *My father will expect you to take me to his side so he can introduce us.*

Following her instruction, he walked alongside her in a direct path to her father. *You know, this talking in our head thing is coming in handy. I really don't want to tick off your dad.*

She released a silent laugh.

Should I say something when we get to him?

Nay. My father will talk for both of us.

Kincaid wasn't sure if that was better or not.

With such a mix of family and non Druids who knew little or nothing of the family's true power, he was anxious to see how Ian would spin Kincaid's presence at Amber's side.

Ian signaled for someone to take his cup as the two of them approached. The man's stoic expression matched every portrait Kincaid had ever seen. He was nearly impossible to read. His family appeared relaxed at his side, giving Kincaid some assurance the man wasn't angry. Truthfully, it was difficult to tell.

The massive hall grew silent, one voice at a time. Even the youngest children didn't shuffle their feet. Amber squeezed his hand. He squeezed back and met his father-in-law's stare.

"I am but a humble servant of God who has been blessed with strong, healthy sons and beautiful daughters. In all the trials of parenthood, none is more difficult than giving the hand of my youngest daughter."

Some of the voices in the crowd mumbled.

"Especially when her hand will follow her husband far away from the hearth of this home."

Ian reached a hand to his wife and beckoned her to his side. She moved beside him and placed her palm in his. "Yet I remember the day I asked for my lovely woman's hand and knew I too would take her from all she knew."

Ian released Lora and stepped toward Amber and Kincaid. Ian gathered their joined hands in his, and Kincaid swore he felt an electrical snap.

"You have brought back the smile to my daughter's face. I trust, Gavin Kincaid you will continue to make her happy and keep her safe. That you will sacrifice your life for hers, if need be."

Kincaid met Ian's stare. "My promise to you."

Ian nodded and turned to his daughter. "As his wife, you will honor him all your days."

Amber turned to Kincaid. "My promise to you."

Their words sealed something inside him and made him stand taller.

Ian reached toward Lora. She handed him a cord and stood back. With slow care, Ian wrapped the cord around both Kincaid and Amber's hands, binding them together. "As laird of this land, I join you both in handfasting, giving blessing to this union until a man of the church can be summoned to give your vows before God."

A cheer went up and Ian stood back.

Kincaid couldn't say he'd ever watched a handfasting ceremony, but he'd been to enough weddings to know what was expected next. And even if it wasn't, he didn't want this moment to end.

With their hands joined, he stepped into Amber's space, pulled her closer with his free arm, and lowered his lips to hers. She softened and leaned into his kiss and, for one brief instant, it was only the two of them in the room.

Chapter Twenty-Seven

Every time Amber looked at her husband, she found him watching her. His adoring gaze made her feel as if she were the only one in the room...or at least the only female in the room.

She sat between Gavin and her oldest brother, Duncan, while they dined. Tables lined the great hall and timber filled the hearths, which would keep the hall warm for hours. So many familiar faces offered their congratulations, shook Gavin's hand, and called him a lucky man.

Once again, Amber felt his eyes and turned toward him.

Why are you staring at me?

We're married.

Was this something he just now realized? *Aye, we are.*

You didn't flinch.

Amber sipped wine from her glass and tried to understand the meaning behind his words.

When I kissed you...you didn't flinch.

The wine caught in her throat with a cough. Gavin placed a hand on her back and rubbed. He leaned forward and whispered in her ear. "I didn't mean for you to hear that thought."

After catching her breath, she laughed and leaned into her husband's arm. The joy of the moment, her family surrounding her and truly happy for her union, filled the moment, especially when she turned her head and kissed the man holding her without an invitation to do so.

She didn't have to ask if he welcomed her bold move, his hand moved to embrace her head and his lips parted to accept the tiny swipe of her tongue.

Someone in the crush of guests called notice to them and Amber reminded herself that her family watched.

Gavin broke the kiss and tucked her head in his arm.

She should have been embarrassed, and perhaps a part of her was, but she couldn't keep that emotion inside her for long. The joy of the hearts around them seeped through Gavin's gift in small degrees. Amber closed her eyes and tried to sense her parents—her father. He was there, slightly detached, but accepting and at peace.

Amber sought out her father and found him smiling. Beside him, her mother watched her with a silent tear streaming down her cheek.

Amber caught both their eyes and mouthed the words *thank you.*

Lora leaned into her husband with a smile.

Ian offered a nod.

Pushing her plate aside, Amber waited for the inevitable. Her sisters didn't make her wait long before they pulled her from her chair and away from Gavin.

What's going on? Gavin asked as the girls swept her away from the hall and up the stairs.

It felt good to be in her element, her life, without the crushing intensity of everyone around her. Instead of answering her husband's question, she offered. *You're a smart man, Gavin Kincaid. You'll figure it out.*

Amber peeked over her shoulder to see Gavin's brow narrow before Duncan and Fin moved in and clasped him on the back.

"C'mon, Amber. Move it," Lizzy slapped her bottom through her dress to move up the stairs faster.

The tradition of escorting the bride to her chambers before her husband followed wasn't something many of the MacCoinnich marriages had the privilege to experience.

Instead of tucking Amber in the chamber she called her own for the past half dozen years, they took her to the room she and Myra often shared as children. The larger room already had a fire burning and the shades were drawn. Candles lit the walls and the coverings of the bed had been turned down…inviting.

Tara, Lizzy, and Myra pushed Amber into the room.

Amber turned full circle and laughed.

Tara and Lizzy stared at her, and started to bust out laughing while Myra held her belly and laughed along with them.

"This has to be the most absurd tradition of this time," Tara said.

Escorting the bride to her room to dress and get her ready for her husband so they could consummate their vows would have terrified Amber to death if she hadn't already shared some intimacies with Gavin.

"The first time is scary enough without everyone downstairs thinking you're upstairs going at it." Lizzy must have realized what she said and promptly closed her mouth. "Not that you should be worried."

Amber waved a hand in the air. "Don't fret. I'm not at all frightened." She wasn't, which surprised her.

Myra moved behind Amber to help her unlace her gown. "I know it sounds strange, but I'm happy you're here so we can share this with you."

"I am, too," Tara agreed.

A knock sounded on the door before Lora tucked inside to join them.

Tara helped Myra pull the layers of fabric over her head leaving her in her underclothes.

"Is he already on his way?" Amber asked.

Her mother smiled. "You have some time. The men are pouring more spirits for him while they boast about their own wedding nights."

"I'm sure that's not all they're boasting," Lizzy said.

One layer at a time, her sisters helped her peel away her clothes before dressing her in a long silk nightdress. The silk was a luxury brought back from one of the many trips in time. It's dusty rose color complimented her coloring and hugged her figure.

Lora bid her to sit so she could remove the flowers from her hair and brush it out. The pampering wasn't something Amber had an opportunity to enjoy when she was last in the Keep.

Tara and Lizzy carefully folded the dress to pack away.

Lora caught Amber's gaze through the mirror. "When you were a child, I would sit for hours brushing your hair. Both of you." She smiled at Myra and continued with long strokes as she talked. "Myra was less tolerant of my hands, but you...you'd sit with me chattering about everything from the barn cats to the meat pies you were so fond of eating."

"I still love meat pies."

Lora smiled but there was a hint of sorrow behind her eyes. Or maybe Amber's gift was once again leaking in.

"I knew there would be a day I wouldn't be able to do such a simple task. I didn't realize the reason why. Such is the way of my gift. I don't always know the why...or the when." Lora stopped brushing and caught her eyes again.

Amber reached a hand to hold onto her mother's. The touch brought a wave of longing. Her mother had knowledge of something and was keeping it to herself.

"What is it?"

Lora kissed the top of her head and stepped back. "You'll be leaving tonight."

Tara sighed.

"I thought we'd stay a little longer," Amber said.

"I don't know why you're leaving, only that by morning you'll be gone."

Amber sighed and resolved herself to what her mother said. Her premonitions were never wrong.

Lizzy walked over and pulled Amber to her feet. "I'm getting really tired of all these goodbyes," she teased. "But seeing how we just did this a few days ago and you're already back, I'm not going to stress out about it." Lizzy pulled her into a hug. "Tell my son we love him and to take care of his wife and child."

Amber refused to feel sad with her impending departure. This day was for happiness, for her future, her marriage. For family. "I'll tell him."

Tara pushed forward. "My turn." She hugged her and leaned in to whisper in her ear. "Bonded sex doesn't hurt the first time. Just thought you'd like to know that."

Amber laughed and said a phrase she'd heard Lizzy repeat more than once. "Thanks for sharing."

Tara pulled back laughing. "I love ya."

Where the other women were smiling, Myra was tearful. Her hug was longer. "I'm so happy he found you and brought my sister back—even if only for a short while. We can move on in life knowing you're happy."

Lora hugged her last but didn't cry. From the pocket of her skirts, she removed the necklace Gavin had taken off her neck when she arrived. Amber pulled her hair back and allowed her mother to join the clasp. "You know where we are should you ever need us."

Amber couldn't help feeling she'd see them all again. Such a contrast from the last time they'd parted ways. "Does father know I'm leaving?"

"Aye. And he wants you to know he trusts the man you've married. You've grown stronger with him by your side, and I can't help but feel that will only improve. Trust your instincts and remember the bonds of this family."

"I will. I wish Cian would accept my husband."

"We all do. Perhaps one day."

Amber couldn't dwell on her brother's grief. Not with her husband waiting to join her.

"Gavin's waiting."

After one more group hug each of them left her room so she could await her husband's arrival.

Only a few minutes passed when the sound of boots and shouting men, well into their cups, escorted her husband to her door.

The tradition really was barbaric.

"Don't keep her waiting!"

"Go on, man."

"Back off!" she heard Gavin shout with laughter in his voice. "Not one set of eyes moves through that door."

Amber hid a smile behind her hand as the door slowly slid open and Gavin looked around it. Seeing her standing well away from the door and any wandering eyes, he pushed at someone and then moved into the room. He locked the door behind him, not that he needed to worry. No one would have entered.

"That was crazy," he said before he turned to give her his full attention.

"Aye. It was."

The grin he had on his face dipped when his eyes swept over her.

She refused to fidget under his stare.

"Wow."

Okay…now she found her feet moving.

"You've seen me in far less," she reminded him.

He approached her slowly. "Yeah, but…not like this. Not here."

She took a moment to soak him in. The plaid of her family draped over his shoulder and around his waist. It suited him as much as it did her father and brothers. His broad shoulders and firm build would match any man in this time. He was the most handsome man she'd ever met, making her a very lucky woman.

"It's me who's lucky," he said when he stopped in front of her.

She tilted her head back and placed the palm on his shirt. "Peeking into my thoughts again, husband?"

"I am."

Her eyes skirted past him toward the bed. The bed they would share.

"W-we don't have to." His words were weak, but his

heart wanted her comfortable. For that, she would gladly give herself to this man.

"I don't believe I've flinched once since you entered the room."

Relief washed through their joined gifts.

He reached for a lock of her hair and brushed it off her shoulder. "No. I don't believe you've flinched for days." His palm moved to her neck and cradled the back of her head.

There was no hesitation when he tilted her head back to accept his kiss. She sighed and pressed into him, his warmth. His lips were soft on hers, tasting and, if she read him correctly, savoring her.

He spread one hand around her waist and pulled the small of her back toward him, bringing her entire body flush with his. Her soft curves met his hard ones with only her thin gown and his kilt separating them. The feel of his tongue sweeping in her mouth distracted her and made her moan.

Gavin angled his head and kissed her deeper.

A roar of laughter interrupted their embrace from outside the door.

Gavin growled and Amber giggled.

He broke their kiss and rested his forehead to hers. "Wait right here."

He stormed toward the door, threw it open, and shook his finger at the men on the other side. "Go! Away! Now!"

Amber didn't dare look to see who stood there, but she did hear Fin's voice. "Time for us to leave, men."

Gavin closed the door again. This time when he stood back, she noticed the blue aura of his gift spread to circle the walls of the room.

"What are you doing?"

"I'm making sure no one out there hears a thing happening in here."

"That's not playing fair," she said with a click of her tongue.

He was back at her side in three steps. "I don't care. I want to make love to my wife, to hear you moan when I bring you pleasure."

His words made her insides quiver, as did his hands as they circled her hips and pulled her back into his arms.

"And I *will* bring you pleasure, Amber." He kissed her briefly. "So much pleasure."

If his kiss was any indication, she needn't worry. The taste of ale on his lips, the smell of the wool of her family plaid mixed with the unique bold scent of Gavin was something she would always remember from this night.

She reached into his hair and returned his kiss with as much fervor as he gave. When he pulled away again, she nipped at his lip, catching him by surprise. "My little minx." Gavin bent down, gathered her into his arms, and walked her to the bed. The soft mattress of straw, plush feathers, and wool met her back before Gavin moved beside her, cradling her.

"I want in here," he said tapping her head.

Amber opened her thoughts. *I'm not keeping you out.*

Yet once she said the words in her head a flood of emotion, of raw feeling had her closing her eyes to embrace the enormity of it. All Gavin...every ounce of the man wanted one thing.

Her.

"Oh, Gavin."

Something inside him had changed since the last time they were this connected.

"Coming here, having the blessing of your parents weighted on you."

"It did."

He stroked the side of her face as he spoke. "When your father joined our hands that weight lifted."

"Aye."

Gavin grasped one of her hands and brought it up between them. "Whatever the future holds, we will work it out together."

There wasn't an ounce of doubt in his mind, and that fact pushed away any that might have lingered inside her. "I will be true to you, Gavin. Always."

And I will protect and cherish you, Amber. Always.

His vow to cherish her began with a kiss. When breathing became difficult, he moved his lips to her neck and rounded his hands down her hip and leg.

I love the way you taste. He pushed aside her gown, licked, and kissed her shoulder.

I-I love the way you taste me.

He released a small laugh. *I'm going to enjoy teaching you what you'll truly love.*

She knew there was more than kissing to enjoy. He'd already taught her that much. *I'll be your willing pupil.*

He ran his hand under her nightgown and caressed her thigh. Everywhere he touched, her skin tingled.

"You like that."

Her eyes fluttered closed. "Aye. Your touch is like a fresh breeze on my skin."

A breeze?

He shifted until his knee rested between her legs.

With a will of its own, her body arched into him, closer. "Oh!" The very center of her body heated and that breeze grew into a wave of heat.

I prefer heat to a breeze, he told her.

You're very good at creating heat.

He licked the lobe of her ear, and she nearly shot off the bed.

"Yes, it's going to be a joy to teach you everything."

She clawed at his shirt, pulling it. *Do that again.*

Demanding little minx.

Her eyes opened and a tiny bit of doubt slipped in. *Is it too bold of me?*

He shook his head and gave a reassuring smile. "Ask me to do anything, and I will. There are no limits here, with us like this. If something doesn't feel right, stop me. I'll never hurt you."

"I know you won't."

Gavin leaned down and nibbled her ear. *Is this what you like?*

I like that very much.

As he nibbled and kissed, her hands found his waist and tugged his shirt away from his kilt.

Gavin reached down and unfastened something on his leg before a loud thump hit the floor.

My weapon.

My warrior is always ready.

God help anyone who disturbs us now.

She laughed. She couldn't help herself. "You really are desperate to have me."

"More than you can know."

Being inside his head, she had a pretty good idea. She envisioned her hands on his backside, felt his desire for her to touch him. Instead of bringing the image into her head she took the liberty of walking her hand down his bottom, loved the taut round feel of it against her palm.

He groaned, or maybe that was her. It didn't matter. The feeling of making him squirm mixed with the electricity of touching Gavin in such an intimate way exhilarated her, made her bolder.

While his hands danced up her leg, she allowed hers to do the same to his. Every muscle rippled beneath her fingertips. When she reached the apex of his leg where it met the bare curve of his arse, Gavin captured her lips in the most soulful kiss he'd delivered yet. She couldn't touch enough of him, couldn't separate her feelings from his. They both had the same goal—give the other complete satisfaction.

Something inside him switched, and he pulled away long enough to strip his shirt and all the finery that went with it. In only his kilt, he lowered his chest to hers and took her lips again.

His strong back was silk beneath her hands. Such a strong capable back. Such a strong man. Hers.

"I am yours."

And I'm yours.

He lifted off her long enough to help her remove the silk that separated them. The gown slid to the floor and Gavin looked his fill.

"You're so beautiful."

Amber lifted a hand and traced the ridges of his shoulder and down his chest. His hard muscles twitched, and she leaned forward to kiss and taste him.

Gavin leaned back against the bed. *Yes.*

Her tentative touch found the sensitive nub of his nipple. It grew into a tight bud, much like hers did when he touched her. When Gavin moaned, she felt his pleasure ripple through her and dampen between her legs.

Gavin filled his palm with her breast before she realized he'd moved over her again. His fingers played and without any warning, his mouth was on her, licking and making all rational thought explode from her head.

You're killing me, Amber.

The thick ridge of him sought her through his kilt with a need to be touched. Amber had no idea what it was like for a woman to have intimacies with her husband for the first time without the bonding link they shared, but she knew it couldn't be as all knowing as this time was for them. Her husband's desire to be touched moved her hands with a will of their own. Her hand traveled higher on his thigh until she felt him.

Yes. Please.

Amber smiled under his kiss and reached for him.

His thickness shocked her. Yes, she'd seen him before, but never like this. Her gentle squeeze brought a moan to his lips and complete abandon to whatever she wanted of him over his soul. He was so much larger than she was.

Before the thought managed to form in her head, Gavin said, "We'll fit. I won't hurt you."

I know you won't hurt me. How can anything so

perfect ever hurt?

She ran her hand along his length and felt the joy it gave him, felt her own excitement grow.

Gavin undid his kilt and swept it from his body.

It was only them, this moment. He pressed her open, wider, and slid a hand between her legs. One swipe of his fingers left her pushing him closer.

Please, Gavin.

No reason to beg, my love.

He moved between her legs and positioned himself over her.

Open your mind. Think of my pleasure.

She gasped as he pressed down. She felt her own sheath closing around him, accepting him into her tight, welcoming home. The intensity of the moment brought the flames in the hearth across the room higher and the candles flickered against her closed lids.

Gavin moved away and back, filling her a little more.

As her excitement grew, so did his, yet she knew he held back, afraid he'd hurt her. Instead of telling him he wouldn't, she pushed the thought of them joined and the feeling of how glorious it would be having him fully embedded inside her.

Gavin leaned up on his elbows and opened his eyes, which she met without waver. An emotion she wasn't sure she wanted to label moved between them as he took her fully. Her body hesitated, but she only felt her husband's pleasure. She was tight, gripping him and making it nearly impossible for him not to move.

Energy circled them both, solidifying their bond in a way only intimacy could.

He kissed her, slowly. *Tell me I can move, Amber...Please God tell me I can move.*

Instead of answering him, she surged against him. The friction forced his name from her lips.

The feel of him within her wasn't something she could have prepared herself for. The emotion of joining him completed her.

With each stroke of his body against hers, all thoughts of anything other than unraveling in his arms fled. "Gavin," she cried.

Thank goodness his gift filtered the sound of them in the room from anyone else in the Keep. When he found the perfect pace, her body fought the climb until it surged over in a stream of fire and heat.

As her pleasure pushed over the edge, she felt a wave of ecstasy crash over her husband like a wave on the sand. The tidal wave swept her up with him, leaving them both rolling back to the earth in slow foamy tremors.

Chapter Twenty-Eight

Gavin enveloped her. The enormity of emotion that welled over him when he claimed her was too big to describe. Even now, as he lay by her side with her leg draped over his, he wasn't close enough.

Tara was right.

Amber's thought drifted in his head. "Tara was right about what?"

"I-I didn't want you to hear that."

He laughed. "Too late."

Amber snuggled closer. "She told me that because we're bonded I wouldn't feel any pain."

A completely male part of him swelled. "It's a perk of our heritage."

"Yet you and I both know you've never used that perk before."

He tilted her head and smiled down at her. "I've never needed it before."

Kincaid felt her pride in knowing she was the only maiden he'd ever taken to his bed. What she probably didn't know was he was the one who felt like a god. He'd made her first time something special, something she'd treasure. Hell, he'd treasure it his entire life. The way she moaned and called his name made him feel more powerful than any gift from his ancestors, whoever they may have been.

Laughter from the great hall drifted up the stairs. "Are there any other crazy traditions I need to be aware of tonight? Anyone gonna rush in for an early morning roast?"

"We're quite safe from anything like that. I'm sure the maids will report the status of our sheets—"

"They'll what?" *Status of the sheets?*

"Aye. Proof of my purity, and confirmation we consummated our union. When I say that out loud I realize how barbaric it sounds."

"Incredibly." Though there was no question in his mind Amber wasn't pure. When he'd breached her thin barrier, he thought for sure he'd hurt her, but when she moved closer and encouraged him to take her, he knew he hadn't. Sex had always been a pleasurable release, but with Amber, it was so much more.

She tucked closer and yawned. "I'm sure my father will be pleased in any account. Not that we will be here to feel his pride."

He closed his eyes and felt the weight of the day's events suck his limbs deeper into the bed. "We won't be here?"

"Nay. My mother said we'll be gone by morning."

"We will?"

"So she told me. But I can't see leaving this bed until the sun is high tomorrow."

Lora's premonition must have been interpreted wrong. Sleep beckoned both of them. When Amber's breathing evened out and her limbs went lax over him, Kincaid pulled her closer and let his mind rest.

****

Static in the air tickled Kincaid's nose as he slept. He rolled into the soft sleeping woman in his bed and heard a snap. A blue light filled the room and he shot up in bed.

Amber was awake in an instant.

Kincaid felt the air change, grabbed his weapon, and threw Amber her gown. "Quickly."

The dark shadow of a man shifted in time and entered their room with hardly a puff of air.

Friend or foe?

Beside him, Amber slid the gown over her head, and he moved to shield her from their late-night visitor. Kincaid leveled his weapon before the man turned around.

267

"Rory?"

His green-eyed friend offered a full wattage smile. "It worked."

"What are you doing here?"

You know him? Amber asked.

"Yes, he's a branded warrior." And he was in their bedchambers in a part of time none of them had ever been told to travel. Which meant only one thing…something was about to go down.

"Time for you to get the hell out of here," Rory said without as much as a hello. His friend's eyes traveled to Amber. Kincaid shifted closer and covered her with one of the blankets.

"Did you come alone?"

"Had to. Now get dressed."

Amber grasped Kincaid's arm. "What's happening?"

"I don't know, love. But if Rory is here, it must mean we're meant to leave." Kincaid shot his eyes to his friend. "Turn around, mate."

Rory wiggled his eyebrows and presented them his back. Kincaid wrapped the kilt he'd had on the night before around his waist while Amber pulled a cape over her shoulders to hide her near-naked state.

"Hurry."

Kincaid found his weapons in the trunk by the bed, and began strapping them on. He handed Amber the clothes he wore when he first arrived.

Noise from the hall was brief and then the door to the room swung open.

"Cian?"

Her brother stood in the doorway, a sword in his hand.

"What are you doing here?" Kincaid didn't like the look on the man's face, nor the stance in his frame.

Cian looked beyond the men and straight at Amber.

Hate boiled from the Highlander. There was no possible way Amber didn't feel his emotion. "Let it go,

Cian," Kincaid told him.

Cain shifted his stare to the bed and cursed under his breath. "I'm too late."

"What are you talking about?" Amber pushed between him and Rory. "Too late for what?"

Stand back, Amber.

But instead of listening, she stepped forward, forcing Kincaid to move closer to her angry brother.

"It isn't what you think...the prophecy can't be about us. Please, Cian, you're my brother. I've loved you since the day I was born."

Kincaid felt her heart breaking when her brother's face didn't soften.

She hesitated and stepped back. "You came in here to take me away."

Cian narrowed his eyes. "And how can you know that, Amber? Your gift only allows you to feel my hate, not my intentions."

"We need to go," Rory said behind them.

"I feel your hate and your sorrow. What happened to the love in your heart, Cian? You don't need to worry about me, but yourself."

Cian took a step forward and lowered his sword. "All of us now need to worry about you. I will see this undone."

"Back off, Cian!"

Kincaid thickened the layer of protection over them and extended his gift to Rory. He pulled Amber close and glared at her brother who was causing her so much pain.

The air sparked and Kincaid shifted time.

The moment they landed in Dawson's Manor, Amber curled into his shoulder and released a sob.

"Shh. It's okay."

"He hates me."

"He's angry and confused. Don't cry."

Rory moved away from the two of them and circled the room. "Are we where I think we are?"

"Mrs. Dawson's home in the twenty-first century."

"It's changed."

Amber pulled out of his arms and lifted her chin. "Thank you for warning us."

"Ah, you're welcome, Miss…"

"It's Mrs…" Kincaid corrected his friend. "Mrs. Kincaid."

Rory's jaw dropped. "Really?"

"Amber Kincaid, formerly Amber MacCoinnich."

Rory went ghost-white. "Holy hell. Colleen told me to be prepared for anything. To grab you and leave. I don't…she didn't say…Holy hell."

Kincaid knew how his friend felt. Good thing Rory only met up with Cian. Although the impression of the family by that one man wasn't a good one.

"Does Colleen need you to return right away?"

Rory shrugged. "I thought we'd both return there."

Kincaid looked at his wife. "No. Not yet anyway."

His friend offered a small smile. "Well then, I guess I'm going back alone." They shook hands and Rory pulled him into a man-hug. "Be well."

Rory took Amber's hand and kissed the back of it. "M'lady. I never thought I'd have the pleasure."

"Thank you."

Rory winked and said, "Good luck with that one."

She smiled though Kincaid knew her thoughts were still on her brother's reaction.

"Until we meet again."

They both stood back while Rory chanted and shifted forward in time.

****

The house had yet to stir. Their presence went undetected. Gavin drew a warm bath and joined her in the scented soap.

"Is this going to be our life?" she asked him as he ran a hand down her arm and chased the bubbles in his path.

"What do you mean?"

"Moving in and out of time, following the path set by the warriors in your time?"

He released a long-suffering sigh. "I don't know, Amber. I can't help but believe we are exactly where we need to be for now. Look how quickly we left your home. I think we both doubted your mother's words."

"My mother has never been wrong."

"Then I doubted her enough for both of us."

Amber laughed and the sound warmed him. "You simply didn't want to get out of bed."

She felt his lips on the side of her neck and she moaned.

"Why would I want to leave my bed with you in it?"

Her head rolled back onto his shoulder and she offered him her lips. He kissed her thoroughly and ran his hand down her body.

She broke away. "I have a feeling we'll be spending a lot of extra time in our bed."

"There are more places to make love than a bed." To emphasize his words his hand slid up her legs and in-between the heated folds of her sex.

"Aye. You've already shown me that."

His hand fell away, and he grasped her hips and lifted her to the edge of the tub. "I have many, many things to teach you."

The chill of the outside air didn't compare to the excitement of seeing Gavin kneel before her and lean in to kiss her breast. She squeezed his shoulders as he worked his way to her other side. This would never get old. She understood now why her sisters were always so animated when they talked about sex.

Gavin slid down farther.

I'm going to taste you now.

She didn't understand, not completely. Yet when she opened her eyes, she saw him hovering over her most intimate parts as if he were about to embark on a feast.

Gavin, no. Embarrassment flooded her mind.

271

One taste, and if you want me to stop, I will.

His feather light touch on her thighs reassured and coaxed her to open for him. *One.*

She couldn't watch him, not while he was so close.

That's it, love, close your eyes and just feel.

Then he tasted her, his tongue sought her tight bundle of nerves and she cried out, *God's teeth.*

More?

Yes. A million times, yes.

He did…a million times more, until she saw stars and climaxed harder than she ever had before.

The world didn't still before Gavin pulled her from the tub and carried her to their bed. He was on her, in her, in seconds. The sensation was different from the first time. He didn't push thoughts of his pleasure into her head, and she experienced more of hers. Where his thickness scared her before, it excited her now.

He touched the very back of her core, finding another spot that made her need of him even stronger.

Gavin's hungry kisses continued as he rolled her on top of him. The change of angle brought on a small burst of his seed.

"I want all of it," she told him as she met his pace and felt her body grow tight again.

"Together," he said and hissed out with each thrust of his hips.

The wave was nearly on her. The desire to feel him release inside her, against her deepest spot, drove her harder. *Now, Gavin. Finish me now.*

Their surrender shattered them both.

Her breath came in short pants, and the walls around them grew silent. "Please tell me no one else heard that."

Gavin laughed beneath her. "Only me."

She laughed a big hearty laugh until Gavin joined her.

"The next time I say no, please remind me of our bathtub."

"I'll do that." Gavin ran his hands down her body that

had collapsed against his. "And then I'll taste you again."

"That really was magnificent. Does it feel the same for you?"

"You mean your lips on me?"

"Aye."

"I've always thought men had the better end of that bargain, but after feeling your pleasure, I'm not so sure."

"You felt my pleasure?"

"Every drop."

She couldn't be embarrassed. Not with him.

"Well, we will just have to see if you feel the same."

Gavin threw his arms to the side. "I've created a monster."

"I think you like the monster."

He rolled her under him in the space of one breath. "I think I love the monster."

Amber's laugh caught in her throat. *You think you love me?*

He placed a palm to her face. "I don't know what else to call the emotion inside of me, Amber. I only know I've never felt about anyone the way I feel about you."

"What if it's just our bond ruling your heart?"

Gavin shook his head. "Then sign me up to say the vows again. I would never have chosen to leave my home for anyone, but I can't think of going anywhere without you. It's as if I found my place in this crazy world, and that place is with you."

"You've taken the words out of my mouth. I thought the knowledge I wasn't to live in my parents' time would bother me, but all I thought of was you. Of us. If this is love I don't want the feeling to ever end."

Gavin leaned down and kissed her softly.

"We'll figure it out together."

"Aye, together."

Chapter Twenty-Nine

Amber chose a pair of black pants and a pull over knit shirt that hugged her body to wear for the day. It reminded her of her husband, of his dress and demeanor. The fabric was flexible and, to add to her mobility, she pulled her hair back into a band so only one long strand fell down her back. She should probably remove some of the length. It simply wasn't practical in this time. Maybe Helen could help her with that later in the day.

She stood by the window and watched the hues of the sun stretch over the horizon.

Those in the house were just starting to stir. She thought of her gift and opened herself up to the emotions of others. Slowly the pulse of Helen and Simon seeped into her. Their anxiety rolled from their images in Amber's head. Giles, if she had to guess, slept with disturbing dreams.

Selma was close as well. Only when Amber thought of her friend, all her emotions were overruled by someone. Jake. Aye, she was with Jake and they were…Amber felt the room warm and turned off her inner voyeur.

Mrs. Dawson slept soundly. Her dreams didn't penetrate Amber's head.

There was two other souls close by. Children. And their sorrow was so deep Amber clenched her shirt over her heart. "Poor babies." They'd lost something and grieved.

Amber tucked away the children's grief and focused on taking a deep breath. Gavin's shield built up around her, one thin layer at a time, until it moved everyone's emotions to the opposite side. *I'm getting better at that.*

Gavin walked up behind her and slid his arms around

her waist. "You're getting much better at that."

"'Tis because of you. Your gift."

"It's because of your strength."

They walked hand in hand down the stairs and into the kitchen. Amber moved about to put water on to boil for tea while Gavin brewed coffee.

Giles found them first.

"Somehow I knew you'd both just pop back up."

Gavin shook his friend's hand. "Just a short trip to meet the in-laws."

Giles nearly dropped the cup he'd just picked up. "You're kidding!"

"Most intense few days of my life."

The librarian blinked, his jaw slacked open.

Amber laughed.

"Ian? Lora?"

"All of them." Gavin removed the cup from Amber's hand and kissed her temple.

"I thought I heard your voice," Helen said as she walked into the kitchen. She headed straight to Amber and hugged her. "You have to stop scaring us. It's giving me grey hair."

Amber chuckled. "No more running off."

Helen looked deep. "You sure?"

"Aye. I'm sure. No matter what happens, Gavin and I will see it through together."

When Simon strode into the room, he lifted Amber off the ground in a hug. "How is everyone at home?"

"How did you know that's where we were?"

"A guess."

"As time would have it, I arrived shortly after they left us here. Hardly an hour had passed. They were surprised, of course. But in the end my father gave us his blessing."

Simon looked at Gavin. "He knows of your ancestors?"

"We told him everything we know. There's yet to be

275

any real evidence of that prophecy being about us."

Helen shoved her husband's arm. "That's what I said. There isn't any proof of anything."

"There is no confirmation I'm not of her blood either. However, neither one of us have noticed anything awful happening inside of us."

"I suppose we'll simply have to let time decide."

Amber sat at the table and reached a hand toward Gavin. He clasped it and kissed her fingers. *We have time.*

We do.

Amber glanced up to see Simon watching her. She smiled. "They send their love and congratulations on your child."

After pouring a cup of coffee, Simon sat opposite of Gavin. "Everyone is well then?"

Amber nearly nodded, then thought of Cian. "Cian didn't approve of our union."

Simon seemed to soak that information in before he said, "I'm not surprised. He's become harder these past years."

We need to tell them, Gavin told her.

The last thing she wanted was to soil her brother's name, but if he were to appear there now, everyone would need to know what he'd tried to do.

"I can't."

Gavin squeezed her hand.

"You can't what?" Helen asked.

"The night of our handfasting, we were awakened by Rory," Gavin made eye contact with Giles. "A warrior of my time. He told us we needed to leave immediately."

"Why?"

"We don't always know why we're sent in time. If we'd left immediately as Rory wanted, we wouldn't have known why."

"What happened?"

"Cian arrived uninvited."

Simon's body tightened. "Arrived?"

276

Amber needed to tell the rest of the story. "He wanted to take me away from Gavin. His anger was thick, Simon. Hateful."

"Did he want to harm you?"

God's teeth she didn't want to believe her own brother would. "I-I don't know. We didn't stay to interrogate him. He vowed to undo what was done."

"Undo?" Helen asked. "Undo what?"

Amber shrugged. "Our union, our bonding? I don't know. Our shield was thick and I couldn't read all his emotions." Yet she knew that wasn't entirely true. Her brother was willing to do anything needed to undo her bond with Gavin. Anything.

"He's changed over the years," Simon said.

"Do you think he's dangerous?" Gavin asked.

"He's a fierce warrior. Our enemies had no mercy at the end of his sword."

Gavin looked to Giles. "I suppose we need to study his history. See if there's anything we need to watch."

Amber wasn't sure what bothered her more, the fact Cian would have kidnapped her to get her away from her husband, or the fact Simon wasn't surprised by her brother's actions.

"What did we miss here? I believe we have new house guests?" Amber changed the subject.

Helen blew out a breath. "Jake's ex and her fiancé were murdered."

"No!" Now Amber understood the level of grief in the home.

"Yeah. We just don't know for sure who did it," Giles said.

"It was an animal attack. But I've yet to find an animal that can open doors and penetrate a home without help." Simon leaned forward on his elbows. "I can't tell if it was mortal or magical."

"How are the girls?" Amber asked, more worried about the children than who was behind the deaths.

"Unharmed. They hid in a closet when they heard their mother's screams."

"Did they see anything?"

"No, thankfully." Helen went on to explain the charms Selma had given the girls and how they'd been found.

They were still talking when Amber felt the children moving closer. "They're coming. Best we change the subject."

You can hear them? Gavin asked Amber.

Aye, can't you?

He shook his head.

A couple of seconds later, two adorable girls walked into the kitchen with Selma and Jake at their side.

"You're home!" Selma rushed forward for a hug.

"Aye, we are."

"It's about time." Mrs. Dawson walked into the room behind the others. "We were getting worried about you."

Amber stood and offered her chair to the older woman. "Tea or coffee?"

"Tea would be lovely, dear."

Selma introduced Amber and Gavin to the girls and put them on the task of mixing a couple of bowls of pancake batter. The twins quietly watched the others in the room and talked amongst themselves.

Amber moved to Jake's side and laid a hand on his arm. "I'm sorry."

He nodded toward his daughters. "It's them I'm worried about."

"We'll keep them safe." He met her gaze, and sorrow mixed into her thoughts of the girls safety. "But that isn't what you're worried about."

"They just lost their mother."

"But they still have you."

Jake gave a curt nod and moved to the place between his girls to help.

****

278

The prophecy lay on the tip of Raine's tongue, yet there wasn't a single crack in the white honor of Kincaid or Amber MacCoinnich. Not one.

She sat next to the fire under the night sky. Her clothing was carelessly tossed to the side as she bared herself to the elements to feel every ounce of energy around her.

The herbs tossed into the pyre billowed in dark smoke and filled her lungs then her head.

She rocked back and forth and stared into the hot flames. When the world around her slid away, she whispered the words, "Show me."

A white flame licked an orange one then merged into a blue ball that spread and filled with the Druid lives she wanted to take. Their souls were chess pieces moving on a board, and she was a dark angel watching from above.

The white light of children played. The call of a wolf screamed as sap slid from the bark of a tree and ignited in the flames. The blue sphere tightened, enclosing the children. All the souls in the Manor cried.

Then before she could see more, the ball exploded.

Yes. Raine needed to move the chess pieces in place for the queen to take her throne. No use destroying a MacCoinnich who had yet to realize all their power. That would be like chewing cake and spitting it out.

No, it wasn't time to kill. It was time to move about the board, collecting power, removing a pawn, a knight, and then removing the queen would reward her as an empress.

The world slowly moved back in place around her and the wind kicked up. Without thought, Raine stood and walked through the flames to reach her discarded clothing. She flicked the soot off her arm and dressed.

As she turned to walk away, the flames behind her died.

****

Kelsey and Sophie had taken to the backyard to

CATHERINE BYBEE

explore Mrs. Dawson's massive yard.

"Todd sends his best," Amber told Jake who watched his girls through the door.

"It's not fair you just saw him."

"He feels the same way. Perhaps one day you'll meet again."

Jake pushed away from the window, and Amber took his place.

The girls were chasing two butterflies and laughing. Then, as if they realized they were smiling they both stopped.

Amber gave a silent prayer for their strength and ability to laugh. The girls continued to move in and out the flower garden talking with each other.

"So the person behind the murder—any leads?" Gavin asked.

"Selma seems to think the wacko that wants a piece of her is behind it, but Simon thinks something witchy forced the dogs to attack."

Amber overheard their conversation, only half listening as she watched the girls. Apparently, two dogs from one neighbor and another one from an adjacent property banded together and attacked.

Amber cracked the window so she could hear the girls. *They need to be guarded. It isn't about the mother; it's the girls.*

Amber?

The window wasn't open enough so she moved to the door and walked outside.

Amber?

She opened her shield and stepped on the porch.

Voices from the adjacent houses filtered in. She pushed them away. The girls were quiet in their grief, and the attention of those in the house were focused on one person. Her.

But she couldn't dwell on that, not now. Someone, two someone's were close. Watching.

Something darted from the trees. Kelsey and Sophie both screamed.

The hair on Amber's nape stood on end. She lifted her arms and pushed her shield around the girls some half an acre away. The blue light surrounded them when several wolves moved out of the trees. Their howls pierced her ears and Jake ran past her.

Amber?

Gavin called to her, but she couldn't answer.

He was out there...the person making the wolves attack.

One of the wolves jumped on Jake. But before the wolf could sink its teeth into Jake's flesh, she reached for a way to fight off the animal from so far away. The solution was there, like a jay sitting on a fence inside her head, mocking her.

She caught her breath and held it.

Stop breathing! Amber pushed the thought into the animal's head. The wolf whimpered and dropped to the ground, its eyes nothing more than a cold, dead stare.

Her mind flooded with a tsunami of knowledge—power resting just beneath the layer of her consciousness.

Jake stumbled away from the fallen animal and moved into the circle with his girls.

Do you feel him, Gavin? He's here...

"Where are you, you coward?" Amber yelled to the sky.

I feel him.

She swiveled toward the house to see Simon standing before Helen, a dirk in his hand. Gavin's weapon was pointing toward the ground. Giles stared directly at her. Mrs. Dawson stood inside the house and Selma was gone.

Selma!

Gavin turned to see the missing member of their family. "Shit."

A scream sounded from the front of the Manor.

Amber grew cold and she started to run.

281

Gavin was in front of her in the space of one breath. They both found Selma being dragged by a man twice her size into a waiting car, a knife to her throat.

Drop the knife! The words came from her husband's head, not hers. The knife shot from Selma's attacker's hand and flew several yards away.

Amber focused on the man. Her body grew rigid and rage swirled in her line of sight.

You stupid man. You can't breathe.

The attacker stumbled, his grip loosened.

You! Can't! Breathe!

The man dropped Selma and grasped his neck.

"Move away, Selma," Amber didn't recognize her cold and calculating voice.

Selma didn't need to be told twice. She stumbled behind Amber and Gavin.

Amber opened her gift, pushed into this man's head. He struggled to breathe while cursing Selma. Called her a witch. He hated her... only her. Wanted to hurt her as much as he'd been hurt.

The man fell to his knees, his face turned bright red.

Amber!

No one hurts my family...my friends!

Gavin moved into her line of sight. "Amber! Stop!"

She blinked several times.

"Let him go!"

She tilted her head. *Let who go?*

Kincaid looked at Amber, saw the darkness swirling in the whites of her eyes.

Let him go. You're killing him.

Amber sucked in a breath. *Oh, God. Breathe.*

He didn't need to turn around to know the man behind them pulled in a desperate breath of air.

Confusion marred Amber's brow. "What did I do?"

Kincaid gripped her shoulders. "Focus. Someone else

is here." As soon as Amber darted outside, the world darkened. Opposing forces with evil intent surrounded them all. He noticed the girls playing and before the first wolf emerged, Amber had covered the girls in the thickest layer of blue he'd ever seen. He couldn't remember, not once, an ability to protect someone from as far away as they were. When the wolf dropped into a lifeless heap, he turned to his wife. Pulsating power surged from her and wouldn't let him in. He couldn't get into her head. He called her name but she didn't respond.

She was looking at him now… his innocent wife.

"Focus."

Amber closed her eyes and envisioned the back of the house. Someone was still there watching them.

"Stay here. Keep him from leaving." Gavin shoved his weapon in her hand and ran to the back of the house.

Jake and his girls were in the center of the yard. One dead wolf lay on the ground, but the others were gone.

The air shifted and a high sulfur scent filled the air.

Whoever had been there was gone.

Shifted in time and gone.

****

The Arizona man, Norman Rock, was led away in handcuffs. The blood of his ex-girlfriend and her fiancé was found all over towels in the trunk of his car.

He mumbled about witches and supernatural power, which simply put him on a medical evaluation list. Kincaid knew, however, if they didn't start placing the right barriers and protection around Mrs. Dawson's home, the kind of finger pointing the man who'd attempted to kidnap Selma would draw attention. Unwanted and potentially dangerous attention.

The entire time the police were at the home, Amber remained silent. Her worry about what happened, why and how it happened was a constant sea of emotion inside him.

Kincaid saw the darkness in her eyes but, more than that, he'd felt the darkness inside them both. His ability to force another to move in any way was limited, yet Kincaid knew he had forced Norman to throw his weapon aside. Worse, Amber tried to destroy him. Nearly did.

Helen and Selma had taken the girls inside while Simon and Jake spoke with the police, and Mrs. Dawson and Giles huddled together in the library. Kincaid and Amber stood on the porch watching the police as they finished talking.

"The prophesy *is* about us," Amber said under her breath.

He wanted to deny her.

"Grainna could steal away one's breath."

Kincaid moved to her side and slid his arm over her shoulders. "You were saving the life of a friend, an honorable friend."

"That isn't the point, Gavin. I nearly killed a man with only a thought. I didn't mourn the animal. And the animal was only acting on the will of someone else."

Gavin stood in front of her and caught her eyes. "You're not evil, Amber. You're human. When the innocent around us are in trouble, we do whatever we can to save them."

"But to kill?"

"Were you not a part of destroying Grainna? It took all of you, but you did. If you could have done it alone, wouldn't you have tried?"

Amber squeezed her eyes shut. "I'm scared, Gavin."

The clear sky above him cracked.

"My father's gift is only a thought. I feel it as easily as I feel yours."

When his insides turned on themselves, the growl of faraway thunder erupted. Gavin thought of the growl again, and the earth replied. *I feel his gift, too.*

A tear fell down Amber's cheek. *We're cursed.*

"No, Amber. We're gifted. We saved innocent lives today."

"But what if we don't? What if the power swallows

us, pushes us to *her* ways?"

"We're in this together, Amber. I *will* keep you grounded, and you *must* keep me the same."

And if we can't?

We will. We have to believe we will.

"Promise me."

"Promise you what?" Gavin asked.

"Promise me we'll leave this world together if the power consumes us. On our love, promise me."

Kincaid met her unwavering eyes. "On our love, I will do anything in my power to remove us both if the power turns us."

****

"It's just going to help them forget…to ease the pain." Selma stood over the stove, her pot simmered with what Amber assumed was tea.

Jake crossed his arms over his chest and grumbled.

"Trust me."

Amber and Kincaid moved into the room filled with their family and friends. Holding hands in unity. Honesty in the home was paramount, and they didn't make exceptions.

If the others weren't comfortable with the changes happening inside them both, they would leave.

The conversation ceased as they walked in.

"We need to talk with all of you."

Selma turned the fire off the stove and moved to stand beside Jake.

Giles stood beside Mrs. Dawson while Simon took the space beside his wife.

"Go ahead, child," Mrs. Dawson. "We're listening."

Gavin smiled at the older woman. "The prophecy…it was right. We don't know what changed to shift what's happening inside us, but we both feel a change in our power."

Amber watched Simon's jaw clench. "We noticed."

"I almost killed that man."

Simon shook his head. "On a field of battle in our time, he would have been dead by the swiftness of a sword."

"But I nearly did it with a thought...*her* thought."

"You're not *her*."

"Nay, Simon. I'm not. But it's here." Amber poked her chest. "And it's dark."

A slight surge of fear washed over the man she thought of as a brother. "We all see the darkness in your eyes. We know it's there. We also know that power, all power has two choices. Good or evil."

Amber didn't think he understood. "I almost destroyed a man today."

"And I've killed many. Your point, Amber?"

"'Tis against my nature."

Simon moved to stand before her. "You have yet to determine what your true nature is. Kincaid's gift has afforded you a real life. Now this dark power, as you call it, will give you even more power to fight the righteous fight. You have never been anything but innocent and careful of all life."

"You saved my girls today," Jake reminded her.

"And instead of keeping your thoughts to yourselves, you're both coming to us," Giles pointed out. "You have nothing to hide."

Mrs. Dawson pushed from the chair she sat in and walked over to them. "Awareness is most important in this time in your life. Awareness and love." Mrs. Dawson leveled her gaze to Amber. "Remember, Grainna lost her love, lost the part that made her sane. Within the bond your father laid was a blessing to keep you righteous. You have to believe that."

Amber leaned into Gavin. *Could it be that simple? Could love be the glue that keeps us on the path of righteousness?*

"Love is always the answer."

Amber glanced at her husband. *Did she just hear my thought?*

Perhaps she's just a wise woman.

"Your husband was a lucky man, lass," Simon told Mrs. Dawson.

"Damn straight he was," she said.

Laughter filled the room.

"Now, enough of all this talk of darkness. I'd like to consume something other than Selma's forget-everything potion. And then Giles and I need to rack his brain about entities that take over animals to accost little girls."

"So there was someone else here."

"Of course there was," Mrs. Dawson said. "You don't think that putz sitting in a jail cell controlled those wolves, do you?"

Giles released a long sigh. "I was hoping."

"Well knock it off. We have work to do." She turned to Amber. "And with all this newfound power, perhaps you can start laying wards over this house to help keep those babies safe. They've seen enough evil, don't you think?"

"Yes, ma'am. I'll try."

"We'll try," Gavin added. "Together."

"Good. Let's get to work."

Epilogue

Raine sat before both Mouse and Clarisse.

"Their power is united," Mouse informed her. "I escaped with my life only because of the human who offered himself as a distraction."

"Who holds the most power?"

"It's hard to tell. Neither one of them were approachable. Their shield wasn't breached by an ant."

"And you, Clarisse? Did you accomplish your task?"

The beautiful blonde lifted her chin, her perfect figure stretched like a cat. "Cian is in my bed. It's only a matter of time."

Raine sat back with a smile playing on her lips.

"Time? We have plenty of time."

About the Author

New York Times best-selling author Catherine Bybee was raised in Washington State, but after graduating high school, she moved to Southern California in hopes of becoming a movie star. After growing bored with waiting tables, she returned to school and became a registered nurse, spending most of her career in urban emergency rooms. She now writes full-time and in addition to the MacCoinnich Time Travel series she has penned the novels *Wife by Wednesday, Married by Monday,* and *Fiancé by Friday* in her Weekday Brides series and *Not Quite Dating, Not Quite Mine,* and *Not Quite Enough* in her Not Quite series. Bybee lives with her husband and two teenage sons in Southern California.

Connect with Catherine Bybee Online:
CatherineBybee.com

Made in the USA
Monee, IL
18 June 2021

71637149R00167